THE
LAST
DRIVE

THE LAST DRIVE

AND OTHER STORIES

REX STOUT

Edited by Ira Brad Matetsky

MYSTERIOUSPRESS.COM

OPEN ROAD
INTEGRATED MEDIA
NEW YORK

This compilation, including the introduction and commentary, copyright © 2015 by Ira Brad Matetsky

The stories in this book first appeared between 1912 and 1918 and are reprinted with the approval of the Estate of Rex Stout. For original publication information, see Appendix, pp. 275–77.

The illustrations accompanying *The Last Drive* first appeared in *Golfers Magazine*, July to December 1916.

Cover design by Neil Alexander Heacox

978-1-5040-1134-1

Published in 2015 by MysteriousPress.com/Open Road Integrated Media, Inc.
345 Hudson Street
New York, NY 10014
www.mysteriouspress.com
www.openroadmedia.com

CONTENTS

—ᴡ—

INTRODUCTION

—ᘛ—

Today, Rex Todhunter Stout (1886–1975) is remembered primarily as the creator of Nero Wolfe and Archie Goodwin, who appeared in 72 murder mysteries published between 1934 and 1975. But two decades before he created Nero Wolfe, "Rex T. Stout" authored at least 46 works of fiction—novels, novellas, and short stories—spanning a variety of genres. These works appeared in at least ten different magazines between 1912 and 1918.

Stout had travelled from his native Kansas to New York seeking a career as a writer. In 1913, he told the newspaper back home in Topeka that he felt an "irresistible attraction" to writing, and that he was "strongly of the opinion that New York City is the field in America for anyone desiring to enter upon a literary career." Stout hit the ground running, selling fourteen stories to a variety of publishers in his first year, and receiving from $18 to $40 for each. Over the next four years or so, he wrote and sold five novels and two dozen more short stories. And then he stopped writing, having concluded that he'd been writing for money rather than for art, and that he needed to make his fortune so as to gain the freedom to write what he wished rather than what publishers would pay for. He stayed away from the typewriter for more than a decade.

Some of Stout's early stories show signs of the literary talents that would later give rise to the Nero Wolfe corpus, and some, frankly, do not. But all of them should be of interest to the many fans and admirers of Stout and his work. During the 1970s, Stout's biographer, John McAleer, sought to locate as many of these stories as possible. It was not an easy task. Though McAleer frequently met with Stout while writing the biography, McAleer told another collector, Judson Sapp, that Stout was "no help" in locating his early stories because "they are too far in the day ago for him. He hasn't seen them or thought about them for almost sixty years."

Instead, McAleer visited and communicated with libraries throughout the country. He was handicapped by the limited number of magazine indexes then available (there were no computerized indexes back then, and the pulps and popular fiction were not included in the *Reader's Guide* or comparable works). Even when magazines containing the stories could be located, some libraries still would not provide copies based on copyright and preservation concerns. The Library of Congress denied McAleer access to the serialization of one early novel until McAleer relayed his request through his brother-in-law—Congressman Tip O'Neill, majority leader of the U.S. House of Representatives.

Despite these obstacles, Stout collectors and bibliographers did ultimately locate the majority of these early Stout stories. The greatest number of them appeared in a popular pulp magazine, *The All-Story*, and its successors, *All-Story Weekly* and *All-Story Cavalier Weekly*, all published by the Frank B. Munsey Company. Others appeared in somewhat more upscale magazines: *Short Stories*, *The Black Cat*, *The Smart Set*, *Lippincott's Monthly Magazine*, and *Smith's Magazine*.

McAleer discussed the stories he had found in several chapters of his magisterial *Rex Stout: A Biography*, later republished as *Rex Stout: A Majesty's Life*. (On reading McAleer's first draft, Stout opined that "I think there is too much detail of . . . the stuff I wrote in my twenties," though he conceded that he was an interested party and "I can't safely trust my judgment.") McAleer also published a collection chosen from the early stories, *Justice Ends at Home and Other Stories*, in which the lead story was Stout's first murder mystery, as well as an edition of *Under the Andes*, a serialized 1914 novel representing Stout's foray into science fiction. McAleer's introductions to the two volumes are required reading for fans of early Stout. Later collectors published two more collections of the early short stories (*Target Practice*, which reprinted the stories from *All-Story*, and *An Officer and a Lady and Other Stories*) and three more early novels (*Her Forbidden Knight*, *A Prize for Princes*, and *The Great Legend*). But no one knew whether all the early works of Rex Stout had yet been found.

Today we know they had not. In this volume, we present eleven more early stories by Rex Stout, all first published between 1912 and 1918. The first story in this volume, *The Last Drive*, was Stout's second murder mystery novel (after *Justice Ends at Home*), published in a completely unexpected place, *Golfers Magazine*. Its rediscovery is the most important development in Stout scholarship in the past twenty-five years. The other stories include a supernaturalistic shaggy-dog story ("Ask the Egyptians"), an ironic tale of local politics ("The Pickled Picnic"), several pulp romance tales, and at least one romance-that-wasn't (to say here which story would spoil it). Although the stories are a century old, all stand up to modern reading.

For the rediscovery of eight of the stories in this volume, we are indebted to the volunteer indexers of the comprehensive and ongoing FictionMags/Galactic Central magazine indexing project (www.philsp.com) under the leadership of Phil Stephensen-Payne and William G. Contento, as well as the editors of Rex Stout's bibliography on Wikipedia, whose addition of these new stories first drew them to my attention. For finding and recognizing the significance of *The Last Drive*, we are grateful to Ross E. Davies and Cattleya Concepcion of *The Green Bag Almanac and Reader* (www.greenbag.org). For encouraging my work on this volume, I thank Rex Stout's daughter,

Rebecca Stout Bradbury; Otto Penzler and Rob W. Hart of The Mysterious Press; the staff of the Burns Library at Boston College, archival repository of the Rex Stout, John McAleer, and Judson Sapp papers; Noah Peters, who located copies of many of the stories at the Library of Congress; and of course my colleagues and friends of the Wolfe Pack, the worldwide literary appreciation society for the many fans of Rex Stout (www.nerowolfe.org).

Despite substantial research efforts to locate all the remaining early works of Rex Stout, of course we may still have missed some. Please bring any new discoveries or leads to our attention at werowance@nerowolfe.org.

—Ira Brad Matetsky

THE
LAST
DRIVE

THE LAST DRIVE

—⚭—

Introduction

The Last Drive is a detective fiction novel—a murder mystery—that was serialized in *Golfers Magazine* in six installments from July to December 1916. *Golfers Magazine* primarily consisted of non-fiction for golfing enthusiasts, but some issues included a piece of golf-related fiction.

Rex Stout was never known as a golfing enthusiast, and the fact that he published fiction in *Golfers Magazine* was entirely unsuspected until 2011, when researcher Cattleya Concepcion came across a citation to this story in a Copyright Office register while searching under Stout's name for something else. (It is fortuitous that the story was listed under Stout's name; everything Stout published in other magazines during this period was copyrighted in the magazine owners' names, not Stout's.)

Stout's earlier novella *Justice Ends at Home* and *The Last Drive* are the two main pieces from Stout's early writing career from which one might have extrapolated important elements of the early Nero Wolfe books written twenty years later. But to say more of *The Last Drive* would spoil the story, so let us hold our thoughts for the afterword.

THE LAST DRIVE

CHAPTER I

There had been a friendly argument before the foursome got started that Saturday afternoon in June. Carson Phillips, retired from the army with the rank of colonel, and possessor of a fortune ample enough to allow him to regard the monthly check from Washington as just a little added pin money, had hotly resented the insinuations of his two nephews, Harry and Fred Adams, concerning the relation between a man's age and his golf score.

"So you'll be kind enough to divide yourselves between us!" he snorted. "Do you hear that, Fraser? A wonder their impudence doesn't choke them. I'm hanged if I wouldn't play their best ball— I've tamed wilder lads in the service—"

Fraser Mawson smiled and nodded his head, held with the poise and air of authority acquired by thirty years of experience at the New York bar.

"As a matter of fact, Colonel," he agreed, "you'd probably give them a run for their money. I'm rather a better lawyer than golf player, but—impertinence! So you want to let us old fellows down easy, do you, boys? We'll show you! Won't we, Carson? Shall we give them a trimming?"

The soldier nodded, and straightway produced a silver coin from his pocket and sent it spinning in the air, with a "Call it, Harry," directed at one of the young men, who stopped laughing long enough to pronounce the word:

"Heads!"

But it fell with the eagle up, and, having thus won the honor, the Colonel motioned to the waiting caddies and turned to lead the way to the first tee.

They found a crowd there ahead of them, for it was a clear, brilliant June day, and the links of the Corona Country Club was one of the most convenient and best patronized within easy motor distance of New York. For the most part they were men, and you might have found among them the possessors of many well-known names in the business and professional world of the metropolis. Not the least prominent were the members of the foursome with which we are especially concerned. Colonel Carson Phillips, fifty-six and straight as an arrow, was a fine figure of a man with his clear-cut, bronzed features, steady gray eyes and military bearing; Fraser Mawson, also a little more than fifty, one of the most popular men among his own profession as well as a welcome addition to a jolly corner in any of the exclusive clubs, was perhaps a little less distinguished in his appearance, but still a handsome man; and Harry and Fred Adams, brothers, and nephews and heirs of the Colonel, twenty-four and twenty-six respectively, were engaging young fellows with a great deal of foolishness still clinging to them, and all their accomplishments so far developed of a purely social nature. They were spending a week at their uncle's country home, not far from the Corona club, back in the Jersey hills; and Fraser Mawson, who had handled the Colonel's business and legal affairs for the past twenty years, was down for the week end.

Silent nods and low-spoken greetings, not to disturb the pair who were driving off, were exchanged as they reached the first tee. Everyone knew Colonel Phillips, open-handed and good-natured old warrior that he was; and there were friendly smiles for him from men like Bolton Cook, the Colorado millionaire who was waking up a section of Wall Street, Harrison Matlin, corporation attorney; John Waring, widely known as a travel lecturer, and Canby Rankin, a wealthy southerner, who had become interested in the detection of crime as a pastime and performed it so well that his talents had more than once pulled the New York Police Commissioner out of a hole. The Colonel and Rankin were old friends, and now they joined each other for a low-toned conversation while most of the others in the crowd swung drivers and irons at blades of grass to limber up.

In thirty minutes or so the foursome's turn came, and Mawson and the Colonel teed up. With a short, nervous swing, all forearm, Mawson got a ball 180 yards straight down the middle of the fairway. Then the Colonel. His style was slashing and business-like; you might have thought he was using a cavalry sword on an adversary in the heat of battle. A slice carried him into a trap on the right, 200 yards away. His two nephews followed, with the gracefulness and assumed carelessness of a generation who plays thirty-six holes in the daytime and dances thirty-six numbers at night; they got long straight drives. As the four men started off down the smooth turf side by side the Colonel turned to call over his shoulder to those assembled at the tee:

"We're going to show these youngsters! The match will end on the fourteenth green!"

And with a wave of his hand and a smile he strode ahead beside

Mawson. With what suddenness would the answering smiles and shouts have died away if they had known what the next hour held in store!

The Colonel's optimistic enthusiasm was reinforced by an astonishing 3 for the first hole by Mawson, who reached the green with his second, a long iron over a trap, and sunk a twenty-footer. The two young men took fours; Colonel Phillips needed six.

"That's alright," observed the old soldier cheerfully as they headed for the second tee. "If I don't do it my partner will. One under par! Do you still think we're too old to make it interesting, Fred?"

"A miracle, sir," laughed the elder of the two young men. "To my certain knowledge Mr. Mawson never made that hole in less than five before in his life. Confess it, Mr. Mawson!"

The lawyer was nervously swinging his putter back and forth, nipping the tops of the blades of grass. "That three was a little unusual," he admitted. "But it's the Colonel I'm looking to. Slicing is something new for you, Carson."

"Been at it for a week," frowned the soldier in reply. "Some devilish trick that's caught me unawares. Totally undiscoverable. I had Mac go around with me yesterday, but he could find nothing wrong; advised me to try my brassie off the tee. I am doing so. You saw. Worse than ever."

"The honor is still yours, gentlemen," came from Harry Adams as they reached the tee. "Let's take this one, Fred, miracle or no miracle."

It was a short hole, a midiron over a lake, and three of them laid their balls neatly on the green. It was a half in three, with the Colonel barely missing a fifteen-footer for a two. On the next, a two-shot hole, the Colonel used his brassie again from the tee, and again he sliced badly, into the rough. No miracle came to assist Mawson, and the elder pair lost the hole four to six. The fourth was something over five hundred yards. Once more the Colonel went far to the right; he chopped out of some underbrush, gritted his teeth, called for his brassie,—and sliced out of bounds. They lost the hole by two strokes, and became one down.

On the way to the fifth tee the Colonel grew highly voluble. "I've been led forty miles on a false trail out in Luzon," he declared in deliberate disgust, "and I've seen twelve-pounders suddenly kick up their heels and grin in your face. Also I've had experience with women. But for pesky, petty, unholy tricks, nothing can equal golf. Incomprehensible. Satanic. All at once, from nowhere, I acquire this damnable slice. Cause not to be found. For fickleness women are hopeless amateurs compared to a golf club."

"Use an iron, sir," suggested young Harry Adams respectfully.

"You should have fought it out with the driver," put in Fraser Mawson, busying himself with the selection of a new ball. "Don't give in to their whims. You see that the brassie is even worse. Something in your stance or grip or stroke."

"I didn't suppose it was the way I combed my hair," observed the Colonel in wrathful sarcasm.

The younger pair had the honor now, and each got a long straight one from the tee. Mawson's nervousness appeared to have increased, and he topped badly, dribbling along into a hazard. The Colonel hesitated a moment, took out his brassie, then handed it back and called for his driver. As he teed up and took his stance his jaw was set and his eyes were grim. He did not take his golf with the poignant earnestness with which the famous Mrs. Battle played bridge, perhaps, but he had sworn to beat "the youngsters" and like a good soldier he put his brave old heart into it. Slow back, an easy, well-timed swing, and away went the ball, straight and true as a bullet, 220 yards down the fairway. The Colonel watched it tensely till it came down, then relaxed, straightened and grinned happily.

"A beauty, sir!" Harry called out.

"Longer than ours," Fred agreed.

The Colonel waved his driver valiantly in the air. "The weapon of a gentleman," he announced vaingloriously. "I retract my remarks of a moment ago. After Fraser recovers from that trap you boys may play the odd. Permit an old man to exult."

They tramped together down to the bunker, on their way meeting and exchanging greetings with another foursome coming back on the fourteenth hole. It might have been thought a pity that their interest in the game kept them from appreciation of the lovely landscape that spread itself out in four directions: woods and a winding ribbon of road to the left, a bubbling merry brook in front, and on the other two sides the gently swelling green hills, smiling in the sunshine, with the smooth turf of the links dotted here and there with thick clumps of underbrush, a solitary tree or a miniature grove; and all made alive by a group of players at a tee here or scattered there along the fairway, the caddies with their bright yellow caps making little dots of color in the most unexpected places, as though a painter had carelessly thrown drops of ochre about from the point of his palette knife.

Fraser Mawson, standing in a sand pit, niblick in hand, was certainly not thinking of the landscape. He took three to get out, and his fifth was played before they came up to the other balls. The two young men took brassies to make the green, just over a deep ditch two hundred yards aways; one reached it nicely, the other hooked a little to the left into some deep grass. The Colonel, with twenty yards less to go, used a driving mashie; again his jaw was set firmly, down came the heavy iron head, and the ball sailed through the air, just clearing the top of the ditch and dropping dead on the sloping green. Again the Colonel grinned.

"Nice approach, sir," came from Fred Adams; and he added to his younger brother in an undertone, "We'll have to go some, Harry; the old boy's back on his game."

Then he turned quickly at a swift expression of alarm in Harry's eyes, and the two young men stepped forward together, calling out:

"What's the matter, sir?"

The cause of their alarm came from their uncle the Colonel. He had let his mashie fall to the ground, and he stood with white face and eyes drawn close in pain, trembling visibly, while a half comical expression of surprised dismay parted his lips.

"What the deuce—what—" he stammered, moving his hands uncertainly upwards to his chest, while his two nephews ran forward, crying out, "What is it, sir?" and Fraser Mawson stood still, opened his mouth and let out in a high-pitched voice the one word:

"Indigestion!"

Suddenly the Colonel straightened himself up with an apparent effort, and made his voice steady:

"Most curious sensation in my chest—no, here, lower down—I don't think—indigestion—quite acute and—and painful—."

By that time the two young men had him by the arm, one on either side, and were trying to lead him toward the seats at the sixth tee, but he shook them off impatiently and stood still on the green turf, swaying a little from side to side with his hands pressed tightly on his breast. Harry turned to Fraser Mawson with a frightened look:

"Maybe it's his heart—I'd better—."

As he spoke there came a cry from his brother, and again they sprang forward as the Colonel suddenly thrust his hands straight in front of him and sank to the ground. They caught him and let him gently onto the turf, while Fred knelt to hold his uncle's head in his arms, calling frantically to the others:

"Run—quick—a doctor! Wortley's around somewhere—for God's sake hurry!"

Harry was off like a shot in the direction of the clubhouse. Fraser Mawson stood as one helpless with astonishment, his eyes staring. The caddies, who had gone on toward the green, came running back at the sound of the young man's shouts, and were speedily scattered over the links in every direction in search of Doctor Wortley, as were several other golfers who hastened over from nearby tees and greens. Their shouts for a doctor soon filled the air over all the June landscape; meanwhile Fred knelt with his arms around the shoulders of his uncle, whose eyes had assumed a glassy, fearful stare, while unintelligible sputterings came from his lips and his fingers tore nervously at the grass. Fraser Mawson had knelt down beside him and was saying over and over, "What is it, Carson, for God's sake what is it?" finally causing the young man to exclaim half angrily, "Shut up, don't you see he can't answer you?"

All at once a great shudder ran through the Colonel's form and his hands were clenched tightly against his sides; a line of white foam appeared between his lips as his voice became articulate, barely so, a mere series of gasps:

"Fred—here, so I can see you—that's right, my boy—goodbye— tell Harry—and you, Fraser—I don't know what this is, but it's the end—all on fire inside—water—cool me off a little, you know—"

The words gave place to meaningless sounds, little noises that escaped the old warrior in his terrible agony despite the tremendous effort he was making to control himself. His eyes were the eyes of a tortured man, rolling from side to side, and froth covered his lips; he had seized Fred's arm with his right hand, and the crazy force of the grip crunched the bones so that the young man had to set his teeth on his lip to keep from crying out. Fraser Mawson had disappeared and now came running back with a pail of water from a nearby drinking tank; they tried to get the Colonel to drink, but he was beyond sensible action and the water ran over his neck onto the grass with little splotches of white in it. Shouts were heard, "The doctor!" and men seemed suddenly to appear from all sides, while from the direction of the clubhouse an automobile was seen dashing over the smooth fairway and leaping across the rough. By the time it arrived a crowd of twenty or thirty golfers had gathered; three or four of them had knelt down to assist Fred in his efforts as the Colonel's body writhed and twisted horribly about in his pain. As the automobile jerked up suddenly with a grinding of brakes they made room for Doctor Wortley and he leaped out toward the group. Just as he arrived a mighty convulsive shudder ran over the prostrate form from head to foot, and then it lay still.

The doctor leaned over with an ejaculation of amazement, and silence fell over the crowd as he knelt to unbutton the old faded army shirt that the Colonel had always worn on the links. Mutterings and whisperings from forty throats accompanied his quick, deft movements, lasting for the space of two long minutes; then absolute silence again as he slowly rose to his feet and turned about. A glance to one side, a clearing of the throat, and he spoke in an undertone:

"Gentlemen, Colonel Phillips is dead."

There was a gasp from the crowd and two muttered words of dismayed unbelief from Fraser Mawson as he stood whitefaced beside the doctor:

"My God!"

Then a boyish cry of despair from Harry Adams as he threw himself down beside his uncle's body and seized the hand that lay there on the grass in his own; his brother Fred was supporting the grey head on his knees and was trying to close the eyes with pathetic little strokes of his fingers. Stammering amazed whisperings passed around, and suddenly a direct question was put to the doctor by somebody. He seemed to hesitate, then turned again to the bareheaded group.

"Gentlemen, you are all members of the Corona club, and you have a right to know; the Colonel was poisoned. I tell you this at once that there may be no gossip about it. The nature of the accident will have to be investigated, and it will be well if no silly rumors are circulated, both for the sake of the Colonel's memory and the reputation of the club. I think you may be trusted in that respect. I'll leave it to you, Matlin, to see that the caddies do no talking. Call it heart disease.—Here, some hands, if you please. Cook, will you kindly run your car a little closer."

There was a tug at Doctor Wortley's arm, and he turned to look into Harry Adams' set face and staring eyes.

"Doctor—did you say—my uncle was poisoned—"

A nod answered him, and he spoke again, stammering:

"But what—what was it—"

The doctor threw his arm across the lad's shoulder. "We'll find that out later, my boy. Keep steady. The thing now is to get him home.—Here, you men—"

Carefully and gently the still body was lifted and carried to the automobile and covered with a robe. The faces of the crowd, filled with the fearful solemnity that always accompanies the presence of death, no matter whose, also bore the finer imprint of the hand of real sorrow, testifying eloquently to the quality of the man who had just left them.

The caddies were permitted to approach now, and one of them, a little brightfaced fellow with his eyes filled with tears, came sidling up with a timid query as to what he should do with the Colonel's bag of clubs, which he carried on his shoulder. Mawson bestirred himself at that and reached out for the strap, but it was grasped by Harry Adams, who tucked the bag under his arm as though it had been some sacred thing. "I'll take it, Harry," Mawson called, but the young man paid no attention to him. The little caddie had meanwhile made his way silently to the automobile, where he stood gazing tensely at the robe over the form in the tonneau; now he suddenly burst into tears and turned away with his hands over his face. Perhaps the Colonel would have appreciated that tribute more than any other if he could have known of it.

The automobile started slowly in the direction of the clubhouse, with the group of golfers trooping silently, heads bare, in the rear. Bolton Cook, the Colorado millionaire, was at the wheel, and beside him sat Fraser Mawson, the dead man's attorney, business adviser and friend. Among those who walked behind there was one face in which the general shocked expression of grief and solemnity was overshadowed by another—a look of keen professional interest and speculation. Throughout the scene at the fifth hole this man had remained silent, in the background, but his steady penetrating eyes had not missed a word or glance or movement among the actors in the tragedy; and now they were fastened on the backs of Harry and Fred Adams, the dead Colonel's nephews and heirs, as the two young men trudged along beside the slow-moving car.

The face was that of Canby Rankin, the Southerner, who had turned detective.

CHAPTER II

At Greenlawn

Rankin did not immediately follow the procession to the clubhouse. Instead, he moved across to the spot where Colonel Phillips had lain on the ground, and stood there for some time gazing at the crushed and trampled blades of grass with an absent expression in his eyes and a wrinkled brow. The Colonel had been one of his dearest friends; Rankin, a man not lavish of his affection, had sincerely loved him; but beyond a shocked tightening of the lips there was no indication of deep feeling on his countenance. He was in the habit of keeping his emotions sternly within; and, besides, a problem was trying to set itself in his mind. Finally he turned with an impatient shrug of his shoulders and strolled off slowly in the direction of the fifth tee, casting his eyes from side to side over the green turf, half curiously.

"Probably absurd," he muttered to himself. "Some constitutional secret, no doubt. Wortley says poison—symptoms, that's all. Indiscreet. Still, he knew the Colonel. And there's this devilish feeling I get, as though out of the air, like a dog with his nose full of fox-smell; it's never yet played me false. Drives me to wonder . . . but who the deuce would harm Carson Phillips? Fine young fellows like those boys! No. Positively no one. It's absurd. I must talk with Wortley."

But for all that, when Rankin had hastened his step somewhat and made his way across the fairway and the rough to the sloping terraces alongside the eighteenth tee he did not go at once to the clubhouse. Instead, he sought one of the smaller buildings set in a group of trees off to the right, around the door of which a number of boys in brown uniforms and yellow caps were scattered, engaged in a general discussion with a show of great animation and excitement. The greater part were gathered in a circle around some central object of interest near a corner of the building, and as Rankin approached he sighted the object of his search in the midst of this group. It was the little caddie who had turned the dead Colonel's bag of clubs over to Harry Adams and later turned away from the automobile in a flood of tears.

"The face was that of Canby Rankin, the Southerner who had turned detective."

The detective beckoned to him. "Come here, Jimmie."

The lad separated himself from the throng, and Rankin led him over toward the terrace out of earshot of the others.

"What are they talking about over there?" he began, abruptly.

"About Colonel Phillips, sir," replied the boy. The excitement of his sudden elevation to supreme importance among the other caddies had evidently somewhat submerged his grief, but the tear stains on his cheeks made two whitish lines down to his chin.

"What are they saying?"

The reply was rather vague, mostly to the effect that they were "just talking."

"I see." Rankin looked down at him speculatively. "You know, Jimmie, Colonel Phillips was stricken with heart disease. Doctor Wortley says so. I want to ask you a question or two, but you must promise not to say anything to the other boys. I think I can trust you. For the Colonel's sake, Jimmie."

"Yes, sir." The lad's brown eyes flashed up. "I'd do anything for the Colonel. I won't say anything, sir. Is he—"

"Well?"

"Is he really dead, Mr. Rankin?"

Jimmie's lips quivered a little as he put the question; then, at the detective's somber affirmative nod, he closed them tight again.

"Yes. I want to know, Jimmie, if you noticed anything at all unusual during the match this morning."

The boy thought a minute. "No, sir, nothing unusual. Except that Mr. Mawson got a three on the first hole."

Rankin smiled a little in spite of himself. "You're sure there was nothing? Think hard."

"No, sir, not as I remember."

"Did they stop at the water tank on the fourth for a drink?"

"No, sir."

"Anybody smoke?"

After a second Jimmie replied that the two young men had lit pipes at the second tee.

"Not the Colonel? Nobody gave him a cigar?"

"No, sir. Nor Mr. Mawson, either."

"And the Colonel seemed well and in good spirits up to the time—up to the fifth hole?"

Jimmie's yes was quite positive, and then he added: "Except that he was mad on account of his driving. He's been slicing awful for a week. Yesterday he used his brassie, and he used it today too; but it wasn't any better. Only on the fifth hole today he took the driver again, and got a beauty. I was so glad because I thought—and then just five minutes later—"

Rankin nodded. "And then drives didn't matter any more. Now, Jimmie, look back and think carefully. Was there anything peculiar about the actions of any of the other three gentlemen? At any time?"

"Why—Mr. Mawson was awful nervous about the Colonel's driving, sir. Of course, he was his partner—"

"No, no; I mean anything unusual, suspicious."

The boy's brow wrinkled in the effort of memory. "No, sir, nothing," he replied at length.

Then, prompted by questions from the detective, Jimmie described in detail the actions of the other three members of the foursome when the catastrophe came. It was necessarily a meager recital, since the caddies had been a hundred yards in front at the time, and on running back had been sent off immediately in search of the doctor; and boys are not observing in the pressure of excitement. The detective got all he could out of him, then handed him a dollar bill and left him with a final warning not to repeat the conversation to the others. Then he turned toward the club-house.

The Saturday crowd was all over the place—in the library, the bar, the dining-room, the piazzas, and, of course, the one topic of conversation was the tragic end of one of their best loved members, whose body was at that moment lying in some room upstairs. Everybody

"Is he really dead, Mr. Rankin?"

had come in from the links; all playing had ceased. In the dining-room members had left their luncheon to get cold on the tables, and then returned to sit and talk in hushed tones. There was a buzz everywhere. The mystery of the thing had grasped everybody. The word "poison" was being whispered around, and there was a rumor that police had been summoned from Brockton, the nearest village. Rankin, with his eye open for Harrison Matlin, the president of the club, was making his way from group to group through the throng in the library, when he suddenly heard his name called from behind and a hand came down on his shoulder.

"Looking for you, Rankin. You're wanted upstairs. Cortwell's room. There's the devil to pay."

It was John Waring, the travel lecturer. Rankin followed him through to the back rooms and up the rear staircase to the floor above. Half way down the long, wide hall they stopped in front of a door and Waring knocked lightly.

"It's Waring. I've got Rankin," he called, and an instant later there was the sound of a key turning in the lock and the door swung open.

As they entered and the door closed behind them again Rankin's quick glance showed him two or three men gathered about a table in the center of the room; others were seated on chairs and on the bed over against one side; Harry and Fred Adams were standing near an open window with their backs turned, talking together in low tones. Harrison Matlin, the president of the club, was there, and Bolton Cook and James Cortwell, and Fraser Mawson and Doctor Wortley. The eyes of all were turned on the door as the two newcomers entered.

"There's a problem here, Mr. Rankin," Matlin began, abruptly, "and we want to put it up to you. Doctor Wortley called us in to show us—you tell him, Wortley."

"Just this," explained the Doctor, "that the examination of the body, together with what I learn from Fred Adams of the nature of the attack—spasmodic rigidity, pronounced dyspnoea—verifies beyond all doubt that Colonel Phillips was poisoned."

Rankin frowned. "It's a certainty, then. What agent?"

"The motor nerves were paralyzed and death resulted from suffocation. Some virulent neurotic, most probably curare. *Strychnos toxifera*."

"Ah!" Rankin's frown deepened. "That must enter through a wound. How—"

"Look here," was the Doctor's answer to the unfinished question. The men about the table moved to one side, disclosing to view a lumpy, oblong form covered with a dark cloth; and Doctor Wortley, stepping forward, removed the covering from the body of Colonel Phillips. The clothing had been cut away, leaving it nude to the waist; and Rankin's gaze, directed by the Doctor, fell on a spot some three inches below the terminal of the breast bone. There was a tiny puncture of the skin, which was inflamed and slightly puffed, with a greenish tinge extending over a circular spot about the size of a silver half dollar.

"So that was the way," breathed Rankin at length, straightening up. "But what did it?"

"That's what we want you to find out," replied Matlin, keeping his eyes away from the table, where Doctor Wortley was readjusting the covering.

Rankin was silent.

"We don't want any scandal about it," the club president went on anxiously, "but we feel—of course, it wouldn't be right to try to hush the thing up, even if it were possible. It must be investigated, but the Lord knows we don't want the village police here. They're no good, anyway. We feel we can trust you to do as much as anyone could do, and there will be no publicity. Colonel Phillips would want it that way himself."

Still the detective was silent. Suddenly another voice came, and all eyes were directed at Fred Adams, the elder of the two brothers. He had turned from the window and was facing them with his countenance pale and grief-stricken.

"I only have this to say," he remarked, quietly and distinctly, "that I don't want publicity and scandal any more than the rest of you, but nothing shall be left undone to punish the man that murdered my uncle."

"I tell you, Fred, we don't know he was murdered," Harry Adams put in, and the sentiment found echo in two or three other voices:

"Yes, how do you know he was murdered?"

They were silenced by Rankin:

"Gentlemen, for my part, I agree with Fred. You have requested me to solve this thing. Very well. I'll do my best, but only on condition that it is left to my discretion to notify the authorities at any time. Meanwhile, everyone of you must keep absolute silence on this affair. There must be no hint of crime in your discussions with those outside. Already the atmosphere is electric all over the place. Dispel it. And now, you will kindly leave me here with Doctor Wortley. You, Mr. Mawson, and Fred and Harry, will remain also, if you please."

There were mutterings as the men began a general movement toward the door, and Harrison Matlin stepped up to whisper in the ear of the detective, who nodded impatiently in reply. Slowly they trooped out, with backward glances at the covered form on the table, and as the last of them disappeared into the hall Rankin stepped to the door and closed it. Then he turned to the four men who had remained behind at his request. Doctor Wortley stood with his hand resting on the table; Fraser Mawson had sunk into a chair, while the two Adams brothers still stood together near the window. The faces of all were lined with gravity.

"You've heard what Doctor Wortley has declared to be the cause of Colonel Phillips' death," began Rankin, abruptly, glancing from Mawson to the two young men. "A virulent neurotic poison, probably curare. Curare is an arrow poison, without serious effect when taken internally, but almost instantly fatal when introduced into the blood through a wound. It was used by South American Indians to infect the tips of arrows; tiny arrows shot from blowpipes. The abrasion of the skin on the Colonel's chest is final proof of the agent. The point is, how did it get there? It must have been done sometime within the ten minutes immediately preceding his collapse. Who did it, and how?"

Silence greeted the detective's pause. Mawson glanced at Doctor Wortley, then at the window; the two brothers had their eyes fixed on the detective. Nobody spoke.

"Did anything unusual happen during that time?" Rankin continued. "Was there anyone about except you four men and the caddies?"

There was a simultaneous "No" from the two young men, and Fraser Mawson shook his head in negation.

"No one," the latter declared. "Nothing unusual occurred,

absolutely nothing, until poor Carson suddenly cried out and fell to the ground. To me, Mr. Rankin, the whole thing is incomprehensible. There was absolutely no way it could have happened. And I can't believe—why, Carson Phillips hadn't an enemy in the world."

"Nevertheless, it did happen." The detective's tone was grim. "And I don't suppose you intend to suggest suicide, Mr. Mawson."

"Good heavens, no!" the lawyer protested. "I simply can't understand it."

"One of the caddies was a West Indian," Fred Adams put in suddenly.

Rankin sent him a quick glance. "Which one?"

"Mine. His name's Joe; that's all I know about him. Never had him before."

"M-m-." Rankin didn't seem particularly interested. "I'll talk to him. You can never tell. But as a matter of fact, I expect to find nothing here. The sooner we're away the better. Doctor, I'll ask you to go with us. An examination should be made of that wound. Telephone to Brockton for a conveyance for the body. It can follow."

The detective paused, then turned to Fred Adams:

"I'll spend the night with you at Greenlawn, if you don't mind. And Doctor Wortley—"

"Very well, sir. But I don't see how you expect to find out anything there." The young man was plainly surprised, as were the others.

"Perhaps I won't. We'll look around a bit, though. Will you do that telephoning, Doctor? It would be best to go down at the rear; no use running past all those curious eyes." He turned to the others. "You came over in the Colonel's car, I suppose. Run it out on the drive and wait for me there. I'll be only a minute or two."

Downstairs again, Rankin observed that the excitement was beginning to quiet down a little. Groups had broken up and scattered, and when he reached the piazza he saw several pairs and foursomes making their way to the first tee. On the lawn he found Harrison Matlin and surprised the club president by informing him of his decision to depart at once for Greenlawn, Colonel Phillips's country estate; then the two men proceeded together to the caddie-house. Joe, the West Indian mentioned by Fred Adams, proved to be one of those indolent, ignorant half breeds who seem to consider the process of breathing an unwarranted tax on human energy; he had been with the club now for more than two seasons, and the caddie-master declared him to be inoffensive and fairly competent. Rankin asked him a few guarded questions, then dismissed him with a shrug of the shoulders; clearly there was nothing to be suspected here.

He found the motor car on the drive near the gateway, with Fred Adams at the wheel and Harry seated beside him with a bag of golf clubs between his knees. To an observation of Rankin's as he climbed in the young man responded:

"They're not mine, sir. Uncle Carson's. I didn't want to leave them. . . ."

The detective seated himself in the tonneau beside Fraser Mawson, and the four men sat in silence, waiting for Doctor Wortley. He soon put in an appearance, with the information that conveyance would arrive from Brockton for the body in half an hour. Rankin merely nodded, sliding over on the cushions to make room for him.

"All ready, Fred."

The engine whirred and the automobile shot forward, with two hundred pairs of curious and sympathetic eyes gazing after it from the piazza and lawns.

Twenty minutes later they entered the gateway of Greenlawn, nestling in a wooded valley among the Jersey hills. Down a long avenue of lindens, with well-kept park on either side, the car rolled smoothly, then curved round a large sunken garden to bring up before the main entrance of the house. It was one of those summer castles that have been appearing throughout the east in ever increasing numbers in the past decade, low and rambling, of grey stone brought from Colorado, with extensive lawns and gardens dotted here and there with fountains, gravel walks in every direction, terraces descending at one side to a miniature lake and a broad driveway leading circuitously to a garage, constructed of the same material as the house, in the rear. Some comment had been excited among Colonel Phillips's friends when he bought the place a few years before, for what use can an old bachelor make of a castle? He had merely smiled good-humoredly at their sly insinuations and proceeded to make Greenlawn one of the show spots of the hills. An old man's whim, he said; and his nature was incapable of guile.

Together the five men left the car and ascended the granite steps of the wide shady portico. From the rear of the house a chauffeur appeared, advancing inquiringly, but Fred Adams dismissed him by a wave of the hand. At the door of the reception room they were met by Mrs. Graves, the housekeeper, and the five men glanced at one another: Here was an unpleasant duty.

"You tell them, Mr. Mawson," Fred pleaded; and the lawyer was left behind to call the servants together and announce the death of their master. The others went on to the library, where Harry Adams finally freed himself of the burden of the Colonel's golf bag, leaning it against a corner of the fireplace. They watched him in silence, with the thought in their eyes: He has played his last game.

"Now if you young men will be good enough to leave me alone with Doctor Wortley," said Rankin abruptly.

Harry turned and started to go without a word. Fred hesitated, and finally blurted out:

"I know you have charge of this thing, Mr. Rankin, but I must say that I don't see why you run away from it. What can be done here at Greenlawn? I know you're older and wiser than I am, and I don't want to criticize, but Harry and I feel we have a right to know—"

"You have," Rankin put in, stopping him with a gesture. "But as yet there's nothing to tell. I hold myself responsible. I am doing what I think best. But of course you're in authority here now, and if you think—"

"No, sir, it isn't that," the young man declared hastily. "I suppose I shouldn't have said anything. But you—you know how we feel."

"I do, my boy."

Fred turned and followed his brother out of the room, closing the door behind him.

The doctor and the detective, finding themselves alone, glanced at each other, and then away again. Rankin's eye happened to light on a large bronze clock above the mantel, and stayed there; the hands of the clock pointed to a quarter past two. Doctor Wortley walked to a window looking out on the garden and stood there a moment, then crossed to a chair near the table and sank down in it, his fingers moving nervously along the arm. Neither said a word.

"Of course, I know what you're thinking, Rankin," the Doctor finally observed, breaking into speech all at once. "I know why you thought there was nothing to be done over there. But—well—it seems preposterous. Fred? Harry? Mawson? Why, it's preposterous!"

The detective turned from his contemplation of the clock.

"If you know what I think you know more than I do," he said at last, slowly. "And you do as a matter of fact know more than I do. That's why I want to talk to you. But certain conclusions are inevitable. We know how the Colonel was killed. A tiny arrow or steel needle cannot be sent from any considerable distance. From the fifth tee to the spot where the Colonel fell there is no shrubbery anywhere, nothing that could have served as a hiding place for the murderer. That is certain. Then it is equally certain that the murderer was not hidden. He was there, and he was not hidden. The caddies are out of the question. They were the two Simpson boys, Jimmie Marks and Joe, the West Indian Fred spoke of. Absurd to suspect any of them. That leaves only the members of the foursome. First the Colonel himself. Suicide must be considered, though the circumstances render it highly improbable. You were his friend and physician for thirty years. You knew him more intimately than anyone else. Your opinion?"

"Carson Phillips did not kill himself," declared the doctor with conviction. "There was absolutely no reason—I knew every detail of his life—and besides, he wasn't the man to sneak out of a thing. No."

"Then the other three are left. The thought is repugnant to us. Admitted. Also, the hypothesis is difficult. It seems impossible that the thing could have been done without attracting notice. They all swear nothing unusual occurred. Can they be in league? I dismiss that as incredible. Then it was done, somehow, without attracting notice. How? And by whom? There motive enters. But the point is, how? If only I had been in that foursome! The blowpipe is out of the question as requiring extraordinary skill. There was some devilish trick somewhere.

"You know," said the doctor slowly, "it's my opinion you're on the wrong track, Rankin. I can't believe—"

"It's the only open track," the detective retorted. "No other way to turn. Disagreeable as it is, we must follow it. There's one other thing I haven't spoken of.—Hello! What's up?"

As he spoke the whirring of an engine had made itself heard, and now, through the window, an automobile, the one that had brought them to Greenlawn, was seen to turn about on the drive outside and head for the outer gate with a sudden leap forward. Fred Adams was at the wheel. An instant later Harry appeared on one of the gravel paths at the edge of the garden.

Doctor Wortley, who had joined Rankin near the window, threw it open to call to the young man:

"What's up, Harry? Where's Fred going?"

"Down to Morton's," came the reply. There was a touch of disapproval in the tone. "Said he'd be right back in case you asked for him."

The doctor had closed the window again before Rankin's query came:

"Morton's? Where's that?"

"Over west a few miles," replied the doctor. "There's a girl. Dora Morton. Rather odd he should run off there just now."

"I know you have charge of this thing, Mr. Rankin, but I must say
that I don't see why you run away from it."

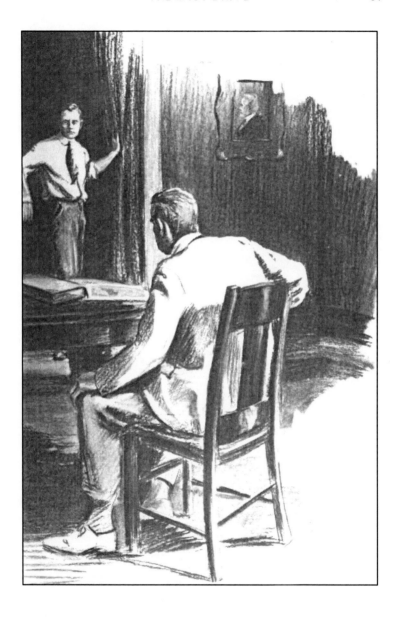

Something in the tone caused the other to pursue the inquiry. "Why?"

"Why—Carson didn't approve of her. There's been a quiet sort of row on about it for some time. She's a daughter of Morton the cheese man, and well—Carson's ideas were somewhat aristocratic, you know. I believe he even threatened to disinherit Fred if he didn't give her up."

"Ah, I see," said the detective softly.

CHAPTER III

But Doctor Wortley did not permit the insinuation in the detective's tone to go unchallenged.

"Good heavens, Rankin," he exclaimed, "you can't believe that Fred Adams would take his uncle's life for such a reason as that!"

"I don't believe anything," the other returned impatiently. "Right now it isn't a question of who did it or why, but how it was done. We don't even know that. But to put it in plain words, I am convinced that one of the four members of that foursome is responsible for the Colonel's death. It's the only possible solution."

As he spoke the sound of wheels was heard on the driveway outside. It was the conveyance that had been sent for to Brockton to carry the body of the Colonel to Greenlawn. Doctor Wortley went out to superintend the removal to the room that had been prepared upstairs, while Rankin went in search of Fraser Mawson.

He found the lawyer in a small room at the further end of the lower hall. This room was the place that Colonel Phillips had set aside for the transaction of business; it contained a desk and a safe and files filled with letters and documents of various kinds, all kept neatly and methodically after the Colonel's custom. As Rankin entered Mawson was in the act of taking a large book from a shelf in the safe, the door of which stood open.

"You seem to be acting on a thought that has occurred to me also," observed the detective, stopping beside the desk.

The lawyer looked up at him inquiringly.

"I was just looking to see if there is anything out of the way," he explained. "You know, I came down here from the city once a week to confer with Carson on his affairs. We were to have attended to it tonight; that was our custom."

Rankin, nodding, found a chair, while the lawyer placed the book on the desk beside another that was lying there open. The fact of his having been entrusted with the combination of the safe, containing private documents of every description, was evidence of the complete confidence in which the dead man had held his attorney and lifelong friend.

"He kept everything here, I suppose," observed Rankin presently.

The other nodded. "Everything. Except, of course, what was needed for any specific purpose, temporarily, in New York. Such were kept in my office."

Silence, while the lawyer compared entries in one of the open books before him with those in the other, occasionally writing something in the latter. From the other end of the hall, through the open door, came the sound of many slow and heavy footsteps, those of the men who were carrying into Greenlawn the body of its dead master. Rankin, craning his neck a little, could see their straining forms framed in the outer doorway, with Doctor Wortley in front directing them.

"One thing I'd like to ask, Mawson," resumed the detective after a moment. "Had the Colonel indicated an intention lately of making any change in his will?"

The question appeared to surprise the lawyer a little.

"None whatever," was the reply. "Why, do you know of any reason?"

"Nothing in particular," Rankin returned, "except that Doctor Wortley tells me that he had been having a difference of opinion with Fred concerning a certain young lady named Morton, I believe."

"Oh." The lawyer looked up from his writing. "Yes, there has been something said about it. Carson was much put out, and Fred was—well—obstinate. There were some pretty warm words, I believe—you know, Carson had a temper—but I don't think he ever seriously contemplated changing his will."

"But Fred might have thought so."

The lawyer frowned. "Of course. He might think anything. But it seems to me a pretty weak thread to hold a suspicion like that against a boy like Fred." A moment's pause, then he added, "If you want my opinion, Mr. Rankin, it appears to me you're pursuing a delusion. If I am a little diffident about speaking it is only because I see that I am included in your thoughts as well as the two boys. Of course, you may have reasons that I know nothing of—"

"I haven't," the other interrupted. "All that I know, you know."

"Then I don't see what you expect to find at Greenlawn, unless you look for something among Carson's private papers. They are all in this room, and I am willing to stretch a point and submit them to your inspection, but I can tell you beforehand that your search will be in vain. As for Harry and Fred, it seems to me absurd even to entertain the possibility of their guilt of so black a crime."

"Then just what is your opinion, Mr. Mawson?"

"One that I dislike to utter," returned the lawyer with some hesitation. "At least, part of it, and that the most likely. It is forced on me by circumstances. It seems to me that there are just two possibilities.

In the first place, I reflect that Colonel Phillips spent several years of his life in the Philippines and other parts of the Far East, and it isn't only in novels that the Orient is filled with strange enmities and mysterious crimes. Some act of Carson's, official or personal, some wrong, fancied or real, of many years ago, may have found its tragic sequel here on the Jersey golf links. Secondly, my long legal experience has taught me that any man's life is apt to contain a secret, a dark and shameful secret sometimes, that remains unsuspected even by his oldest and dearest friends, and that may drive him to any desperate deed, even the most desperate of all, to bury it."

"Then you admit the theory of suicide?"

"Merely because as a possibility it cannot rightfully be excluded. Before Fred and Harry I rejected it, not to wound their sensibilities; and to me also the thought of self-destruction in connection with Carson Phillips is—well—distasteful. But reason requires me to admit it. The point is, the motive."

"There is nothing here?" Rankin waved his hand about the room.

"Nothing. Everything is in the best possible condition, with the exception of one unfortunate financial deal, and that was hardly a serious inconvenience; it certainly was not vital enough to serve as the cause of tragedy. There is a lawsuit on with an estate in Connecticut; nothing serious."

"What was the financial deal? A speculation?"

"Yes. Against my advice. United Traffic. Of course, you know the circumstances; the bottom fell out of it two weeks ago. I just got rid of the last of it yesterday; you see what it amounted to."

The lawyer pointed to an entry in one of the books before him, on which the ink was scarcely dry:

2000	United Traffic	57	$114,000.00
1000	United Traffic	56	56,000.00
2000	United Traffic	52	104,000.00

"He bought around a hundred and twenty, so the loss amounted to something over three hundred thousand," Mawson explained. "But, of course, it was only a temporary inconvenience."

"Of course." Rankin agreed. "Mighty imprudent, though, for Carson Phillips—but financial difficulties are beside the question. There is nothing else?"

"No. The best way, perhaps, would be to look yourself, but I know every paper in the room, and there is nothing. That isn't to be wondered at. If there were anything in Carson's life that might have led—as it did lead—to this, he wouldn't have left evidence of it lying around where even I could see it. No, if my theory is correct, Mr. Rankin, the mystery of our friend's death isn't going to be easy to solve. For my part, I am not even convinced that it came from that little green spot that Wortley showed us. I'll have to have better proof than that little spot on his skin."

"The symptoms were conclusive."

"In a way. Second-hand. Wortley didn't get there till it was over."

"The examination of the organs will settle it."

"By Wortley?"

"Yes. He's at it now."

"Of course, that will settle it," agreed the lawyer. "I don't dispute the probable correctness of his diagnosis, but I wait for proof. Anyway, you have my theory. You understand my position in the matter. As the representative of the Colonel's heirs, I feel it my duty to defend them against what seems to me unjust suspicion. I thought it best to be entirely frank with you . . ."

"Then you think I am merely wasting my time here at Greenlawn?"

"I do. Not that I regard the time as particularly valuable. I doubt if any direct evidence will be discoverable anywhere. It is my opinion that if the mystery is solved it will be only after a most minute and thorough examination of the Colonel's life. I feel that the roots of this tragedy are buried somewhere deep in the past."

"I wouldn't be surprised if you're right, Mr. Mawson." The

detective got to his feet. "But as you say, in that case the present time is of no peculiar value, and I believe I'll use some of it snooping around here just to satisfy an idea I've got. You've no objection to my looking through the safe?"

For reply the lawyer handed him the bunch of keys to the several compartments. Rankin prosecuted his search in a leisurely and deliberate manner, still his eye was alert. Mawson turned to his books and resumed his writing.

The search revealed nothing. In these papers and books that the detective examined the simple straightforwardness of Carson Phillips's life was revealed logically and in order, like the lucid march of a geometrical proposition to its Q.E.D. The mistakes of his youth were chronicled in letters of thirty-five years ago by his father; the brilliancy of his early army career in medals and copies of dispatches; his one affair of the heart in a bundle of blue-tinted envelopes; the generosity and charity of his maturity in innumerable letters and receipts and documents of various kinds. Here, too, were copies of affidavits, since proven forgeries, on which a famous breach of promise suit had been based; Rankin knew of it, though it had been before his time. The only note of hardness was a reminder here and there of the sternness with which the Colonel had insisted on the same standard of strict loyalty in others as he imposed on himself. To him treachery and deceit had been the deadly, unforgivable sin; his detestation of these qualities had at times smothered his charity.

Rankin had about finished when a servant appeared at the door with a message that Doctor Wortley wished to see him in the library. He went at once, leaving Mawson still poring over the account books. In the hall he saw the two Adams boys at the foot of the great staircase; Fred had returned from the Mortons, then. They were talking in low tones with Mrs. Graves, the old housekeeper, whose eyes were red with weeping.

Doctor Wortley was alone in the library, standing by a window overlooking the garden. As he turned at the detective's entrance the latter saw at once by the expression of his face that he had made some new discovery. Immediately and hastily he came forward, holding out some small object in his hand.

"I've probed," he said, abruptly. "See what I found."

Rankin took the small object and examined it. It was a tiny steel needle, little more than an inch in length, with the blunt end filed off square; there was no eye. Rankin tried the sharpness of the point against his finger.

"Take care!" called the Doctor sharply, stopping him. "There may be poison left on it."

Dusk was coming on, and the detective moved nearer the light of the window. "So this is what did it," he breathed slowly. "A little thing like that to bring a man like Carson Phillips to the ground! You found it beneath that spot on the abdomen?"

The Doctor nodded. "Straight in, buried half an inch beneath the skin, but pointing a little upward toward the breast bone. It must have entered at that angle, for there was nothing to deflect its course. Its velocity was not very high, or a sharp pointed needle like that would have penetrated much deeper."

"You say it pointed *upwards*? Are you sure of that?"

"Absolutely. An angle of about twenty degrees from the horizontal."

The detective seated himself and thoughtfully turned the needle over and over in his hand. During a long silence his brow was wrinkled and his eyes half closed in speculation.

"It is incomprehensible that it should have been pointing upwards," he said at last, turning to the Doctor.

Admitting that it was difficult to understand, the other maintained that such was the fact. "To tell the truth," he added, "it takes a load from my mind. In spite of my conviction to the contrary, I have been forced to confess inwardly that it might have been suicide. This removes that possibility. That needle was shot from a gun of some kind—possibly a blow-gun—it must have been noiseless—"

"Undoubtedly. A report would have been heard. But that doesn't explain—" The detective got up from his chair. "See. You stand there. I here. Now how would it be possible, with any kind of a gun, for me to fire that needle at you so it would enter your breast pointing upwards?"

"If you were on the ground, and a little closer—" the Doctor suggested.

"But I'm not. Remember, concealment was out of the question. There was no place for it."

"It might have been deflected by something—a button on his shirt, for instance."

"A bullet, yes. But hardly a thin sharp needle like this. The deuce of it is, we can't know the exact moment it happened. It's evident that the Colonel didn't feel the thing at all when it struck him. You say it would take from five to fifteen minutes for the poison to work. Then it might have been anywhere from the fourth green to where he took his second on the fifth. What I can't understand is how it could possibly have been done without one of those men seeing it—or one of the other two, if one of the three is the murderer."

Again the detective thoughtfully turned the needle over in his fingers, as though he would extract the stubborn secret somehow from the slender piece of steel. There was a long silence. Doctor Wortley, wandering to the closed fireplace, found himself regarding the Colonel's golf bag, left standing there by Harry Adams on their arrival at Greenlawn. The Doctor took out the driver and passed his hand slowly up and down the shaft. "Poor old Carson, he's had his last drive," he breathed. At that moment the dinner bell rang.

At the table the subject of Fred's visit to the Mortons was brought into the conversation by a remark of Harry's and the elder of the two young men defended himself by explaining that he had had an engagement to play tennis with Dora Morton that afternoon, and had driven over merely to break it. Furthermore, he announced his intention of remaining away from her for a time, out of respect for

"You found it beneath that spot on the abdomen?"
The Doctor nodded.

his uncle's memory. Fraser Mawson and Doctor Wortley signified their approval of this. Nobody ate much, and the conversation was by fits and starts. Fred, grave and thoughtful, seemed a different person from the young man who had so gaily chaffed his two elders only that morning; Harry seemed to be irritable and nervous, to an extent that caused the old doctor to turn a solicitous eye on him. At the end, over the coffee, the Doctor announced that in accordance with the boys' request he had made the preliminary arrangements over the telephone for the funeral to be held on Monday morning; the services were to be military. The young men acquiesced with silent nods.

Afterwards—and it was quite dark when the meal was finished, for they had not sat down till late—Rankin and the Doctor went to the piazza with their cigars, while Mawson, observing that he wanted to have everything straightened out that night, returned to his books and papers in the little office at the end of the hall.

Half an hour later the detective, having left the Doctor below on the piazza, made his way upstairs to the room at the front of the house where the blinds had been closed since early in the afternoon. The door was shut. He turned the knob softly and entered; then, as he heard the sound of smothered sobbing from the further side of the room, where a dim light burned above the motionless form on the bed, he would have turned back. But already he had been seen: the young man who was kneeling there had lifted his tearstained face to gaze at the intruder. It was Fred Adams.

"I'm sorry," Rankin apologized. "I didn't know you were here."

"It's all right, sir. It doesn't matter." The young man barely managed to control his voice.

Rankin moved across to the bed and stood there looking down at the face to Colonel Phillips, set in death. The other remained on his knees beside him.

"I haven't prayed for ten years," said the young man presently, in a voice now almost calm. "And I can't now. I don't know what to pray for. I suppose you think I'm a baby, Mr. Rankin, but you don't know . . . Only yesterday I had a quarrel with him . . . I said things . . . I'd give anything in the world to have those words back. And he was so good. He let me have my way. It was about Dora—Miss Morton. He was going with me to see her tomorrow."

Rankin looked at him, and nodded. "Then it's no wonder you feel badly, my boy. Your uncle was a noble and good man. Tears for him are nothing to be ashamed of."

"No, sir. I know how good he was. He was father and mother to Harry and me. Better than we deserved. And we didn't—we treated him—"

The voice broke again, and silence followed. Rankin felt vaguely uncomfortable, and after a minute he turned and tiptoed silently out of the room.

He left the house by a side door and strolled into the garden. The night was cool, with a fresh breeze from the east, and the light of a full moon shed its silvery radiance everywhere. The fragrance of the blossoms, stirred by the breeze, filled the air; the soft music of the fountain came from the terraces at the other end. Rankin, lighting a cigar, wandered about the gravel paths for a time, and finally sat down on a bench in the dark shadow of a great spreading laca bush.

His thoughts were for the most part confused. Try as he might, he could fasten on no theory that would fit the circumstances of Colonel Phillips's mysterious death; he could not even evolve a satisfactory explanation of the manner in which the crime had been committed. For the twentieth time he pictured to himself the scene on the golf links that morning, trying to discover some possible combination of events that would answer to the known facts. He, himself, had seen the foursome drive off from the first tee. He went over again the answers of the Colonel's caddie to his questions. He tried to deduce the solution from what was known; he tried to arrive at it by elimination; he tried to visualize it. Without success. His brain whirled. Finally he rose to his feet with a sigh, pulling out his watch, and was surprised to see that it was past eleven o'clock. Probably the others had gone to bed, with the exception of Doctor Wortley, who was to sit up with the dead. He had been in the garden over two hours. A glance showed him that all the windows on that side were dark.

He turned toward the house, but before he had taken two steps he saw something that caused him to draw back hastily into the shadow of the laca bush. Someone was moving on the piazza, and this someone suddenly leaped over the rail onto the driveway and stood there in the moonlight glancing furtively about him in every direction. It was the furtiveness in that look that caused the detective to draw back.

Suddenly the man turned and moved swiftly down the driveway. Rankin thought it looked like one of the Adams boys. He waited till there was a hundred yards between them, then followed, being careful to keep on the soft turf at the edge of the drive. The man ahead moved so swiftly that he was forced to trot to keep up. Down the length of the driveway he was led, until finally the great entrance gate was reached; there the man turned to the right without hesitation and continued on down the road. A moment later Rankin emerged from the gateway and, seeking the shadow of the trees along the opposite side, followed warily. The man ahead kept to the center of the road, full in the moonlight, pounding along at a rapid walk.

They had gone perhaps two hundred yards from the gate when the detective, happening to glance back over his shoulder, saw the figure of still another man emerge from the entrance of Greenlawn and turn up the road toward him.

He, too, was being followed!

CHAPTER IV

As Rankin turned he saw the man in the rear dodge hastily into the shadow of a tree. With a mental shrug of the shoulders the detective turned again and strode on. His chief concern was with the man in front; if the other came along, so much the better.

In the bright moonlight the straight macadam road stretched ahead like a pale silver ribbon, embroidered at more or less regular intervals with the bunchy shadows of bordering trees; and so still was the nocturnal countryside that the footsteps of the man two hundred yards in front rang sharply out, staccato. Rankin, keeping to the turf at the edge of the macadam, followed noiselessly. An

automobile passed, honk-honking at the man in the road, its lamps
piercing the moonlight with two cones of yellow fire; and they had
gone perhaps a mile when a dog came out from a gate and ran bark-
ing after the pedestrian. Rankin crossed to the other side of the road
to escape the dog's observation, and got safely by.

At the crossings, a little further on, the man turned to the east.
This, Rankin knew, was the detour to Brockton, three miles away. He
kept straining his eyes ahead in an effort to guess the identity of the
man he was following, but all he could certainly discern was that the
youthfulness of his figure and gait made it probable that it was one of
the Adams boys, if anyone who belonged at Greenlawn.

A mile beyond the crossing a quick glance over the detective's shoulder showed him the man in the rear trudging doggedly along. Thus the queer procession wound its way along the country road. Now and then, even at that late hour, an automobile whizzed by in one direction or the other; in the tonneau of a big touring car Rankin fancied that he recognized Harrison Matlin, president of the Corona Country Club, which was not improbable. Finally lights shone ahead, and the houses began to come closer together; they were entering the village of Brockton.

Rankin quickened his step and drew a little closer to the man in front, who kept straight ahead as one who knew where he was going and wanted to get there. Reaching the main street of the town, he turned swiftly to the right and went on past a block of business buildings to the next corner, where stood an old three-story frame hotel, the only one in the place. It was past midnight now, and save for one or two stragglers the street was deserted, with the bright moonlight over everything, like sunshine strained through a silver cloth. In front of the hotel stood a racy-looking roadster. Rankin was on the heels of his man as he sprang up the steps of the hotel porch and entered the door; but there the detective stopped and tiptoed to a window a little distance to the right, through which he could observe the interior.

The man was indeed one of the Adams brothers: Harry, the younger. He advanced a few steps into the room, a typical country hotel office, with wooden chairs and a fly-specked cigar case, then stopped and turned at sound of a voice.

"Harry! Thank God!"

Rankin, too, heard the voice from his vantage-point outside the window. It came from a man who had been seated in one of the chairs by the windows at the front of the room, and who now sprang forward toward young Adams with an eager and anxious countenance. He was a young fellow about Harry's age, but of a very different mould. The quick, shifty eyes, the whitish cheeks, already too

He turned toward the house, but before he had taken two steps
he saw something that caused him to draw back hastily into the
shadow of the laca bush.

often shaven, the nervous oiliness of his manner even in his excitement, were all quite familiar features to one who had had opportunity to observe a certain type of young man who infests Wall Street.

"Have you got it?" came from his eager lips before the other had time to return his greeting.

Harry Adams shook his head.

"No, I haven't. I—"

"You haven't! But, man, you must have! You promised! Why, I came—my God! You promised, Harry!"

Young Adams took him by the arm. His voice was commanding:

"Don't shout so. I'll explain. I don't want to talk in here. It was risky your sitting in here where everybody could see you from the street. Come outside."

As they turned toward the door the detective retreated hastily from the window and dropped noiselessly over the porch railing onto the grass below. As he crouched there in the shadow he heard their feet descending the steps and saw their shadows on the lawn. The unknown's voice came:

"I've got my roadster. Shall we—"

"No," came Harry's reply. "We'll walk a little."

He continued in a lower tone, and Rankin, straining his ear, couldn't catch the words. The two young men turned down the sidewalk to the left. Rankin prepared to follow. As he straightened up he caught sight of a form disappearing in a doorway a little down the street. "Probably the man that followed us from Greenlawn," thought the detective. "Who the devil can he be and what is he up to? Well, we'll attend to him later."

The two young men continued on down the street, talking earnestly in low tones; their voices came, but not the words. Rankin stepped cautiously after them at a distance. If only he could hear what they were saying! He drew a little closer; the sidewalk here, flanked by trees, was in heavy shadow, which made it less risky; but though he got within thirty feet of them he could only catch a meaningless word now and then. Otherwise, the silence of the night was almost unbroken; the call of insects sounded occasionally, the hoot of an owl came from the woods toward the river, and the horn of a motor car tooted faintly somewhere far down the road. Subconsciously the detective noted the curious resemblance between the two latter sounds, as if one were answering to the other.

At length the two young men halted and, half turning, stood still talking. The detective crept closer. The nearest street lamp was a block away, and the moonlight tried in vain to penetrate the thick foliage of the trees. Rankin moved cautiously and silently from one protecting trunk to another; he was quite close now. One more advance—his foot bent a twig, but it was unheard—and he stood behind a tree so close that he could almost have put out his hand and touched the unknown, who was nearest him.

Harry's voice came, scarcely more than a whisper.

"I simply don't see how I can help you, Gil, but as I say, I'll try. You can see it's not my fault. It's a horrible mess, and that's all there is to it. I'll telephone you tomorrow morning, at Migg's at ten o'clock. You go back there and stay there, and whatever you do don't show your face anywhere, or you're a goner; they may be after you now. I've been thinking it over—"

The interruption came from the street. An automobile had come up from the other end of the village and through it with dimmed lights. Here it was approaching the country again, and the lights, turned on suddenly, blazed forth with startling brilliancy. Like two monstrous flaming eyes they glared down the road and, as the wheel turned a little, in among the trees flanking the sidewalk; and the form of Canby Rankin, behind one of the trees, was revealed as in the light of noonday.

Young Adams saw him, not ten feet away, stopped, and sprang forward.

"What the—who—why, it's Mr. Rankin!"

Feeling profoundly foolish, the detective stepped out. The

unknown, who had leapt away like a scared rabbit, halted and turned, holding himself in readiness for flight.

"Who's Mr. Rankin?" he demanded in a voice that rasped.

"Why—" Harry stammered "— he's a friend of Uncle Carson's— that is, he's a detective—"

"A detective—damn you, Adams!"

With the first word the unknown was off down the sidewalk at a bound. Rankin leaped after him. Harry called out:

"It's all right, Gil! Come back! He's not after you!"

The last was a rather absurd remark, since as it was uttered Rankin was quite obviously after Gil in the most literal sense of the word. Heedless of Harry's shouts, repeated from the rear, the unknown rushed madly down the street, his feet pounding on the brick side-walk as he leapt forward like a stampeded steer; and fifty feet behind was the detective, running low on his toes, almost silently. A window went up in a house as they passed, doubtless that of some sleeper awakened by Harry's shouts, and a call came through the night, unheeded. A block ahead shone the lights of the hotel; at sight of them the unknown bounded forward with fresh energy, increasing a little the distance from his pursuer. He made for the front of the building, where stood the racy-looking roadster; and Rankin, guess-ing his purpose, strained every muscle. Reaching the roadster, the unknown jumped to the seat; almost instantly came the buzz of the engine; a lever clicked; the car started, jerked, and started again. But too late. Rankin, leaping through the air, was beside him.

There was a short, sharp struggle over the levers, and the car jerked to a stop and stood still with the engine whirring madly. Yell-ing an oath, the unknown stooped and, rising again with a heavy wrench in his hand, swung it at the detective's head. Rankin par-ried the blow, catching his arm, but in doing so lost his balance and tumbled from the car to the ground, dragging the other with him. At that instant Harry came running up.

"It's all right, Gil—for God's sake, Mr. Rankin, let him go!"

But Rankin's blood was up now, and even if he had heard he would not have heeded. The murderous look in the other's eyes as he struck with the wrench had roused him to fury; and he loved a fight. He got one.

He had landed on his knees on the pavement, with Gil, pulled after, tumbling on his shoulders. The impact knocked Rankin prostrate, with the other on top, raining wild blows on his face and neck. With a mighty heave of his body the detective half unseated him, twisted about and caught his arms. Holding with a grip of steel, he worked to his knees, then one foot to the ground, then both. He was upright. With a desperate effort the unknown got an arm loose and swung, but Rankin sprang forward to clinch before the blow could land. Breathing heavily, grappling fiercely together, they swayed back and forth over the pavement; and with the superhuman strength of fear in him, Gil was holding his own. Harry Adams stood on the sidewalk, starting forward and then halting again, as if unable to decide which man to help; and all the time calling frantically to Gil that it was "all right," and to Rankin to let him go.

They lurched back and forth across the sidewalk, struggling silently; then suddenly Rankin's foot caught on the edge of the curb and he stumbled, loosening his hold. On the instant Gil jerked away, then hurled himself forward and bore the other to the ground, knocking the breath out of him; and then jumped to his feet and sprang for the car with a triumphant oath. Swiftly Rankin was back on his feet and after him, dragging him from his seat, though his head was dizzy and stunned from the impact of the pavement. Gil clung to the edge of the car; Rankin tugged at him, and when the hold was suddenly released they tumbled backwards together. Gil was up first; his eye caught something on the ground; a quick swoop, and he straightened and turned with the heavy iron wrench in his hand. "Now, damn you!" he screamed, and rushed forward.

Rankin dodged swiftly, and got a glancing blow on the shoulder. Again the wrench was raised, but the detective leaped forward and caught the arm before it could come down. There was a sharp pain in his shoulder, but he grappled and held on, jerking at the wrench with one hand, and finally got it loose and sent it spinning through the air. Then he drew back and swung his clenched fist at the others' jaw, unexpectedly and successfully. He felt his knuckles crunch on the flesh and bone, and the unknown went down like a log. Rankin sprang astride of him and sat on him; and then Harry Adams's agitated voice came:

"Let him go, Mr. Rankin—please let him go. He's done nothing—that is, not what you think. You must let him go, sir."

The detective merely grunted, pinning down his captive's arms.

"You must, Mr. Rankin—he meant no harm to you—"

"Of course not," panted the detective. "He just wanted to see how close he could come with that wrench without hitting me."

"You were after him."

"And I got him."

"You must let him go."

"Don't be a damned idiot, Harry. Of course I won't let him go."

The unknown stirred a little. The detective tightened his hold, resting for breath.

"But I say you must." Young Adams moved so that he stood directly over the two men on the pavement, and spoke rapidly. "Listen, Mr. Rankin. It's a question of my honor. Gil came down here to see me. It would be the same as if I'd betrayed him, when I'd promised to help him. You must let him go. It's a matter of honor."

"Your honor is your own lookout, my boy. As for me, I'm going to have a good long talk with your pleasant-mannered friend and find out why he's so free with his wrenches."

"Mr. Rankin, let him go."

Silence. The detective shifted his hold a little and, leaning over, saw the shifty eyes open, and simultaneously felt a reawakening of the muscles of the man beneath him; and then he felt something else: two strong hands gripping him from above.

"I'm sorry, sir—"

"Keep off, Harry!"

The detective sat harder. Gil's body twisted feebly about. Young Adams seemed to hesitate an instant, then he stooped swiftly and encircled Rankin with his arms. The detective struggled, but in vain; he was still all but exhausted, and the strength of the young athlete was too much for him. Inexorably he was dragged from his captive and across the sidewalk; he tried to twist about, but the arms held him in a grip of steel. The unknown, left free, stirred and turned, lifting himself to his knees; there he stopped for a moment, swaying as if dazed, then hastily scrambled to his feet. Young Adams was calling to him quietly:

"Get in the car, Gil, and beat it. Quick! Come on, pull yourself together! Beat it, I say! You might have known—I'll phone you in the morning. Lay low till you hear from me."

The unknown lost no time, nor wasted breath in speech. For a second he stood uncertainly in the attitude of a man who asks "Where am I?" then turned without a word and staggered to the roadster and pulled himself in. The engine was still running. A jerk of a lever, and the car leaped forward into the night.

Harry waited till the red light had completely disappeared in the darkness, then released his hold on the detective and stepped aside.

"I'm sorry, sir—"

Rankin made no reply. He was feeling gingerly about his shoulder for broken bones, and moving his arm cautiously up and down. It seemed to work all right. Now that the passion of battle was leaving him, he felt a little silly as he looked at the young man standing there quietly before him in the peaceful moonlight.

"Who the deuce is Gil?" he asked abruptly.

Then as Harry hesitated with his reply the detective looked at his watch, shook himself together and brushed the dust from his clothing.

"Nearly one o'clock," he observed. "No use standing here. Let's get back to Greenlawn. You can tell me about it on the way."

So it was as they trudged back along the moonlit country road, side by side, that Harry explained. Until they reached the border of the village he was silent, and when he began to speak his words came jerkily.

"I'll have to tell you about it, I suppose," he said slowly, "so you'll understand my position. Not that there's anything really wrong about it as far as I'm concerned, but I—well, I'm not very proud of it."

They walked on a moment in silence, then he continued:

"Gil—Gil Warner—was a classmate of mine at college. He did me a mighty good turn one night—in fact he saved my life and more, too. But that hasn't anything to do with the worst part of the business—that is, my worst part—the beginning.

"I never really liked Gil, but I was under a great obligation to him, so when he came to New York I saw more or less of him—got him invited places and so on. Finally, about four months ago, he started after me to go in on a stock speculation with him. At first I wouldn't listen, but he talked it up and it really sounded good. He wanted me to interest Uncle Carson in it, and at length I consented; but I didn't have much success. Uncle looked into it a little and turned it down cold; said it wasn't worth a cent."

"Did the Colonel meet Warner?" the detective put in.

"No. I didn't mention Gil's name. Then Gil got after me to go in on my own hook. You know, I have—*had*—about a hundred thousand left me by father, in good securities. I refused twenty times, but he kept after me, and at last I gave in. That's where I was a blanked ass. But it really looked good to me. I went to Mr. Mawson—"

"What did you go to Mawson for?"

"He handled things for me. He has since father's death. I told him all about it, and he agreed to help me realize on the securities without telling uncle. I got it and put it all in United Traffic. We—"

"In what?"

"United Traffic. What's the matter? Oh, you've heard how it blew up, of course. I said I was a blanked ass."

The detective had stopped short with an expression of surprise on his face. Now he whistled a little, as the surprise deepened into perplexity.

"Yes, I've heard how it blew up," he replied as he moved on again. "But it wasn't that. It was—nothing. Go on."

"That's all. It blew up. The bottom fell out. And then Gil came to me and said he had embezzled a big sum from the brokers he works for and sunk it in United Traffic. He was frantic. This was only day before yesterday. As I said, I was under a great obligation to him. I promised to see uncle and try to get a loan to help him out. I meant to do it tonight—and this afternoon—and uncle's dead. I had an appointment to see Gil at Brockton. He's—you saw what condition he's in. They're onto him and he's laying low. I don't know what to do—I'm all broken up about Uncle Carson and I can't think anyway. I thought maybe I'd see Mr. Mawson in the morning."

The young man finished and the detective began to ply him with questions. All of them he answered readily and consistently. About them was the soft silence of the countryside, broken only by their voices and the rhythmic pat of their feet on the macadam as they swung along side by side; the moon was dropping to the horizon now, and there was a new ghostliness in the long narrow shadows of the trees as they stretched into the fields and moved their lazy fingers to and fro over the quiet grass. The two men became silent, walking more swiftly; an abrupt question now and then, and its answer, was all that was heard for half an hour.

"The best thing you can do is to drop this Gil Warner entirely," Rankin observed as they came within sight of the gate of Greenlawn. "Obligation is one thing and common sense is another. He's a crook anyway, and the more you do the more you'll have to do. You say you think he's not been in this neighborhood before. I'll find out about that. He may know—"

The detective stopped short.

"By Jove, I'd forgotten!" he exclaimed after a moment.

Harry turned inquiring eyes on him.

"There was a man following me," Rankin explained. "He came out of the Greenlawn gate and followed us all the way to Brockton. I saw him there in a doorway. In the excitement I forgot all about it."

"He came out of Greenlawn?"

"Yes. Not far behind me. He followed all the way." Half involuntarily the detective wheeled and looked back down the road. The next instant he grasped Harry by the arm.

"There he is now!" he cried.

CHAPTER V

Harry turned and gazed back down the road.

"Where? I don't see anyone."

"No. Not now. He jumped into the shadow—that clump of trees on the right."

"But who can it be?"

"I don't know." The detective stood peering intently toward the clump of trees two hundred yards away. "It looks as though you'd got mixed up in a dirtier piece of business than you bargained for."

"What—you don't mean Uncle—"

Rankin interrupted him:

"Ah, there he is!"

With the words the detective was off toward the trees with a bound, and without an instant's hesitation Harry was at his heels. Back down the road they raced at the top of their speed; and when they had traversed half the distance, in the dim glow of the waning moonlight they saw a figure dart suddenly out of the shadow across the road, scramble over the fence and start at a dead run across the fields like a startled rabbit. Rankin swerved aside, squeezed between the wires almost without halting and took after him. Harry, not far behind, was calling as he ran:

"Cut across! He's making for the woods!"

Rankin had already seen and was straining every muscle to intercept the maneuver, but Harry, with his youthful athletic stride, soon passed him. The man ahead bounded frantically across the furrows without looking back; his goal was evidently the fringe of woods bordering the river some five hundred yards from the road, and the advantage was his, as the two converged at a point half a mile down. Rankin, seeing himself outdistanced by Harry anyway, took it easier, as his injured shoulder was causing him considerable pain; then, seeing their quarry finally reach the edge of the woods and disappear, he pushed forward again. When at length he reached the spot he could see nothing, for the waning moonlight stopped at the barrier of the thick foliage and left all in darkness. Young Adams, too, had disappeared.

From the woods, some distance within, came the sound of rushing footsteps and rustling branches, and the detective pushed forward in that direction, calling meanwhile:

"Harry! Harry! Where are you?"

An answering shout came:

"Here! This way!"

Rankin went on, stumbling over hollows and fallen trees and scratching his face and hands on the low-hanging branches. The sounds ahead of him grew fainter, then suddenly swerved to the left and seemed to be approaching. Here in the midst of the woods the night was black, though now and then, through the interstices of the leaves, could be seen the faint shimmer of the last rays of the moon on the surface of the nearby river.

"Where are you, Rankin?"

The detective answered and thrust his way blindly toward the voice. The sounds of commotion had ceased. Two minutes later he came suddenly upon Harry at the edge of a small clearing.

"Is it you, Harry? Have you lost him?"

The young man nodded. "Keep still a minute."

They stood there motionless, listening, enveloped in darkness and silence. The woods were still as the tomb; there was not so much as the sound of a rustling leaf; from a distance there came faintly on the air the murmur of the river in the shallows half a mile below.

"He got through the thicket to the bank," said Harry at length, "and started downstream. Then he dived into the underbrush again and I couldn't tell which way he went. I thought I heard him again, but it was you. He's lying low not far from us right now."

They listened another while, but no sound came.

"No use; he's given us the slip," the detective finally observed.

They turned reluctantly and made their way back through the woods. A match showed Rankin the face of his watch; twenty-five minutes past two. When they got to the open they found that in the short interval of their search the moon had dropped below the edge of the hills to the east, leaving the sky light and the earth dark. Tramping across the stubble, they crossed over the fence into the road, and five minutes later were at Greenlawn.

"You're sure the fellow came out of here?" Harry was asking as they turned in at the gate.

Rankin replied that he was.

"That's funny. I thought it might have been Fred, but of course he wouldn't have run. I can't understand it."

A dim light could be seen in one of the upper windows of the house, in the room where Dr. Wortley was keeping his lonely vigil with the earthly remains of the dead Colonel.

All within the house was quiet. Rankin and Harry mounted the stairs together, without speaking; after the excitement of the past four hours the gloom of the house of death had dropped its heavy mantle over them at the threshold. At the first landing they parted, Harry to mount another flight and the detective to continue down the hall to his own room at the further end.

There he halted with a sudden appearance of alertness. He heard Harry's footsteps traversing the hall above, and the soft opening and closing of a door. Then, instead of entering his room, the detective stepped noiselessly back down the hall and stopped before a door near the stair landing. He stood there listening intently for a full minute, then all at once raised his hand and rapped softly on the panel. When a second knock brought no response he noiselessly turned the knob and entered.

He stood there listening intently for a full minute, then all at once raised his hand and rapped softly on the panel.

The room was pitch dark. Rankin stood motionless just inside the door, without having closed it, straining his ear. When the utter silence had convinced him that the room was unoccupied he moved to the electric switch and turned on the light. One quick glance at the bed showed him that it had not been slept in, and with a gleam of satisfaction in his eyes he turned the light off again and left the room.

He stood hesitating for a moment at the top of the stairs, then turned down the hall to the door of his own room, and entered. The first thing he did after turning on the electricity was to take off his coat and shirt and have a look at the injured shoulder. An examination convinced him that it was nothing worse than a painful bruise. His movements were slow and mechanical, like a man lost in thought; and at length, with his hand stilt moving slowly back and forth over the bruised shoulder, he stood and stared fixedly at nothing with wrinkled brow.

Finally he pulled himself up. "Yes," he muttered to himself, "but how the devil did he do it?"

Then, instead of undressing for bed—though it was nearly three in the morning and he had had no sleep—he turned with sudden decision and put his shirt back on, and his coat. A snap of the switch, and the room was in darkness. Placing a chair just inside the threshold (he had left the door open), he sat down to wait.

At the end of a minute or two he fancied he heard a sound in the hall, but peering cautiously out toward the dim night light at the other end, saw nothing. He settled back in his chair. It was upholstered in leather and very comfortable; after all the exertion and excitement of the preceding four hours his muscles found it restful and soothing. He twisted around to an easier position and stretched his feet out till they rested on the jamb of the threshold. He yawned. The sharp pain in his shoulder subsided a little and became a dull ache, throbbing rhythmically and not all unpleasantly. There seemed to be something restful even in that throbbing. He allowed his head to fall back against the soft leather and stay there. A dozen times he closed his eyes and opened them again . . . and closed them . . .

The next thing he knew he heard himself snoring.

He came to with a jerk and a snort, and got to his feet, telling himself that he had dozed off a second and that he mustn't do it again. Perhaps he'd better look at his watch . . . it was twenty minutes to four! He had slept nearly an hour.

Cursing himself inwardly, he pushed the chair out of the way and entered the hall. Not a sound was to be heard—but yes, a faint, almost indistinguishable murmur of voices came from somewhere at the front of the house. Rankin stepped softly down the hall to the stairs; the murmur became louder, though still faint, drifting up the corridor leading to the right wing. Down it he went, less cautiously now, until he reached an open door through which a dim light shone from the interior. It was the same room in which he had found Fred Adams, early the previous evening, kneeling beside the body of his dead uncle and guardian. Rankin entered. By the light of the candles at the other end he saw the silent figure shrouded in white stretched out on the bed; and nearby, seated in easy chairs drawn side by side, and conversing in low tones, were Dr. Wortley and Fraser Mawson.

They looked up and nodded as the detective entered.

"Up so early?" the little doctor wanted to know with an air of relief at sight of him. To those who watch with the dead anything is a relief.

Rankin nodded and sat down.

"Couldn't sleep. Soon be morning now." He turned to Mawson. "You been up long?" His tone was that of one who makes conversation.

The lawyer had taken out his eyeglasses and was rubbing them with the corner of a handkerchief as he replied that he had been unable to sleep. "So I thought I might as well come in and keep the Doctor company," he continued. "Though when I got here—it was three hours or more ago—a little after midnight—I found him dozing very well alone."

"To tell the truth, I had dozed off," Dr. Wortley put in somewhat shamefacedly.

"It was inexcusable. But it's been a strenuous day, and I'm not as young as I used to be. I suppose I should have allowed Fred to divide the night with me—he wanted to—but the boy was completely worn out, and anyway I felt I owed it to Carson ... And I went off like a log. When I woke up half an hour ago Mawson was sitting there."

As the Doctor spoke Rankin was regarding Mawson from a corner of his eye. The disarranged hair, the soiled collar, the general air of untidiness about his attire, all these were natural enough in a man who had been up all night in a house of bereavement; but what was the explanation of those two long scratches, one on his forehead, the other on his cheek, from which the blood had been carefully wiped away? Such scratches as might come, for instance, from low-hanging branches when making your way hastily through the woods at night.

For a while the three men conversed together, turning naturally to the virtues of their departed friend whose still form lay there beside them. The windows became grey squares as the dawn arrived, and when the light began to dim the rays of the candles the Doctor arose and pulled down the shades. At length Rankin left them and returned down the corridors to his own room; from below came the faint stirrings of the waking household.

"Yes, but how the devil did he do it?" muttered the detective once more as he took off his coat and shoes and got into a dressing-gown. Then he stretched himself out on the bed and slept.

When he awoke it was broad day. Going to the window and letting up the shade to look at the sun, he saw that the morning was half gone. In the rear of the grounds near the garage a man was playing a hose on an automobile; nearer, in the driveway, a dismal black conveyance proclaimed the presence of the undertaker. The blossoms of the garden were smiling in the sunshine, all unconscious of anything but beauty and virtue and happiness in the world they adorned. The detective turned away, his mind attacking freshly the problem of the day before as he began to dress.

Downstairs he found Fraser Mawson and Fred Adams and Dr.

Wortley still at the breakfast table. Over the steaming coffee they discussed the details of the military ceremony to take place on the morrow; an officer from Governor's Island was expected sometime during the day to confer with them. Mawson entered into the discussion with a naturalness and freedom that caused Rankin to wonder a little. Could he be mistaken? Had the lawyer really been sitting in that room upstairs during the chase in the woods the night before? If only he had gone there at once on his return to Greenlawn!

After breakfast the detective went in search of Harry Adams, and at length found him seated on a bench in the gun room with a bag of golf clubs at his side and an assortment of emory paper, cloths and oil; he was industriously polishing a midiron. The detective's surprise at finding him thus occupied must have been apparent on his face, for the young man explained:

"They're Uncle Carson's, sir. I wanted—I just thought I'd polish 'em up a little. Don't you remember how he always said a good soldier could shoot better with a clean gun? He used to keep after Fred and me because our irons were always rusty."

The detective nodded and stood watching the gritty paper slide to and fro over the shining metal. But he had sought out the young man for a purpose, and presently broached it. Harry was surprised at first, and then, as he caught the other's meaning, incredulous. Readily he agreed to follow instructions.

A little later, accordingly, the two men went in search of Fraser Mawson. They found the lawyer in the room at the rear of the lower hall that had served as Colonel Phillips's office, arranging some papers, spread over the desk in confusion. It was with an expression of amiable inquiry that he turned to them and waved his hand toward chairs near the window.

Harry began abruptly:

"Mr. Mawson, I've come to see you about that United Traffic."

The lawyer sent him a quick glance.

"What about it? I thought that unfortunate affair was settled."

"It is as far as I'm concerned, sir. As far as I'm directly concerned. But you remember I told you about a chap named Warner that got me in on it in the first place."

"Well?"

"Well, he's in trouble. He got in too far and in trying to get out again he used some money that wasn't his. Then the whole thing collapsed, and he's up against it. They're onto him."

"What has that got to do with you?"

The young man explained, telling of the obligation he had been placed under to Gil Warner at college. He recited the circumstances in detail, while Mawson sat regarding him impassively and the detective gazed absently at nothing.

"I've got to do it, that's all," Harry finished. "Of course if I help him out of this scrape I'm through with him, for I see now he's nothing but a crook, but I was mixed up with him in this United Traffic thing, and it's up to me to stick—not of course that I knew anything about his using money not his own."

"What do you want me to do?"

"Why, sir, I thought you might advance me enough cash to fix the thing. It would take a little over fifty thousand."

The lawyer was silent, frowning. He turned his keen eyes first on Harry, then on Rankin, and finally let them rest on the papers before him. With the fingers of his hand lying on the desk he was lifting a lead pencil an inch or so and letting it fall again with a series of sharp clicks.

Suddenly he demanded:

"What has Mr. Rankin got to do with all this?"

Harry replied imperturbably that he had gone to the detective for counsel and had been advised to make an appeal to Mawson for the necessary funds. Another silence, shorter than before, and the lawyer turned eyes that had suddenly grown hard on the young man, and said abruptly:

"Either Rankin is extremely clever or you're an awful fool, Harry. It doesn't matter which, since the result is the same. I had feared this—the fact, not the discovery of it—and yet it stuns me."

The young man looked at him in puzzlement. "What do you mean, Mr. Mawson?"

The lawyer shook his head. "It's useless, my boy. I can't understand why you ever—did you think Rankin was so blind he wouldn't see the coincidence between your urgent need for a large sum of money and the—the means of getting it?"

"What—you don't mean—"

"I mean that if you attempted to leave this house now, or even this room, Mr. Rankin would probably insist politely but firmly on accompanying you. I don't blame him. That's his business. You have asked me to advance you fifty thousand dollars. That's my business. Inasmuch as your uncle is dead, and as one of his heirs you are worth more than fifty times that amount, I can easily do so. I can get the money for you tomorrow morning in New York."

Harry had risen to his feet and then sank back again into his chair as one stupefied.

"What—" he stammered, speechless at the horror of the thought, "you can't mean to accuse me—my uncle—"

"I don't need to. You accuse yourself."

"But I—why—"

Another voice interposed, the voice of the detective. With a gesture of command he motioned Harry to be silent, then turned his eyes on the lawyer authoritatively. They were the first words he had uttered since entering the room:

"Mr. Mawson, let's understand just what you are driving at. Do you accuse Harry here of murdering Colonel Phillips?"

The lawyer's answering gaze was steady.

"I didn't say that," he replied calmly.

"Do you accuse him of being implicated?"

Mawson swung around in his chair.

"I'll answer your question with another, Mr. Rankin. Do *you* accuse him of being implicated?"

"I'll waive the precedence. I do not."

"Then I don't either," replied the lawyer abruptly, and swung back to his papers as if the subject were closed.

"But I think I know who is implicated," the detective went on, and stopped. Mawson kept his eyes on his papers, and Rankin resumed:

"This whole United Traffic deal looks suspicious, though I believe Harry to be innocent. It's United Traffic we came to talk about. First, to relieve Harry's mind, you will advance that fifty thousand dollars?"

"I've said I would," replied the lawyer without looking up.

"That's all right then. Now, Harry says he came to you for assistance in realizing on his securities for that speculation, and that you helped him. That's right, isn't it?"

Mawson shoved his papers aside and raised his head to meet the detective's eyes. There was a second's pause.

"That's right," he said finally.

"Good. Harry also told me that he had previously gone to his uncle for assistance, and that Colonel Phillips had firmly refused to have anything whatever to do with United Traffic. Also, he advised his nephew to follow his example. That's right, isn't it, Harry?"

The young man nodded. "Yes, sir."

"Harry also told me that when he came to you for assistance he informed you of his uncle's position in the matter and asked you to keep the transaction a secret. He did so inform you?"

"I don't remember."

"Well, it's unimportant anyway. Here's what I can't understand. If the Colonel was so firmly convinced that United Traffic was a worthless speculation, why did he invest over half a million in it himself?"

A murmur of surprise came from Harry. Mawson's eyes flashed into those of the questioner with a gleam of something that may have been anger. He made an evident effort to control himself, and succeeded.

"I'm sure I don't know," he replied calmly.

"You told me yesterday that he lost about three hundred thousand dollars," pursued the detective. "You showed me the entry in one of those books recording the loss. Was that entry made by Colonel Phillips himself?"

"It was not." Again the lawyer's eyes flashed, and again he visibly restrained himself. "All the entries in those books for the past twenty years, with very few exceptions, were made by me. This one also."

"I see. Now, Mr. Mawson, I'd like you to tell me one thing. When was that entry made?"

This time the restraint failed. Mawson rose swiftly to his feet, pushing back his chair so violently that it teetered and nearly upset. His face was pale and his eyes flashed fire, but there was nothing exactly threatening in his attitude to account for the suddenness with which the detective also got to his feet and advanced to the desk, just across from Mawson. The eyes of the two men met, and it was like the crossing of steel blades. They stood, silently . . .

At that instant the telephone bell rang.

CHAPTER VI

Conclusion

Mawson and Rankin both started a little at the jingling of the bell, but it was Harry, who stepped to the instrument and picked up the receiver.

"Hello. Yes. This is Harry Adams speaking."

During the time that Harry talked into the telephone the two men remained silently facing each other from opposite sides of the desk. Harry's part of the conversation consisted mainly of monosyllables and ejaculations. Finally, he asked the other end of the wire to "wait a minute," and placing his hand over the transmitter turned to Rankin with a worried countenance and an air of excitement:

"It's Gil Warner. They've got him—this morning, on Broadway. He wants me to go bail for him."

"Nothing doing," the detective replied, with instant decision. "No use. Nothing can save him now. Drop it. You're done. Tell him so."

The young man hesitated a moment, then turned again to the instrument and followed the other's advice. This evidently provoked an explosion at the other end, but Harry remained firm, and at length banged the receiver on the hook with a gesture of finality. The look on his face as he turned away showed plainly how little he had relished it. He was ·still young. He started to return to his chair near the window, but Rankin's voice interposed:

"Good riddance. You've done all you could for him. Now, if you'll leave Mr. Mawson and me alone a few minutes—"

"Certainly, sir."

"And say nothing to anyone of what has passed in here—"

"Certainly, sir."

The eyes of the two men met, and it was like the crossing of steel blades.

No one spoke as the young man passed out of the room and closed the door behind him, and for a long moment after he had gone the two men stood regarding each other silently. At length the detective turned, pulled a chair up to the side of the desk and calmly seated himself. When he spoke his tone was easy and amiable.

"To go back to where we were interrupted, Mr. Mawson, would you mind telling me when that entry was made?"

The lawyer, too, had reseated himself, and seemed to have entirely recovered his composure. He sat for a moment as if calmly meditating his answer, then moved his eyes to meet the other's gaze with a look that would have been a challenge if it had been less quiet and unconcerned.

"You remember, Mr. Rankin, that I showed you that entry yesterday morning?"

The detective nodded.

"Well, I had just finished blotting it. The entry was made not five minutes before you entered the room."

Again Rankin nodded, and for an instant his eye gleamed. He was silent a moment before he replied.

"You seem pretty sure of yourself, Mawson?"

"Sure of myself? I'm afraid that remark is too cryptic for me. You asked when that entry was made. I told you."

"Perhaps you will also be good enough to tell me," replied the other, abruptly, "just when that poisoned needle entered Colonel Phillips's stomach."

There was a quick movement of Fraser Mawson's hand and a sudden flash of his eye—then suddenly he was calm again. He replied quietly:

"But I thought that was what you were trying to discover."

"It is."

"Discover it, then."

"I intend to. I ask you."

"And I regret my ignorance."

These words passed back and forth with the speed and crack of rifle shots, and left the two men leaning forward in their chairs a little toward each other, their eyes meeting like those of two boxers in a prize ring. Those of Mawson were confident, with a little excitement behind the confidence. The detective's gaze was steady and determined. There was a short silence.

"You're pretty sure of yourself, Mr. Mawson," repeated Rankin, at length, slowly. "When I do discover it I am certain you will be much interested."

"I will," agreed the lawyer. He suddenly pushed his chair back a little and threw one leg over the other in an easy position. "I suppose I know what you mean when you say I'm sure of myself," he continued, amiably. "The legal mind is accustomed to piercing obscurity. But for once I feel that I would enjoy plain words. It rather amuses me to hear myself say that I am accused of being a murderer. I take it that's your meaning?"

Rankin frowned a little. "I haven't said so."

"But it is?"

The frown deepened, and there was a pause. "It is," said the detective, abruptly.

The lawyer's mouth twisted into a grimace. "That's pretty good," he said slowly. "And frank. I must say, Mr. Rankin, you shift your attack in a manner that leaves me breathless. First, it was Fred—because he wanted to get married. Then Harry, because he made a foolish speculation. And now me. I suppose poor old Wortley will be next—but, of course, he wasn't there."

"What makes you think I suspected Harry?" asked the detective, quickly.

"Why—" The lawyer's eyes shifted, and he hesitated. "You had evidently been questioning him—"

"And I followed him last night?"

"I don't know. Did you?"

"I did." Rankin stopped, opened his mouth to continue, then closed it again. "And you know I did," he went on at length. "You see, Mr. Mawson, I do intend to be frank. For a moment yesterday I did suspect Fred, but I was groping in the dark, then, and grasping at straws. Last night, when I saw Harry leave the house in a furtive and suspicious manner, I followed him to Brockville. There he unwittingly led me onto another false trail—this man Gil Warner. Warner is a crook, but evidently he isn't a murderer. And Harry is neither. I say I intend to be frank. Can you explain these two facts: First, why did you follow me to Brockville last night, and second, why did Colonel Phillips sink half a million in United Traffic, after warning his nephew to keep out of it?"

The lawyer's eyes were on a paper weight on his desk as he turned it over and back again with long, white fingers that seemed somehow, without actually trembling, to lack a little in steadiness. At length he looked up.

"What makes you think I followed you to Brockville last night?"

"I don't think you did. I know it."

"Well, you're mistaken. I followed Harry. The fact that you were between us was not of my choosing. The boy is my client, my ward in a way now—and I knew he was mixed up with this Warner."

"And your excursion into the woods?"

The lawyer frowned. "You know, I don't relish this questioning, Mr. Rankin. I submit to it as a matter of courtesy, though you stretch the bounds yourself. Naturally I didn't want the boy to know I was trailing him about the country at night."

"So you ran and hid in the woods."

"I—yes, I ran and hid in the woods."

Was Rankin's shifting movement one of surprise at this admission? His face remained expressionless. Through the open window came a faint rustling sound, rapid and rhythmical—it was Harry returned to his task of polishing his dead uncle's golf clubs.

"And the deal in United Traffic?" asked the detective.

Mawson frowned a little. "It seems to me," he observed slowly, "that you forget you are asking a lawyer for confidential information of his client."

"I am," the other agreed. "You may withhold it if you choose."

"And not only that, but you are asking for information I do not happen to possess. My client instructed me to invest a certain amount in a certain stock, and I obeyed."

"Have you the order—or a check or draft to cover it?"

At that the lawyer rose to his feet with a violent push of his chair. "Mr. Rankin, you are going too far," he exclaimed angrily. "I have borne your insinuations—"

"You may refuse to answer whenever you choose," was the tranquil reply.

"There is only one answer to an insult!"

"Then you do refuse?"

Their eyes met, and all at once Fraser Mawson was calm again. He resumed his seat. There was a new air about him as he did so—an air of resolve that seemed to have in it something of bravado; and it was reflected in his voice as he spoke:

"No. To both questions. You do not understand the nature of the relations between Colonel Phillips and myself. It has been ten years and more since he gave me any kind of an order in writing; that statement may be verified in a hundred ways. I had his power of attorney, and I myself drew all checks against his account in the National Park Bank—his personal account, of course, was separate. I handled all his business, speculations, investments, everything— directly, subject of course to his advice and instructions, which were always verbal. The United Traffic deal was handled the same as many others; he simply instructed me to take on a certain amount of that stock, and I did so; and when he finally told me to unload—I obeyed. That was last Wednesday. The loss was the figure I showed you yesterday in this book."

The lawyer laid his hand on a loose-leaf volume, bound in leather and canvas, on the desk.

There was a moment's silence.

"I see," observed Rankin at length, slowly. "Carson trusted you implicitly, then."

"He did."

"And he has paid for it."

There was no resentment, almost no feeling, in the smile with which the lawyer met this remark. And there was even a touch of indifferent condescension in his tone when he spoke after a moment:

"If you choose to think he has paid for it, Mr. Rankin, I shan't argue about it. I am even willing to help you get the case a little clearer."

He stopped, cleared his throat, and went on:

"What you are trying to do is to discover the murderer of Carson Phillips and bring him to justice. Very well. It is a difficult task. I know you have been successful in a few minor cases which interested you, but to speak frankly, Mr. Rankin, I'm afraid you're in a little beyond your depth here. To get to the bottom of this will require something more than a curious dilettantism.

"Why do I say that? Look at the facts. Neither Fred nor Harry, according to your own statement, is to be considered. I will say in parenthesis that I agree with you. Leaving myself also out of it for the moment, you then have eliminated everyone who was present at the scene—and you are lost. The mystery is buried in a darkness which I think you would find impenetrable. Quite naturally you turn from that darkness to what you consider a ray of light. You suspect me."

The lawyer paused to recover a sheet of paper that was being blown across the desk by the breeze from the open window, through which still came the sound of emory paper on steel as Harry Adams rubbed away at the golf clubs.

"Well?" said Rankin dryly.

"You suspect me," the lawyer repeated. "But it seems to me your ray of light is obviously deceptive. Granting as a postulate that your suspicion is just, that I am in fact guilty, what then? As a motive you accuse me of embezzling half a million dollars. But granting that I did so, you can't possibly prove it. What I have just said of the manner in which the Colonel and I transacted business has shown you that. There would be one hope left—if you could connect me with the actual deed. But you don't even know how it was committed; all you know is that a poisoned needle was found in the Colonel's abdomen; you have no idea how it got there, and no likelihood of finding out."

The lawyer stopped abruptly, deliberately seeking the other's eye. "And so," he finished calmly, "admitting—which of course I do not admit—that I am the criminal, how the devil are you going to prove it?"

The detective returned his gaze without replying.

"By Jove, Mawson," he said at length, "you've more nerve than I gave you credit for." Suddenly his lips came together. "It won't save you," he added grimly and rose to his feet.

"Nerve? Merely logic."

"Nor will logic save you."

"I am not aware of being in danger."

"We shall see."

With that Rankin turned abruptly and left the room.

The question remained as before: "How the devil did he do it?"

Rankin pounded his brain with it for two hours.

Returning to the house, he encountered Harry Adams in the hall with a bag of golf clubs under his arm. The detective wanted to know where Fred was, and was answered by a voice from above on the stairway.

"Here, sir. Did you want me?"

"Yes. You two come with me to the library a moment."

When they were inside, with the door closed, Rankin asked them to recount once more the incidents of the foursome on Saturday afternoon. Again they went over each detail, and back and over again, from the time they had driven off at the first tee until the Colonel's second at the fifth, when all had ended in abrupt tragedy. Rankin bade them cudgel their brains for the minutest recollected fact, the slightest suspicious circumstance; every shot, every movement almost, of each member of the foursome was repeated, and considered—and it all came to nothing. They could recall no unusual action on the part of Fraser Mawson at any time; at the fifth hole he had taken four to get out of a bunker, just before the catastrophe, so all they could remember of him at that particular moment was a marked indulgence in profanity. He had not been near Colonel Phillips, then, just before the attack? As they remembered it, no.

Rankin at length falling into silence, the two young men began discussing the poisoned needle and the curious fact that it had entered the Colonel's abdomen pointing upward; Harry appeared to hold some absurd theory in the matter and Fred undertook to explode it.

That done, they too became silent. Fred strolled across to a window. It was swinging open, and from the garden the hot summer breeze brought a mingling of heavy odors sifted through the sunshine. From somewhere in the rear of the grounds came the sound of a whirring engine, and a moment later an automobile rolled down the driveway—one of the men going to Brockville to meet the officer from Governor's Island. Fred turned away from the window, moved across to the mantel and idly began to inspect an old portrait of some former Phillips that hung there; then his eye fell on the Colonel's bag of golf clubs which Harry had set in a corner as he entered the room. Fred crossed to it and passed his hand back and forth over the shining irons. Mechanically he pulled out one of them and waggled it back and forth in front of him; and then, with a glance overhead and to either side to make sure of room, he swung the club far back of his head, raising on his toe, and brought it around with a mighty swing.

As he did so two things happened.

Canby Rankin leaped swiftly to his feet with an ejaculation of astonishment and triumph.

The door of the room opened and Fraser Mawson appeared on the threshold.

Rankin, who had started forward, his eyes flashing with excitement, stopped abruptly. Harry and Fred regarded him in inquiring wonder. Mawson glanced at each of them, then came quietly forward.

"About that loan, Harry," he said to the younger of the two brothers. "I'm going to town for an hour in the morning. Since your friend—I didn't know—"

"He won't need the loan, Mr. Mawson." It was Rankin who spoke, in a voice that seemed to tremble a little. He had turned to face the newcomer with gleaming eyes.

"You're just in time," he went on more evenly. "To witness the lucky achievement of a curious dilettantism. Fraser Mawson, you are under arrest, charged with the murder of Carson Phillips."

There was a gasp of amazement from Fred Adams, and Harry got excitedly to his feet. For one swift instant the color left Mawson's face—then he smiled and bowed.

"Ah! You try to force your way through the darkness then. What can I do but humor you?"

"Quite commendable," replied the detective grimly. "I'll begin forcing my way by searching you. You may have another of those little needles in a handy pocket. Better still, I'll fix you so you can't use it."

He stepped forward swiftly, seized Mawson's arms from behind, and pinioned him.

"Mr. Rankin!"

"Fred! Harry! Help me here."

And despite the lawyer's protests his arms were tied firmly behind him and he was led to a chair.

The detective, crossing swiftly to the bag of golf clubs in the corner, paid no heed to him. One by one he lifted out the clubs and examined the butt of the shaft. Next to last was the driver. He glanced at it, held it closer, then straightened up and turned with an expression of triumph.

But the look on Fraser Mawson's face made it unnecessary to say anything. During the few seconds that Rankin had been inspecting the clubs the lawyer's countenance had gone from purple to white; the blazing light had gone from his eyes and left a dead despair; his whole form trembled, and though his lips moved no words came. As Rankin turned to face him he got halfway to his feet, then sank back again into the chair, ashen grey, limp, inert.

Two hours later he was lodged in the Brockville jail, and the New York dailies were preparing extra editions with sensational headlines six inches high across the front page.

That night Canby Rankin was explaining the mechanism of the driver to Doctor Wortley.

"Devilishly ingenious, Doctor. The spring concealed in the shaft was so arranged that it could be released only by the impact of the ivory inset in the face of the club against the ball; and the force of the released spring ejected the needle from the upper end of the shaft. Of course at the moment of impact the butt end of the shaft was aiming at the Colonel's stomach, upwards, and the needle found its mark."

"Then why didn't it happen at the first tee?" demanded the doctor.

"Because he was using his brassie. Harry told us that yesterday. He took out the driver for the first time at the fifth tee. Mawson of course had contrived this thing as an exact replica of the Colonel's own driver and substituted it in his bag. Staying here at Greenlawn, he wouldn't lack an opportunity for that."

The doctor was silent, examining the tiny hole in the butt of the shaft with speculative eyes.

"I don't see how you ever got onto it," he observed finally.

"Nor I," admitted the detective. When I saw Fred swinging that iron the idea simply struck me from nowhere." He smiled a little as he added:

"Perhaps it was curious dilettantism."

AFTERWORD

The Last Drive revolves around the killing of a well-respected figure on a golf course. Before identifying the murderer, the detective must first identify the murder weapon itself. It turns out to be a poison dart that entered the victim's chest while he was golfing.

Anyone familiar with the Nero Wolfe novels will recognize this as the same murder method used in *Fer-de-Lance*, Stout's first book featuring Nero Wolfe and Archie Goodwin, written and published in 1934. There is no evidence that anyone made the connection, however—any more than anyone remembered how Nero Wolfe and Archie Goodwin were dimly prefigured by Simon Culp and his office boy in *Justice Ends at Home*. As Professor Ross Davies has observed, "there is a pleasing symmetry in the fact that publishing history suggests that the primary literary inspiration for Stout's greatest characters (Wolfe and Goodwin) was his own earlier story, *Justice Ends at Home*, and that the primary literary inspiration for the plot of his first great detective story (*Fer-de-Lance*) was his own earlier story, *The Last Drive*. Stout was, in other words, demonstrably his own best source of inspiration."

The Last Drive seems to have been completely forgotten by 1934. It was certainly forgotten by the 1970s, when McAleer wrote Stout's biography. The two men never discussed *The Last Drive* or *Golfers Magazine*. But although McAleer knew nothing of *The Last Drive*, he did speculate that elements of *Fer-de-Lance* might have been inspired by earlier works of mystery fiction. Perhaps, he suggested, Stout might have drawn the idea of a golf-course killing from Agatha Christie's *Murder on the Links* (1923), or Ronald Knox's *Murder at the Viaduct* (1926). Now we know it was not so. Stout came up with the idea himself, used it once, and consciously or otherwise, memory-banked it to use again two decades later. The second time was the charm.

THE PAISLEY

—ww—

This short romance story, one of Stout's first, features three main characters: a lonely man, a lonely woman, and a paisley dog who helps bring man and woman together, at least to the point of sharing tea at the Plaza. The story appeared in Young's Magazine, *a general-fiction pulp magazine aimed primarily at a female audience.*

*S*ammis Thrawn was lonely. Anyone who knew Thrawn would have declared this to be impossible; but it was true. As he sauntered aimlessly along an unknown path in Central Park he made a lazy mental survey of the possibilities of an amusing afternoon, and heaved a deep sigh at the hopelessness of it all.

It was four o'clock of one of those days which June holds up to the remainder of the calendar with an air of serene superiority. By its witchery the clanging of street cars is made musical and the smoke from automobiles becomes fragrant. Everything is as it should be.

But still, Sammis Thrawn was lonely. It is all very well to have a host of friends and a disgracefully large income, but there are times——

Thrawn heaved another sigh, glared angrily at a robin perched on an overhanging branch, and, I am ashamed to say, even went so far as to strike at it with his walking stick. Of course, he was careful to miss; and the robin, retreating hurriedly to a little grassy mound, barely removed from the path, turned her back on poor Thrawn, every feather on her plump, round body expressive of resentment.

Thrawn eyed the robin with severe disapproval, clenched his stick more tightly—and then, sighing once more, continued on his way down the path.

"What the devil!" he mused. "I am bored! Actually bored!" He poked his stick lazily toward a little blue terrier that had stationed itself directly in his way and stood blinking up at him in the sunlight.

Thrawn suddenly turned and surveyed the path to the rear, then to the front. No one was in sight. He stooped deliberately, took the terrier in his arms, and hanging the stick over his wrist, proceeded down the path with an almost eager step.

As he turned a rounding corner in the path, and saw a girl seated on a park bench some dozen paces ahead, the idea that had been dimly revolving in his brain crystallized into a definite intention.

The girl's face, shaded from the sun by a large, filmy, lacy hat and a still more lacy parasol above that, was turned directly toward him. Its creamy whiteness was half hidden by a coat of tan that reached clear to that delightful curve where the top of the lacy collar appeared as a jealous shield; and the effect was one of which Thrawn thoroughly approved.

As he approached nearer and read on her face the expression of a mood that exactly matched his own, Thrawn hesitated. Then, with a reflection that sympathy would perhaps serve as well as gayety, he stopped directly in front of her, bowed politely, and smiled sadly.

"Is this your dog?" he asked.

The girl regarded the terrier with an impersonal curiosity, and then looked up at Thrawn.

"Yes," she answered, "it is. Where did you find him?"

Thrawn sat down on the bench at her side, still holding the terrier. This was rather more than he had bargained for. He had expected the dog to serve as an introduction, but he had not expected to find a claimant in this charming brown and white nymph. He looked first at the girl, then at the terrier, perplexed. They certainly did not seem suited to each other.

"Are you sure he is yours?"

The girl looked slightly amused. "Do you doubt it?" she asked. "See!"

She held out her arms, and the terrier leaped into them and nestled cozily in her lap. That, of course, was convincing.

"He will soil your dress," said Thrawn, indifferently.

The girl was silent, running her slender white fingers through the terrier's silky hair.

"What—what sort of a dog is he?" asked Thrawn.

"A—a—Paisley," answered the girl. "English. You must forgive me," she continued after a pause, "if I don't thank you for finding him for me. The truth is, I am not thankful."

Thrawn looked uncomfortable.

"Don't do that," said the girl abruptly. "That's the way I feel."

"Good Heavens!" exclaimed Thrawn. "So do I."

They smiled at each other sympathetically. Then, as a flush slowly appeared under the coat of tan, the girl turned her face away.

"That," said Thrawn almost cheerfully, "was what I needed. I suppose I should go now. What would you do," he continued, "if I should insist on sitting here and talking to you?"

"That depends," answered the girl. "Are you ever amusing? You see," she went on, without giving him time to answer, "that is the only thing that matters. For you are evidently quite harmless."

At this Thrawn was almost indignant. To be called harmless by a pretty girl is anything but comforting.

"I'm not a pirate," he said, "if that's what you mean. Nor a murderer. But there are times—" He hesitated.

"There are just two kinds of men," said the girl, speaking to the terrier, "that are dangerous. First, the impossible kind."

"Well?" asked Thrawn.

"Oh, one merely calls a policeman. Of course," regarding him critically, "you are not impossible."

"Thank you," said Thrawn gravely.

"Then," the girl continued, "there is the masterful kind. Like the heroes of novels. There *are* such men, you know."

"And I, of course, am not one of them," said Thrawn foolishly.

The girl laughed. "Never!" she declared. "Can you imagine such a man walking in Central Park with a fuzzy terrier in his arms, at four o'clock on a Friday afternoon in June?"

"It was *your* terrier," said Thrawn, with just resentment.

"That only makes it worse," declared the girl. "No; you are too safe to be interesting."

"You are taking an unfair advantage," Thrawn asserted hotly.

The girl smiled sweetly. "Do you know," she said thoughtfully, "you ought to be a school teacher. You talk just like one. Are you?"

Thrawn turned and faced her squarely, and saw the teasing smile, the roguish tilt of the head, the dainty whiteness of her hands resting half hidden in the terrier's coat.

"For the first time in four months," he said evenly, "I am thoroughly angry. The last time was—but that doesn't matter. What I wanted to say was that since I am safe, it naturally follows that anything I do is proper."

He bent his head swiftly over the terrier in her lap, and on one of those hands imprinted a well-directed and unmistakable kiss.

The girl remained motionless and silent. "Of course," she said, finally, "I can't very well be angry, since it was my own fault. But it is really too bad, for now you must go."

"You know perfectly well," protested Thrawn, "that within five minutes from the time I leave you will be frightfully bored. And so will I."

The girl was silent. Thrawn rose from the bench and beckoned with his stick to a taxicab that was passing on Central Park West. The taxi circled back to the park entrance and stopped on the drive some twenty feet from the path.

"Of course," said Thrawn," you are probably right. Discretion is the better part of valor. Like all sensible people, you realize that it is wiser to avoid danger than to overcome it. It is rather curious that you should have been so mistaken when you first saw me. Only one other girl was ever unfortunate enough to tell me I was harmless."

"I suppose," said the girl scornfully, "that she died of a broken heart."

"No," said Thrawn, with a reminiscent sadness, "she is still living. You see," he continued, "there is no good in your feeling mortified, because your asking me to leave is a confession of weakness. It's universal. Not, of course, that I am irresistible."

"But you think you are," declared the girl. "You have more conceit with less reason than any man I know. Where are you going?"

Thrawn hesitated. "To the Plaza, for tea," he hazarded.

"I'm not surprised," the girl declared. "The palm room at the Plaza is exactly suited to you."

"Should I carry the parasol?" asked Thrawn.

"No. You may take the dog."

Thrawn took the terrier in his arms and led the way across the lawn to the taxi.

"What was it," he asked, as the taxi swept through the park, "that first made you like me?"

"Your hat," said the girl, after a careful scrutiny. "Yes, it must have been your hat. It is so flat and ugly."

"Thank you," said Thrawn.

As they were passing into the tea-room from the outer corridor at the hotel the girl halted suddenly.

"Where's the dog?" she asked.

Thrawn stopped and gazed at her blankly.

"Lost," he said simply.

For ten minutes they tramped through corridors and ante-rooms—all in vain. The little Paisley had completely disappeared. Thrawn had lifted it from the taxi, turned to pay the chauffeur, and forgotten all about it.

"It was extremely thoughtless of me," said he, as they sat down on a divan to rest. "I am dreadfully sorry."

The girl was silent.

"You see," continued Thrawn presently, "its all your own fault. If you hadn't said I was harmless we would be sitting in the park in the sunshine talking about Browning or something, instead of running after a confounded dog."

"It isn't," the girl contradicted. "It *isn't* a—a—that kind of dog." She was either laughing or crying.

"Beside," Thrawn continued, "how could I help forgetting? You should have known that a creamy white face with a coat of tan, a little nose and funny twinkly eyes is to me the most beautiful sight in the world. The dog demanded too much attention. I'm glad I forgot him. I'm glad he's gone."

The girl put up her handkerchief to catch a tear that was just ready to fall. I have said that she was either laughing or crying. Thrawn saw the tear, and gasped.

"Did you love him so well?" he asked.

The girl nodded, and again pressed her handkerchief to her eyes.

"Was he—did you have him long?"

Again the girl nodded. "That is the reason I care," she said. "He could never be replaced. We all loved him so."

She gazed tearfully at the spots left on her gown by the terrier's muddy feet. Thrawn followed her look commiseratingly.

"Hello, Thrawn!" came a voice.

Thrawn looked up, startled. Standing directly in front of them was Billy Du Mont, the ever-smiling and never-working, hat in one hand, and in the other—the lost Paisley, struggling for freedom.

"Good afternoon, Miss Sargent," said Billy to the girl. "Here's your pup, Thrawn. Knew you must be around when I saw him."

Thrawn sat as one stricken dumb, while the girl moved over on the divan to make room for Billy.

"Sorry," declined Billy, "but I haven't time. My revered mother is waiting for me at Suzanne's. Besides, you two look so thoroughly chummy."

"Is—is that Mr. Thrawn's dog?" asked the girl.

"Sure," answered Billy. "Don't you think it looks like him?"

When he had gone Thrawn looked at the girl and tried to laugh. She did not join him.

"Your heard what he said," said Thrawn timidly. "We're chums."

"I suppose," said Miss Sargent, icily, "you are speaking of yourself and your dog."

A long silence.

"It seems to me," Thrawn observed, "that I have as good a right to be angry with you for saying it was yours as you have to be angry with me for saying it *wasn't* mine."

"You have. Go on and *be* angry."

"But I'm *not* angry. I feel friendly and charitable, and—and happy. This is the most wonderful day of my life. I would lie twice as often for an equal pleasure."

"Or, perhaps, *with* an equal pleasure," suggested Miss Sargent.

"It's the same thing."

"I'm not surprised at *your* thinking so."

"Besides, it saved you from a most horrible attack of *ennui*."

"My only feeling is one of annoyance."

Thrawn colored hotly. "I beg your pardon," he said, and bowing stiffly, disappeared down the corridor.

He turned a corner to the left. Then he missed the terrier, and started to retrace his steps.

And then—this Thrawn was anything but a fool—he turned back in the original direction, and shortly approached the divan where he had left Miss Sargent, from the opposite side to that of his departure.

Miss Sargent was leaning forward, gazing intently down the corridor where he had disappeared. Held tightly in her arms was the Paisley.

Thrawn coughed.

"Oh!" cried the girl, and jumped to her feet. The terrier landed on the floor in a heap. "You—you forgot your dog!"

"That is what I returned for," said Thrawn, with never a smile. "I am sorry to have been forced to *annoy* you again."

He picked up the Paisley, and prepared to leave.

"I shouldn't have said that," the girl declared hastily—embarrassed. "You—you must forgive me."

"Good Lord!" exclaimed Thrawn. "Forgive you!" He bent over and touched ever so lightly with his lips the hand she held out to him.

"Let's go in to tea," he said.

BILLY DU MONT, REPORTER

—✦—

A novice journalist gains a story, and perhaps a spouse, by a strata-gem that Nero Wolfe or Archie Goodwin might have been proud of (if either of them had ever desired to gain a spouse). From Young's Magazine.

Billy Du Mont sat on the edge of the stenographer's desk, swing-ing his legs in a crisscross fashion carefully copied after a young Frenchman he had met at Nice. Finding this monotonous, he added a few bizarre variations of his own.

"Stop that," commanded his father, gruffly.

Billy thrust his hands in his pockets, and sliding down till his feet touched the floor, began drumming on it with his toes. The elder Du Mont eyed him with growing disapproval.

"Well?" said Billy, encouragingly.

His father grunted. "How long do you think it will last?" he demanded.

Billy looked grieved. "There's no use asking me questions like that," he declared. "It's very discouraging. You know very well I've decided to buckle down and work."

There was a silence, while Billy walked over to the mirror to smile approvingly at his carefully nurtured but scarcely perceptible moustache, and his father turned around in his chair the better to observe this modest proceeding.

"Well," said Du Mont, Senior, with a sigh, "go on down and report to Allen—God help him."

He turned to his desk in a manner which indicated that the interview was ended; and Billy, properly ignoring the implication in the prayer for Allen, left the room and proceeded down the hall and stairs to the office of the city editor.

"Hello," said Allen, cordially, as Billy entered without knocking. "On the job, eh?"

Billy nodded and seated himself on a rickety cane chair, while Allen fumbled among a pile of little yellow slips, with an amused smile.

Billy saw the smile, and resented it—inwardly. But no hostile feeling could long survive in the cheerful and optimistic breast of Billy Du Mont, and when Allen looked up from his desk he met a smile even broader than his own.

"Allen," said Billy, "you've been listening to the voice of the siren—in this case my revered parent. Go on and have your fun. But give me a chance, and I'll show you all up."

Allen laughed—a privilege he had earned by dandling Billy on his knee on several occasions some eighteen years before.

"I hope so, Billy," said he. "We need it. For a starter, here's a run up Riverside Drive to see a beautiful heiress and make some casual inquiries concerning the whereabouts of her heart."

Billy frowned. "Must I go where you tell me to?" he demanded.

"Of course."

The frown deepened. "All right. Go on."

"It's this," said Allen. "There's a rumor that the Count de Luni has come to America solely for the purpose of marrying Cecily Lyndon, daughter of the banker. He landed yesterday on the *Morania*. It's said that it's a love match, only old man Lyndon has interposed a firm and gentle nix. The Count is staying at the Ritz-Ritz, and I want you to see both him and Miss Lyndon, and get a story out of it. If there's any—"

He stopped abruptly. Billy's face had during this brief recital undergone a series of remarkable changes. It had gone from pale to red, from red to splotched, from splotched to rosy pink, shaming his moustache. He had risen from his chair and advanced toward Allen threateningly.

"Who told you that?" he demanded.

Then, realizing that he was making a fool of himself, he sank back into his chair, embarrassed.

Allen regarded him with surprise. "You'd make a fine chameleon," he observed. "What's the row?"

Billy recovered quickly. "Nothing," he said, calmly, rising to go, "only the Count is an old friend of mine. I'll get the story, all right."

Allen was curious, but time was precious, and Billy gave him no time to answer.

"Good luck!" Allen called, as Billy was closing the door.

"Thanks!" said Billy.

Five minutes later he was seated in an uptown subway express, his forehead puckered into a frown, his lips compressed in a thin line, his hands clenched tightly. Clearly, he was thinking—a most unusual occurrence in the life of Billy, his friends would have told you.

Billy was richer in friends than in anything else. A year previous he had graduated at Harvard—barely; he had then tried the brokerage business, thereby adding to his own amusement and subtracting more from his father's bank account; and when his distracted parent had sent him on a sixty days' tour of the Mediterranean he had calmly altered the carefully arranged program into a six months' visit to Paris.

He had been the most popular man of his class at Harvard; he had won the good will of every broker on the street in five months; and there was a certain crowd of students in Paris who loved him well, and drank to his health whenever they thought of it—or had anything to drink. But these are acquisitions which are hardly calculated to gain the commendation of a father; which fact was impressed upon Billy in terms more forcible than elegant on the day that he arrived home from Paris.

Du Mont, Senior, owner and editor of the New York *Clarion*, had been unwilling that his son should become a journalist; but with Billy's insistence and his mother's tears he had been forced to acquiesce. For Billy had written from Paris that nothing else would bring him home; and when the elder Du Mont received a letter informing him that his only son was about to become a waiter at the Café Sigognac, and soliciting his patronage in the event of his coming to Paris, he cabled two hundred dollars and an uncomfortable surrender at once.

On the morning after his arrival, accordingly, Billy had reported at the *Clarion* office for duty. He had informed his father that he had decided to begin with editorials and special articles. Any one else would have been disconcerted by the torrent of sarcasm which this statement elicited; but not Billy. He smiled cheerfully at the assertion that the only articles he could write were the advertisements of haberdashers, and agreed willingly to the course of reportorial work proposed by his father.

As the subway express roared into Grand Central Station and out again, Billy's look of gloom changed into the dreamy smile of one who was recalling sweet memories. A certain afternoon on the Seine, and a fair laughing face that had looked out at him from the cabin of a luxurious motor launch, as he lay stretched on the bank while a student friend belabored him for going to sleep over de Musset; the subsequent meeting at the Club House at Argenteuil, when he certainly had not appeared to the best advantage; the round of drives and theatres during the remaining week of her stay in Paris, necessitating a hurried amalgamation of funds among his friends at

Lampourde's; these things flitted across his mind with a distinctness that spoke highly of their importance.

As for the Count de Luni— But before Billy could decide on the particularly horrible fate to be reserved for that gentleman, the train reached Ninety-sixth Street, and he found himself again in the open air, with an April breeze coming caressingly up the hill from the Hudson, directly in his face. He sniffed it with the air of a *dilettante* and with an evident appreciation.

As he entered the imposing marble hall of the Elemara, on Riverside Drive, a feeling of timidity assailed him. With Billy timidity was so rare a visitor that he paused for a moment to enjoy the novelty of this strange sensation. Then, with a shrug of the shoulders and a reflection that what was worth getting was worth going after, he sent up his card.

Seated in the reception room in the Lyndon apartment, Billy felt an apathy and indifference steal over him which he strove vainly to drive away. This, after all, was not Paris. The sunny Seine of Argenteuil was very different from the sullen Hudson, obscured by the smoke of a thousand chimneys. The glaring magnificence of the decorations and hangings of this commercial castle were in unpleasing contrast to the genuinely artistic tawdriness of Lampourde's and the Café Fracasse. Billy hated show.

He was stopped in the midst of these reflections by the appearance of Miss Cecily Lyndon, about whose slender form the velvet curtains seemed to cling lovingly as she passed through them. Billy rose at her entrance, and as she crossed the room to where he stood, regarded her with frank approval.

This was not the Cecily whose frank friendliness had been so thoroughly charming, but she was as fair. That look of detached politeness could not hide the witchery that lurked in the blue of her eyes and the curve of her lips.

"Good morning, Mr. Du Mont," said Miss Lyndon, with some dignity.

Billy extended his hand, smiling, refusing to be impressed. Miss Lyndon took it languidly, let it drop almost meaningly, and remained standing, politely attentive.

Billy regarded this studied ceremony with mild amusement, and was stubbornly silent. Finally, when she felt that another second would make her ridiculous, Miss Lyndon asked coldly:

"Have you been in New York long?"

"Not long enough to find my way around," said Billy, exasperated. "I started out this morning to call on a friend—a dear friend—and I find that I have somehow made a mistake and intruded on someone I don't know."

Miss Lyndon started to answer, then bit her lip and remained silent.

"I beg your pardon for annoying you," continued Billy, rising to go. "As an excuse I can only plead an invitation which I thought sincere."

"That was the night before," said Cecily, without thinking.

"Before what?" demanded Billy.

Miss Lyndon was silent.

"Before what?" Billy repeated

"Before—before you annoyed me by *not* coming," said Cecily, because she couldn't help it.

Billy stared at her for a moment, not understanding.

"Good Heavens!" he exclaimed, and dropped back into his chair. He had forgotten all about his promise to go to her train in Paris, and his failure to keep the promise because of the financial impossibility of a sufficiently glorious parting gift.

"I was sorry," he said, "sorrier than you would believe. Really, I had the best excuse in the world."

"It's of no consequence," said Cecily, with elaborate indifference. "One always has excuses."

"It isn't an excuse. It's a *reason*. And it is of consequence—to me."

"It's hardly worth discussing, is it?" asked Cecily, dryly.

Billy regarded her for a moment in angry silence. But then, she had a right to be offended.

"Miss Lyndon," he said, "I am sorry. I—if you knew my reason—but I can't tell you. Will you forgive me?"

This was more than Cecily had bargained for. She looked uncomfortable.

"Will you forgive me?" repeated Billy, humbly.

It puts a girl in a sad dilemma to ask her forgiveness. It is sweet to forgive—but it is also sweet to refuse. If she could only have both pleasures at once!

"You don't deserve it," declared Cecily, holding out her hand.

"Of course not," agreed Billy, holding the hand tightly.

"I don't believe you're a bit sorry."

"Not now."

"Haven't you held my hand quite long enough?" sarcastically.

"Not quite," calmly.

Cecily withdrew her hand abruptly and walked to the window.

"I'm going for a drive," she announced, after a brief silence. And as Billy looked at her inquiringly she added, "with my mother."

"Oh!" said Billy, thoughtfully. "Is your mother very—er—fond of driving?"

"Why?"

"Because—if she isn't—I thought we might bring her back some violets or something, and she wouldn't need to go."

"You're a silly goose," declared Cecily.

"We could go to Larchmont, for instance," continued Billy, ignoring the compliment, "and pick some goldenrod and stuff."

"Goldenrod! In April!"

"Why not, in April?" demanded Billy.

Cecily laughed. "You are very ignorant," said she, pityingly.

"You are trying to make me vain," Billy asserted. "First, silly goose; second, ignoramus. I can't possibly live up to it. Besides, I didn't mean goldenrod, really. I was merely referring to your hair."

Cecily greeted this assertion with contemptuous silence.

"How soon are we going?" asked Billy, presently.

Cecily gasped at his impudence.

"I shall never forget," continued Billy, "that wonderful evening at Argenteuil, the cool garden, the—everything. And how surprised I was when you called me 'Billy' without my even suggesting it! And on the way back to Paris you—your—"

"Please stop," Cecily implored.

"Well," said Billy, magnanimously, "we'll forget that. Beside, the night *was* cold. But on Monday afternoon you broke two engagements to visit the quarter with me. On Tuesday evening at the Opera Comique you admitted that I was more interesting than the play. On Wednesday afternoon at the Louvre when Lord Hailes insisted on carrying your scarf you handed it to me. On Thursday evening you put three lumps of sugar in my coffee *without* tongs. On Friday morning, in a retired spot in the Luxembourg Gardens, while your mother had gone ahead to feed the swans, you put—"

"Stop!" commanded Cecily, her hands to her ears.

"Well?" demanded Billy, sternly.

"I hate you," declared Cecily. "We shall start at once. The sooner it's over the better."

"Do we pick goldenrod for your mother?"

"Yes."

"And go for a sail on the Sound?"

"Yes."

"Very well. Then I forgive you," said Billy, generously.

"I have decided," said Billy, as the touring car sped up Seventh Avenue, "to tell you my reason for not going to the train."

"It's of no importance," said Cecily.

"At that time," continued Billy, ignoring the remark, "I was living on a monthly allowance from my father. When I met you the month had nearly ended. That last dinner at the Sigognac was contributed to by no less than fourteen of my devoted friends. I was, in short, completely strapped."

"You could have walked," said Cecily, trying not to smile.

"Certainly," agreed Billy, "and I did. I am shameless enough to admit that I watched you board the train from behind the friendly shelter of a protecting post. But nothing less than the most beautiful flowers in Paris would have suited you, and that was—impracticable."

There was a short silence.

"I had the bouquet made up," said Billy, reminiscently, "by Vidalinc of the Haussamn. It was most gorgeous. My friends admired it immensely. It was wonderful."

"But I thought you—I thought it was impracticable," said Cecily.

"So it was," agreed Billy. "But I wanted to see how it looked. I had thought the thing out so carefully, and I wanted to see if it met my expectations. Vidalinc was most accommodating. Only, of course, I had to—"

"Do you mean to say," Cecily interrupted, "that you had that bouquet made up without intending to buy it?"

"Why not?" asked Billy. "It was for you. I would do anything for you."

Cecily laughed. It was a silvery, musical laugh.

"Billy—," said she, and stopped short.

"There!" said Billy, sternly. "You're at it again. You know what that does to me."

"I am sorry," said Cecily, with averted face. It was positively red. "Mr. Du Mont," she added.

"It's too late," said Billy, gloomily. "I love you."

"Mr. Du Mont!" exclaimed Cecily, as severely as possible.

"I couldn't help it," declared Billy, "but I'll try."

Silence.

"Not to say it?"

"Not to love you."

"Oh!" said Cecily. "You—you probably won't find it difficult."

"Probably not," agreed Billy, almost cheerfully.

Cecily should have been gratified by this sincere effort to obey her wishes, but she wasn't. She looked out across the swamps toward the Sound without seeing them, and then turned and glanced at Billy curiously. His lips were puckered into a round and unmistakable O.

"Oh!" cried Cecily.

"Well?" demanded Billy, surprised.

"You were going to whistle," said Cecily, accusingly.

"Yes. 'Love Is a Jolly Good Fellow.' Have you heard it?"

"I hate you!" declared Cecily.

"Thank you. I was afraid you pitied me."

"Not I," scornfully.

"*May* I whistle?"

No answer. Billy hesitated for a moment, then began to whistle a lilting, catchy tune that sailed out over the fields and seemed to arouse even the sleepy violets tucked away in their modest beds. They had just passed New Rochelle, and the car had left its rough brick pavements for the long stretch of smooth, oily road that leads to Larchmont. Cottages and bungalows appeared at either side of the road at frequent intervals. To the right lay low meadows, reaching to the Sound; to the left and north, miniature hills and undulations that gave only an enticing hint of Mother Earth's great breasts. Over all lay spring's fragrant mantle, alluring, transparent, a continual reminder of the blazing passion of the summer to come.

As Billy whistled tune after tune, seemingly unconscious of all the world save his own agreeable self, Cecily was far from comfortable. There was every reason in the world why Billy should be sad, even sullen; instead, witness his heartless mirth. She turned away in vexation.

Billy, having completed his repertoire of happy tunes, and disdaining the mournful ones, turned to her with the air of one about to divulge an important secret.

"I forgot to tell you," said he, "that I have become a journalist."

Cecily gazed at a bungalow they were passing, with deep interest.

"I am beginning at the bottom," continued Billy, "as a reporter. I began work this morning."

"Aren't you afraid you're working too hard?" Cecily asked, sweetly.

Billy shifted himself a little to a more comfortable position.

"Well," he said, thoughtfully, "to tell the truth, no. I think hard work is good for a fellow. This morning, for instance, I have been successful where any other man on the paper would have failed."

A pause.

"Would you care to hear about it?" Billy asked.

"No," said Cecily, shortly.

"It was this way," continued Billy; "the papers have all printed reports that the Count de Luni has won the heart of a certain Miss Lyndon, and Allen—that's our city editor—wanted the rumor confirmed or denied."

Cecily caught her breath with indignation, and her eyes flashed dangerously.

"Am I being interviewed?" she demanded.

"No. The interview is ended."

"Then we may return, I suppose?"

"As you please."

"But I—but you—" Cecily hesitated.

"That's the same as 'but *we*,'" explained Billy, kindly. "But we what?"

"Oh!" cried Cecily. "How I hate you!"

"That's three times you've told me that," said Billy, "and it's getting monotonous. Once more, and I'll believe it. Besides, I am not hateful. If you don't believe me, ask Cecile—a most charming girl who admired me."

Cecily smiled contemptuously.

"Who *admired* me," repeated Billy, with emphasis. "She admitted it. It would do you good to know her. She is the dearest and sweetest girl in the world. Perhaps she didn't love me, but once in the Gardens she told me that she would never—"

"I didn't say 'never,'" interposed Cecily, hastily.

"You did," Billy contradicted. "Twice. You said: 'I will never, never forget this—'"

"No! No!" cried Cecily.

Billy stopped obediently, and there was a short silence.

"Why do you always stop when people tell you to?" Cecily demanded. "Haven't you any tongue?"

"Did you say 'never'?" demanded Billy, exasperated.

"Yes."

"Did you *mean* 'never'?"

"I—I've forgotten."

As she spoke, the car drew up at the Larchmont Yacht Club. At a word from Billy the chauffeur descended from his seat and, disappearing into the Club office, returned shortly with a telegram blank.

Billy placed the blank against the back of the chauffeur's seat, and wrote on it.

Then, holding it before Cecily's eyes, he commanded:

"Read that."

The message was short:

"M. L. Allen,

New York, *Clarion*,

New York.

Rumor of engagement positively false. Best authority.

WILLIAM DU MONT."

"Is it true?" asked Billy, as he handed the message to the chauffeur. Cecily was silent.

"Is it true?" repeated Billy.

"Yes," reluctantly.

"Yes—Billy."

And then; "Billy! Stop! He's looking!"

"Can you blame him?" asked Billy, shamelessly.

BARNACLES

—〰—

Before he began publishing short stories, Rex Stout served for two years in the United States Navy. Stout's period in service could hardly be called typical—he spent much of it as pay-yeoman on President Theodore Roosevelt's yacht—but it gave him enough Navy background and terminology to lend some verisimilitude to this story. From Young's Magazine.

Since Annie is still living, it would hardly be fair to tell you the name of the town. It is enough to say that it contains about three thousand inhabitants and is somewhere between Albany and Buffalo. It was here that William Brownell enlisted in the Navy; it was from here that he shipped to the receiving ship *Franklin* at Norfolk. Also, it was here that he bade a tearful good-by to Annie, though Annie knew nothing about it, and cared less.

William's first six months in the navy were full of novel incidents, but they were more troublesome than exciting. Then, having successfully survived the somewhat painful instruction of the training school, and having rubbed out, on his hands and knees, the disgraceful stiffness of his recruit's outfit, he was assigned to a berth on the deck of the *Kansas*, and began to criticise the Bureau of Navigation and revile the commissary according to the most approved rules and precedents.

Friendships in the navy rarely have anything to do with caste. A coxswain is as apt to open his heart to a coal passer as to anyone else, or a quartermaster to an apprentice seaman. There is even a case on record where a marine—twelve-eighty and a horse blanket—became the bosom friend of the captain's writer. Therefore, there is really nothing surprising in the fact that within three months William was the acknowledged chum of the equipment yeoman.

The equipment yeoman's name was Jimmy Spear. He was on his second cruise, and he spent most of his time swearing to the Deity that he'd "take one a yard long" before he'd ship over for "a third one." He was, in short, of the stuff of which C. S. C. men are made.

William and Jimmy spent many a pleasant hour together in the little store-room just forward of the pay office, or walking to and fro on the forecastle. They rehashed all their experiences and exploited their opinions with endless enjoyment and ceaseless repetition. Jimmy, whose choice for a liberty port was, first, New York, and, second, Aden, Arabia, recited over and over incredible tales of conquests both bacchanalian and amorous, while William was forced to devote himself chiefly to humble pastorals and glowing descriptions of the County Fair.

It was nearly a year before he mentioned Annie. The corner she occupied in his heart was so deep and sacred that it seemed a sacrilege to expose it even to the sympathetic Jimmy. But it is hard to suffer in silence when a willing ear is waiting to hear your woes; and the time came when William felt an irresistible impulse to lay bare his soul. He was surprised and pleased at the eager interest of Jimmy, who squatted on a ditty box and gazed long and earnestly at the little framed photograph William had handed him.

"She's a peach," declared Jimmy in a tone of authority. "Who is she?"

"Annie."

"Who's Annie?"

William walked over to a box of salt water soap and sat down thoughtfully. "Jimmy, I've never spoke about this before." His voice was filled with sadness. "She's the only girl I ever loved. For as long as I can remember I've loved her. I wish you could see her."

Jimmy tapped the photograph with his finger. "Do you mean to say you left *that* to join the outfit?"

William, unable to speak for emotion, nodded.

"You're a blooming idiot. But, of course, there are always explanations. Tell us about it."

"I guess you won't understand," said William, timidly. "You see, I never knew her. She used to go past the store where I worked on her way to school. There was always two or three guys with her; sissy guys, you know, mamma's boys. I used to catch 'em when they was alone and beat 'em up, but I never had the nerve to speak to her. You see, I was in a different class. Then afterward I delivered groceries to her house, till one day she—she—"

"Well?" said Jimmy, encouragingly.

"That was when I enlisted. She insulted me. I did it just to get away from her. Because, of course, she'd never look at *me*."

"For the second time," Jimmy's tone was emphatic, "You're a blooming idiot. Say!" he tapped the photograph again, "show me one like that, and in two weeks I'll have her rigged to the davits and both the masts down. Delivered groceries to her! Best chance in the world. Why, don't you go in at the back door just like the rest of the family?"

At this William smiled weakly and sighed hopelessly.

"Forget it," continued Jimmy. "Wait till we get to San Juan, and I'll show you the original and only genuine antidote for unrequited love. Who *wants* to eat canned willie and red lead? Forget it."

It was soon sadly apparent that Jimmy's advice was useless. For days, which rapidly extended into weeks, William consistently and absolutely refused to consider any topic for discussion except Annie. Having once opened his heart, he poured into Jimmy's sympathetic ear all the pitiful details of a mad and hopeless passion. And Jimmy, who had seen William's indifference in the combined fire of a thousand eyes on the Prado, and who had studied Annie's photograph, began to take an interest in the affair on his own account. But he succeeded in convincing himself that it was purely through friendship that he evolved and proposed a plan which met with William's instantaneous and unqualified approval.

The first letter, composed by Jimmy, read as follows:

"Dear Annie:

"I am writing this because there is something I want to say which I never had the courage to tell you. I won't write it now, but I will later if you want to hear it. I am now a sailor on the battleship *Kansas*, and we are going to start on a cruise to the Mediterranean in July. My address is U. S. S. *Kansas*, care of Postmaster, New York City.

"Yours sincerely,

"William Brownell.

"P.S.—I will send you postcards from Paris and Rome and other places if you want me to.

"W.B."

In two weeks came the answer, and, though very short and rather discreet, it raised William to the seventh heaven of delight. His eyes were filled with tears of gratitude as he tried to express his thanks to Jimmy in a faltering voice.

"Nothing to it," declared Jimmy. "It was bound to come. It was the postcards that got her. She'll get 'em, all right, and more, too."

"We must answer it to-night," said William, "so the orderly can take it ashore on his first trip."

Jimmy regarded him with contempt. "Lothario, you leave this to me. You know as much about this game as a rookie does about a marlin hitch. We *may* answer it in a week—not a minute sooner. The first and only rule is, keep 'em guessing."

This policy met with strong objections from William. He was afraid Annie wouldn't like it, and he knew he didn't. It was only when Jimmy threatened to desert the ship that he agreed to obey orders and wait for the tide before weighing anchor.

Annie's second letter was distinctly encouraging; the third began "Dear William," and the fourth was almost reckless. By the time they sailed for Lisbon she was signing herself "Your loving Annie," and William was sheenying on the berth deck and making endless computations of the cost of furniture for four rooms.

Jimmy pursued his labor of friendship, seemingly with the constancy of a Pythias and the zeal of a Jonathan. He appropriated Annie's photograph for his own use, claiming he needed it for inspiration in the composition of William's weekly letter. And even considering William's innocence and ignorance, it is remarkable that his confiding breast felt no touch of suspicion when he had a daily opportunity of viewing the green lights in Jimmy's eyes as they rested on Annie's likeness.

The cruise in the Mediterranean was twice as long as anybody had expected. Their first orders had been for Genoa, where they took part in a naval celebration, but subsequently they were told to proceed to Manila and the Asiatic, there to leave half their own crew and bring home an equal number of short-timings. By a miracle William escaped the danger of being buried in a Japanese "take-it-and-leave-it," but even then eighteen months had passed before the *Kansas* found herself at Cherbourg, carrying a three hundred-foot homeward-bound pennant and a happy crew.

Long before this Annie had finally and unconditionally surrendered. It had been arranged that William should apply for a furlough immediately upon arrival at New York, and spend it in Annie's arms. And William, who had conducted the most brilliantly successful bumboat operation of the cruise at Iloilo, and was therefore rolling in untold wealth, gave himself up to so excessive a jollification the night before sailing that he spent the first five days of the trip across in the ship's brig.

On the morning of the day that the *Kansas* tied up at the Brooklyn Navy Yard, Jimmy Spear, whose enlistment had expired in the middle of the Atlantic, walked down the gangway with his canvas bag on his shoulder and his ditty box under his arm. Close behind was William, with the hammock. Arrived at the Naval Y. M. C. A. on Sands Street they deposited their burdens on a settee in the lobby and shook hands solemnly.

"Remember," said William, "you promised to write. Of course, I'll be on furlough for two weeks, but I want to hear from you as soon as I get back to the ship. I ain't going to try to thank you for what you've done. Some day, maybe, I'll tell Annie, and she'll invite you to call and rock the baby."

"Forget it," said Jimmy, roughly. "You probably won't ever see me again. It's the Pacific for mine. I'll send you my address from 'Frisco. And say," as William turned to go, "give Annie my love!"

William returned to the ship to wait for the approval of his furlough. With Jimmy gone it was horribly lonesome, and, since they had not yet received the expected orders to go into dry dock, even furloughs were uncertain. He sent a telegram to Annie, advising her of the delay, and swallowed his impatience with difficulty. It was the second day after Jimmy's departure that he was called to the cabin and advised by the captain's writer that his leave would commence at four o'clock of that day. He was ready to go in fifteen minutes, thanks to the simplicity of his wardrobe, and promptly at eight bells he went over the side with a joyous heart.

His first act after he got ashore was to array himself magnificently and expensively in a suit of "cits." Then he proceeded to Nolan's, and after an hour of selecting and bickering became the possessor of a diamond solitaire ring. Thence to the Y. M. C. A., where, having hung the suit carefully on the back of a chair, and having placed the ring reverently under his pillow, he slept the sleep of the unrighteous, healthy and happy. To-morrow he would see Annie.

As his train pulled into the old familiar station in the middle of the following afternoon, William stood on the car step with a shining new suit case in his hand and tears in his eyes. He was about to enjoy the triumph which had for years been his fondest dream. The pride and joy that filled his h eart were i ndescribable. He h ad not told Annie the time of his arrival, and an expectant smile parted his lips as he pictured to himself her glad surprise. He quickly made his way through the knot of loungers around the station door and started down Main Street.

"Ship ahoy!" came a voice.

William turned. Coming toward him with a rolling gait, his eyes red, his face pale, was Jimmy Spear.

"What in—" began William.

"Hello!" Jimmy interrupted. "It took you a devil of a time to get here. For forty-eight hours I've been hanging around this blooming station to head you off."

"Head me off from what?"

"Wait till you see it! But first I want to admit that I tried to double-cross you. I intended to take Annie for myself. What you said about her, and that damn picture—"

"Where is she?" demanded William, his face white with fear.

"Port your helm," said Jimmy. "Lead me to Snyder's soda fountain. I've been drunk for two days and couldn't tell one from an iceberg. I'm sorry I tried to hand it to you, but I got what I deserved."

William turned as one dazed and, with Jimmy at his side, started down the street. The whole thing was incomprehensible to him, and he didn't even try to understand it.

As they turned in at Snyder's Jimmy caught his arm and directed his gaze toward the soda fountain. What he saw was a girl incredibly fat and unmistakably German, with straw-colored hair and a nose buried in the ample folds of flabby cheeks. The only thing doubtful about her was whether she was above or below four hundred pounds.

"That's her," said Jimmy.

William leaned against a counter for support. Notwithstanding the frightful change, there could be no mistake. It was Annie.

They had reached the station before William found his tongue.

"For Pete's sake," he demanded, "how did she get all that in three years?"

"That," said Jimmy, as he laid down a twenty dollar bill to pay for two tickets to New York, "is more than I can say. By George, she'd make a fine anchor!"

"And yet," mused William, "there was a time when—"

"Forget it!" said Jimmy, sternly.

THE PICKLED PICNIC

—m—

In this tale of local politics, Stout muses on the theme of idealism versus practicality. This was one of several stories Stout contributed to The Black Cat, *a literary magazine published in Boston.*

Cyrus Hamlin sat at his breakfast table ostensibly reading the *Morning Clarion*, but in reality watching his son James. James was reading the *Morning News*. He was reading with an intense avidity; his eyes shone with eagerness; his cheeks were flushed with excitement. For a full week this phenomena had been regularly recurrent, and Hamlin Senior was beginning to grow uneasy. There could no longer be any doubt that something had aroused James' interest. This was incredible. James the silent, James the incompetent, James the hopeless!

James had never done anything exactly wrong. The correctness of his morals was unquestioned, nor did he seem to be without a certain ability. His university career had been, if not brilliant, at least respectable, and had led his father to entertain high hopes for the future. He had been placed in a confidential position in the office of Hamlin & Company, and the gods began to grin. His first achievement was the dumping of a fifty thousand dollar shipment into the maw of Hilton's of St. Louis, who failed for a million three days later. He next proceeded to get into a very righteous and somewhat heated argument with Captain Voorhees of the navy, which resulted in the loss of the government contract and its acquisition by Hamlin & Company's most hated rival. This— all in a single month—was too much for Hamlin Senior. More in sorrow than in anger, he ejected his son from the home offices and sent him up to the mill somewhere in Massachusetts to learn the business from the ground up.

At the mill James outdid himself. He hadn't been there a week when he discovered that the mill hands were not being treated as a twentieth century mill hand should be treated. He protested to the foreman, and was told to mind his own business. He then expressed his views—somewhat forcibly—to the superintendent, who told him that he would look into the matter, and wrote to the elder Hamlin complaining of the invidious activity of the company's heir.

Within two days James got a letter from his father repeating the foreman's advice, with one or two added observations, unpleasantly blunt. James, far from succumbing to this show of authority, decided to manage the affair for himself, since he could get no help from the proper sources, and accordingly organized the employees into a union, arranged a strike, and proceeded with such energy that old Hamlin himself was forced to come up from New York to settle. He acceded to all the strikers' demands but one, that his own son be made superintendent.

Feeling perhaps that he had sufficiently distinguished himself for a man barely twenty-four, James, after the settlement of the strike, had allowed himself to sink into a state of innocuous desuetude. By dint of continuous application and unequalled opportunity, he became in a year the laziest man in New York, and acquired—or assumed—an attitude of utter indifference to the practical affairs of life. Indeed, this indifference reached a degree that alarmed his father almost to the point of anger. "Is it possible," thought the elder Hamlin, "that the fool is an idiot?" But having in mind the cost and outcome of James' previous efforts, he forbore to disturb the calm, and allowed himself a polite smile when James took occasion to make observation on the potential power of a dormant intellect.

Thus James developed a personality that deserved to be called the very flower, the last expression, of indifference. He was not exactly melancholy; his real lack was enthusiasm, not interest. Still, it cannot be denied that gradually he began to look and act more like a monk and less like a man than is allowable in one who is expected to perpetuate a name and an enterprise.

After this explanation, you will easily understand why Hamlin Senior felt a positive thrill when his son came to the breakfast table six mornings in succession with a springy step and a bright eye, and eagerly devoured all the newspapers in sight before he would even so much as look at his grapefruit and jelly. Clearly, there was something in the wind. The first morning, Hamlin Senior had thought little of it; it might be a murder, a race—any one of those passing sensations that are dished up for the daily entertainment of the people. On the second morning he was mildly curious, and on the third he decided that it was unquestionably a divorce, and that James had made a somewhat late discovery of the fact of sex. But divorce suits rarely last six days, and by this time the elder Hamlin was frankly astonished.

As James sat reading the *Morning News*, an expression of firmness came over his face. Hamlin Senior eyed him silently. The young man turned to the editorial page, glanced over it for a minute, then carefully folded the paper and laid it beside his plate. Then he arose, placed his hands, palms down, on the table after the manner of an orator, and said in an impressive tone:

"Father, I've decided to enter politics."

Hamlin Senior sat up straight in his chair, while the *Morning Clarion* fluttered from his hand to the floor. "Good God!" he exclaimed weakly.

James, not heeding the interruption, continued:

"Of course it is unnecessary for me to state on which side I intend to align myself. I shall be the champion of the people—the downtrodden masses—and against the base conspiracy of the bosses, of which I have been reading. The time has come when the predatory interests—"

Hamlin Senior waved a hand for silence. "James," he said, "as a father, it is my duty to tell you that you're a blamed fool. Predatory jackrabbits! What do you know about politics?"

"Enough," said James, with the air of a statesman who is considering the advisability of entering upon a dangerous war. "I assure you, enough. It is no wonder the people have been powerless to assert and maintain their rights, lacking, as they do, an able champion. I intend," he glared at his father, "I intend that they shall no longer be without one."

"And you, I suppose, are it?" asked his father.

James, being dreadfully in earnest, ignored the sarcasm. "If I am honored by being chosen as their leader, I shall not flinch," he said resolutely. "The industrial pirates must be shown that it is the people who rule. Of course, I make no allusion to your personal—er—record."

"Thank you. And what is your present ambition?"

"I shall begin in my own district, where I shall organize the masses. Reform, like charity, begins at home."

"I see. And what about the—er—the sinews?"

"Oh, as to that," said James loftily, "I shall of course expect your financial assistance."

"Of course," said the elder Hamlin, rising from his chair and starting to leave the room. "Of course—I don't think. Your damned insolence is really admirable. If you think that I—that you—if you think—" He was still spluttering with wrath when the door closed after him, leaving James standing in a Bismarckian attitude which was still very grand and solemn, despite the fact that his only audience was a mangled grapefruit and an empty chair.

The scene between father and son was in itself really unimportant. It has been recounted in order to show the depth and strength of James' purpose, in which he could not be made to falter even by the stern refusal of an angry parent. He knew very well that the people were being exploited by selfish interests—as who does not—and he knew also that the people, being honest, needed only honest leaders. And modest as he was, he felt pretty well assured that he could select one of the chosen without straying far afield.

He was going, he told himself, to build his campaign on the inherent good sense of the people. His disinterestednesss was really astonishing. He not only said that he wanted nothing for himself—he meant it; or at least he believed that he meant it, which is perhaps as near as a human is ever allowed to approach godliness. But the wonderful thing about it is that, for all his high-flown generalities, he kept his personal aspirations strictly within the limits of common sense.

In the course of the following week, James suffered from a series of shocks, minor, but still distressing. His was a fastidious nature, and he really had no idea that anyone but rogues could frequent some of the places into which he was led by his search for the people. The people, he found, were unbelievably elusive. In the first place, they were hard to find; and in the second, they seemed more inclined to laugh at than to listen to an exposition of their woes. Some of them even went so far as to deny that they had any.

It was about a week after the commencement of activities, in the back room of Doherty's saloon, that James met Shorty Benson. Here, at last, he found some encouragement. Shorty listened to him with flattering attention, the while he consumed uncounted schooners of beer.

"Well," said he, when James paused for a breath, "that sounds mighty interestin'. You made no mistake comin' to me. And what do you want? Th' assembly?"

James was almost angry. "No!" he shouted. "Good God! Why

does everybody think I want something? I want you to understand once for all, Mr. Benson, that I am in this fight for the people! I want nothing! Assembly! Bah!"

"All right," said Shorty, soothingly. "I know it ain't much. But I thought for a starter—well, we'll talk about that later. Now to get down to business. In the first place, my name ain't Mr. Benson—it's Shorty. In the second place, there's only one guy that'll cause us any trouble—and that's Mike O'Toole. This district was mine till he butted in two years ago. Since then there's been hell to pay. Last year he got me by three hundred."

A week previous such a statement of the case of the people would have filled James with grief and astonishment; but being hardened by a week of interviews, Shorty's picturesque language brought only a mild grimace. He thoroughly intended to make drastic reform in this respect later, but wisely decided that for the present the best thing to do was to ignore it. He tried to keep his tone from showing disapproval as he said:

"What we want to do is to let people understand that we are on their side. We are *for* the people."

"Right-o," said Mr. Benson, into his schooner of beer.

"And," continued James, "in spite of their honesty, it must be admitted that they are ignorant. We must educate them."

"Educate hell!" roared Shorty, without thinking. Then, at the look of pained surprised on James' face, he quickly recovered. "What I meant, Mr. Hamlin, was this: you can't educate 'em. Me and Red Barber's been tryin' it for years. You got to lead 'em."

"Perhaps so," James mused thoughtfully, "perhaps so. We'll see about that later. And now, Mr.—er—Shorty, how can I get together a crowd of—say, five hundred—to talk to?"

"You can't," said Shorty decisively.

"Can't?"

"Not till they get to know you. Maybe not even then. First you got to get acquainted."

"But how?" said James helplessly. "I've been trying that for a week, and they don't seem very anxious to—get acquainted."

"Sure, that's where I'm the handy guy. Listen: come around with me for three days and nights, and you'll call every mick and dago in the district by his first name. That's the way to start. Are you on?"

James was certainly becoming cosmopolitan. He held out his hand and grasped that of Mr. Benson firmly as he said: "We'll begin tomorrow, Shorty."

The ensuing ten days were hard ones. James spent them mostly in livery stables, saloons, and barber shops, and acquitted himself with a degree of aplomb and tact that was positively impressive. By the end of the week he was ordering beers by the dozen with a charm and frequency that won universal admiration. Shorty's confidence rose by leaps and bounds, and even then found it difficult to keep pace with James' enthusiasm; for James found a fresh stock with each new adherent. His father, who had at first considered the affair as one of James' whims, to be dismissed under his frequent and inclusive term of "damned foolishness," was surprised by this unexpected constancy into a donation to the campaign fund that was more than ample for present needs, and which bid fair to make every saloon-keeper in the district independently rich, and release the people for-ever from the degrading bonds of thirst.

Still, without Shorty, success would have been impossible. With all the good-will in the world, James would have found it more than difficult to establish direct communication between his philosophic principles and the people's practical desires; but with Shorty always at hand in the role of interpreter it was no task at all. True, if James could have heard Shorty's popular translations of his dearest doc-trines he would have been grieved and astonished; but he didn't hear them, so there was no harm done.

By the first of June Mike O'Toole was begging for mercy. His followers were deserting him in droves; literally by the dozen. His pleadings and promises were all in vain; the combination of James' principles, Shorty's diplomacy, and free beer was too much for him, and he was barely able to hold the fort—otherwise known as district organization headquarters—with a small band of personal friends and true believers. It began to be rumored in Fourteenth Street that he was done for, and the first week in June found him fighting desperately for a foothold where he had once been king.

Despite this apparent success, however, James was far from satisfied. He was a good deal of a fool, but he saw plainly that his hold on the people was of too fluid a nature to be either sincere or enduring. He knew very well that the only right relation between the people and their leader is the ideal one which he had proposed to himself at the beginning of his career, and he knew how far short of that ideal he had fallen. This thought worried him considerably; he fell to thinking of what would have been Abraham Lincoln's opinion of this compromise with the unrighteous powers; he even felt, as did Lady Macbeth, that he was permeated with the odor of his crime—only in his case it was nothing worse than beer. Studying the thing impartially, he was forced to admit that he had no reason to be proud of a victory won by such questionable tactics, and he resolved to purge his leadership of all taint at the earliest opportunity. He neglected, however, to say anything about it to Shorty.

The opportunity was not long in coming. It was only a day or two later that Shorty arrived fifteen minutes later for a meeting at Doherty's, with his face exhibiting the first sign of worry it had known for two weeks.

"Mr. Hamlin," he said, "it's up to you. The boys are gettin' restless. I've been waitin' for you to speak, but I guess you've forgot. We can't wait any longer. When's the blowout?"

Now, James knew very well what Shorty meant. But the increasing brusqueness of Shorty's manner was beginning to disturb his dignity. Besides, being on the edge of the Rubicon, he hesitated.

"Blowout? What do you mean?"

"Why, the picnic," said Shorty, surprised at this ignorance. "The annual. The boys are beginnin' to ask questions about it, and I don't know what to tell 'em."

"Still I fail to understand you," said James, with perverse pomposity. "Who is going to have this picnic?"

"We are," said Shorty, a little uneasily.

"Ah!" said James, with uplifted eyebrows. "At last I perceive your meaning. But you are mistaken; you take too much for granted. We are not going to have any picnic."

Only those who have either studied or participated in New York politics can appreciate the awful significance, the incredible folly, of this statement. A king can easier rule without an army or a woman without her beauty than a district leader without his picnic. Shorty knew this, so it is no wonder that he leaped to his feet and roared:

"Good God! Are you crazy?"

"No," said James, "I am not crazy. But I am through with pandering to the low appetites of the people. I was wrong ever to begin it. My true appeal is to the intellect, and not to the senses; and in the future, I shall make it there. I do not fear their disloyalty."

For a full minute Shorty was silent with horror and astonishment. Such sublime folly left him speechless. There was no doubt that James was in earnest. Never had he spoken with more firm decision. With a resolution born of despair, Shorty began to plead, cajole, and threaten; his eyes filled with tears; the foam on his schooner of beer was sadly melting away unnoticed. James was as immovable as the Rock of Ages, and refused to recede a step from his uncompromising position.

Then, suddenly, James was struck with an idea. It was more than that; it was an inspiration. He revolved it slowly in his mind, while Shorty continued his gloomy prophecy of the political future of Mr. Hamlin, and then, having decided, held up his hand for silence.

"Very well," he said, "we'll have the picnic."

"What!" gasped Shorty.

"We'll have the picnic," James repeated.

"Thank God!" said Shorty fervently. "And believe me, Mr. Hamlin, you won't regret it."

"I don't expect to," said James shortly. "And now—"

"First," Shorty interrupted, "where'll it be? There's Hiebstein's Casino, and Kelly's Grove, and Murray's Bay Park, and—"

"That," said James, "I'll take care of myself. The only thing you need to be interested in is the inviting. I'll attend to everything else. Tell them to meet me at Columbia Hall on—what's the date?"

"The twenty-second. Mike O'Toole pulls his off on the twenty-ninth—that's a week from today."

"Just the thing. We'll have ours on the same day. We'll meet at Columbia Hall at 10 A.M. on Saturday the twenty-ninth."

"But—" Shorty hesitated.

"Well?"

"See here, Mr. Hamlin, why don't you let me manage this for you? They'll at least want to know where they're goin'. And what's the use of meetin' in a hall? Why not at the ferry or the station? I tell you they won't like it."

"Then they don't need to come," declared James.

"Oh, they'll come all right," said Shorty. "But I hope to God you know what you're doin'. It don't look good to me."

James arose from his chair and looked down at Shorty. "See here," he said, "I'm getting tired of your insolence. Kindly remember who I am. Now go and tell Dan Murphy that I want to see him here at once." And Shorty went.

By the following evening the district was in the midst of a hot discussion as to the probable plans for Hamlin's first annual picnic. Shorty had been in error. It was the universal opinion that the element of uncertainty—almost mystery—was so far from being obnoxious that it was a positive attraction. Many were the conjectures, and they were as wild as they were numerous. Pink Russell declared that the whole district was to be taken in automobiles to Palisades Park, which was to be rented in its entirety for the day; but though this thrilling flight of imagination was heartily applauded, it was generally believed that Pink's optimism was running away with him. Most of the guesses were much more modest, though all were agreed that, considering Mr. Hamlin's well-known generosity, almost anything might happen.

Mike O'Toole was in despair. He had decided to make one last grand effort to regain his supremacy, and his arrangements for June twenty-ninth has been advertised from one end of the district to the other as the most elaborate and wonderful ever attempted in its history. And James, by arranging for his own outing on the same day, had killed Mike's last hope and spiked his last gun.

Shorty's entreaties for details of James' plans were in vain. If James had been trying to qualify for the title role in a clambake he couldn't have been closer-mouthed. Shorty finally gave it up in despair and fell to organizing potato races and greased pig contests.

By the morning of Saturday, June twenty-ninth, the tension had stretched almost to the breaking point. At half-past eight Columbia Hall was beginning to fill; by nine o'clock it was crowded. The air was full of suspense. Wild rumors flew around and evoked protests and applause in turn. Never before had the district been so much aroused; even the excitement of election day was nothing to this.

In the past few days the district had become definitely divided into two groups. One of these declared Pelham Bay Park to be the destination; the other, College Point. Now the dispute waged hot and furious; bets were made at odds of two to one on College Point, it being the favorite; and Tim Dorgan and Ham Keefe even went so far as to necessitate their being carried into the street to end their argument, where Pelham Bay Park, represented by Dorgan, won by a knockout in the first minute. At half-past nine the door opened to admit Shorty.

"Where is it?" yelled Dan Murphy. "Now open up, ye oyster!"

"Go t'ell!" shouted Shorty. "I know more than you do, but I don't know that."

"You're a liar!" said Murphy calmly. "You've known all along."

Shorty started for him. "Ye black-faced, yellow-backed—" but he was held back by a dozen encircling arms, whose owners insisted on his remembering that he was a gentleman in the presence of ladies, though not exactly in those terms.

At a quarter to ten the crowd, which had been merely noisy and happy, began to grow impatient. Five minutes later Shorty, in answer to the growing demand, started for the door on a hurry call for James Hamlin. He had gotten only halfway from his seat when the door opened to admit James himself.

"Speakin' o' the devil," growled Murphy.

"Shut up!" said Shorty.

James was not alone. Through the door behind him came first one man, then another, then another. They grouped themselves silently at the door, then, still following James, marched solemnly onto the stage and seated themselves near its center. James advanced to the edge of the platform and stood with one hand behind his back, the other thrust into the bosom of his coat.

By now the crowd had recovered from its surprise at the appearance of the strangers. They vaguely resented this intrusion of visitors on the district's most intimate day, but at least their leader had not disappointed them. There he was, ready to take them—God knows where. Shorty was already on his feet.

"Three cheers for Honest James Hamlin!" he shouted. The crowd responded nobly. James turned to the three strangers on the platform with a satisfied smile, then turned back to the cheering throng and raised a hand for silence.

His speech was short; so short, in fact, that it can be reproduced in its entirety:

"Ladies, gentlemen—and children: It is needless to tell you how gratified I am by the noble manner in which you have responded to my invitation to be with me today. However sanguine were my expectations, I assure you I had no hope of seeing such a multitude as is assembled here before me. There are, I should say, at least eight hundred persons in this audience—"

"Nine hundred and sixty-five," said Shorty.

"Thank you. Nine hundred and sixty-five persons in this audience, who have thus taken occasion to honor me and the cause I represent.

"Now, I know you are all eager and curious concerning the surprise I have in store for you, and I have no desire to continue your suspense. In past years it has been the custom of leaders in this district to select a day at this season of the year and invite you to spend it with them, mostly at their expense, in amusement which, though probably innocent, is certainly neither instructive nor profitable. All this I have altered. I believe you to be honest, serious men and women, and I believe you would greatly prefer spending this day in a manner that will suit better your dignity, and increase your value, as citizens."

James paused for a breath. The hall was silent—ominously silent.

"I have therefore arranged for a program which I am sure will meet with your enthusiastic approval. First, Mr. Henry Hightower, of Philadelphia, will address you on 'The Power of the Individual in Politics'; second, Mr. John Clay Brown will deliver his famous lecture on 'Honest Government: Why Not?'; third, Professor Carlton Carlisle, of Columbia University, will talk about 'Self-Reliance as a Power for Good'; and lastly, I myself shall have a few words to say about the future welfare of this district.

"One thing more: owing to the length of the speeches, there will be an intermission of one hour between the second and third. This hour will be spent in the consumption of a little refreshment, for which I have arranged, and in the promotion of good fellowship among us all.

"I now have the honor to introduce to you Mr. Henry Hightower, of Philadelphia."

At the conclusion of this remarkable speech the feelings of the district, in Columbia Hall assembled, can hardly be imagined; they certainly cannot be described. Uppermost were wild rage, blind anger, and unreasoning fury, in order named. They were betrayed, insulted, cheated, and outraged.

Mr. Henry Hightower, of Philadelphia, arose from his seat. He advanced to the front of the platform. He cleared his throat. What would have happened to him, to Honest James Hamlin and Mr. John Clay Brown and Professor Carlton Carlisle, will forever remain unknown; for at that very moment there sounded through the open windows from the street below the strains of "Wearing of the Green," in loud-toned brass. Mr. Henry Hightower, looking through a window from this point of vantage on the platform, saw some twenty or thirty men marching down the avenue behind a brass band. In their midst was a huge banner reading:

Third Annual Outing and Games
of the Mike O'Toole Association
At Kelly's Casino, Whitestone, L. I.

But though Mr. Henry Hightower was the only one who could see, everyone could hear. For a moment there was intense silence. A quiver like an electric shock ran through the throng. Then Dan Murphy leaped to his feat and started for the door.

"It's O'Toole!" he shouted. "Come on, boys!"

Immediately the hall was in an uproar. The door was jammed by the sudden onslaught of struggling, pushing humanity. James, on the edge of the platform, was shouting something nobody heard. Women fought with men in the mad stampede for freedom.

Shorty Benson, standing by the window, saw, in the street below, Mike O'Toole greeting with outstretched hands the first to get down the stairs. He heard the band strike up with renewed vigor. He turned to the door inside and saw the last of the nine hundred and sixty-four rush for the stairs; also, he saw Honest James Hamlin running toward him with frantic gestures.

"What shall we do, Shorty?" wailed James helplessly. "What shall we do?"

Shorty looked once more at the throng on the street below. They were forming to march. The band was going stronger than ever. Now they moved forward.

It was more than Shorty could bear. "Do what you damn please!" he yelled as he ran for the door. "Go to hell! I'm going to the picnic!"

TWO KISSES

—m—

This romance was the only Stout story to appear in Breezy Stories, *which was published by the C. H. Young Publishing Company, the same publisher as* Young's Magazine, *from which it was spun off. Though it is largely forgotten today, a pulp historian describes* Breezy Stories *as "one of the most successful fiction anthologies in the history of American magazines."*

It is difficult nowadays to write a story about a princess, because no one believes in them anymore. Formerly it was all right to begin, "Once upon a time there was a beautiful princess," and a thousand ears would open for you. But if anyone should try it now he would probably be brought up with the socialistic statement, "By July 15th, 1942, there will be no kings, and therefore no princesses, left in the world." Or, what would be still worse, by the realistic query, "Did she have indigestion?" It is the modern spirit, and it is called "getting to the bottom of things."

Anyway, Veronica Tellon was a modern princess. She lived in the winter in a palace in a great city, and in the summer in another palace in a smaller city by the sea. She had beautiful clothes and a checkbook that replenished itself automatically, like the fabulous pitcher, as soon as she emptied it: she never went anywhere unless in a luxurious automobile or private car, and every necessary action except breathing and swallowing food was performed for her by servants.

Her person was neither beautiful nor plain. Her neat, medium-sized figure was raised to distinction by the art of the dressmaker; she had an interesting face, with eyes a little too large for the delicate and well-formed nose and mouth, and the contrast between her mass of dark hair and white transparent skin was somewhat startling. She was aware of the latter fact and took advantage of it now and then to make an impression. Even princesses are not above a projection of personality now and then, especially when they are only a year or two beyond twenty.

Miss Tellon sat in front of her dressing-table mirror one evening uttering blasphemies against herself. Her mode of expression was inelegant and forcible.

"Absurd little fool!" she said aloud to the reflection in the mirror.

Then, after an interval of silence, she turned to the waiting-maid who hovered in the background.

"Jennie," she declared resolutely, "you may take this off. I am not going down this evening."

There seemed to be something remarkable in this statement, for the maid's pretty little round eyes opened in astonishment. Then, quickly aware of her involuntary impertinence, she lowered her lashes and murmured in acquiescence:

"Very well, mademoiselle."

Her mistress looked at her for a moment, then burst into laughter.

"It amused even you," she observed with bitter amusement. "It would be amazing, wouldn't it, if I dared to act as I please. Of course I'm going down. Here, fasten this pin."

Jennie snapped the brooch in place, added a last touch here and there, and Miss Tellon's toilet was completed. She arose with a sigh, patted her hair on the sides, looked again in the mirror and left for the drawing-room.

She found it full of men and women conversing in the jerky, desultory manner of those momentarily expecting interruption—in this instance, the call to dinner. She knew them all, from her father and mother down to little Lucille Cowan, who had had her coming-out dance at Sherry's two nights before. There was old Morton Crevel, associated with Veronica's father in the Street, and his wife; Sir Upton Macleod and Lady Macleod; the two Payne girls; Tommie DuMont and his Russian cousin with the explosive name; Albert Crevel, whose approaching marriage with Miss Veronica Tellon was looked forward to as the most important nuptial event of the season; and, to finish, two or three other young ladies and half a dozen scientists, authors and musicians—for Mrs. Henry Tellon ran to celebrities.

At dinner Miss Tellon found herself between Tommie DuMont and his Russian cousin, and directly across the table from Albert Crevel, her fiancé. Thus she could not avoid looking at him, nor did she want to; she was glad of the opportunity. Throughout the weary succession of courses she kept her eyes on him without seeming to do so; what she saw was a good-looking young fellow with premature lines of experience around the fine dark eyes, a straight, ordinary nose above full lips, and a firm round chin. But the thought in her mind was this, that she saw nothing more. And isn't a girl supposed to see something more than a mere set of passable human features in the face of the man she is about to marry?

This was one of the questions, though not the most important, that Miss Tellon was asking herself as she rose with the other members of her sex to leave the men to their cigars. But in the drawing-room little Lucille Cowan claimed her to talk over her party, and they were still discussing gowns and favors when the men entered half an hour later.

"Talking shop?" came Albert Crevel's voice.

Lucille looked up.

"How mean of you!" she giggled. "Oh, I know what you mean."

"It doesn't matter," replied Crevel, seating himself. "I'll be glad to listen anyway. Old Mannerton's been riding around the dining-room on the Will-to-Live and anything would entertain me after that."

They talked, but Veronica was silent. She was telling herself that Crevel had come over to them only because he thought it was the proper thing to do, and she was irritated by his presence; the sound of his voice annoyed her. She even allowed a smile of bitterness to appear on her lips, then, remembering that other people saw such things and made gossip of them, she speedily erased it. Her attention was caught by a movement in the opposite corner of the room, and presently she saw a man with a violin under his arm emerge from the group and walk toward the piano. It was the celebrated virtuoso Cammini, who was to play for them.

In another moment she was under the spell of his music, and it was with a feeling of gratitude that she gave herself up to his caress of the emotions. Listening with lowered head and downcast eyes, she was filled with a sense of something indefinable, of freedom and joy combined with a painful restlessness, and she felt the tears come to her eyes, then, as the music came to an end and a sound of politely subdued applause ran over the room, an indecipherable, powerful longing arose in her breast and threatened to choke her. She raised her head to look at the musician. He was a young man, not older than herself, with white face and black hair and eyes that glowed.

"It is certain that he has loved," thought Veronica. "Or, at least, that he can love. And why not me? It can't be that one must be superior to inspire it. Why haven't I the strength to do what I want to do? Weak little fool!"

She began to study the musician as he stood talking with his accompanist. "Of course he would have the face of a poet," she said to herself. "He has love, and he has his art, and I—I have a checkbook. And that is why I can never, never know."

Lucille's voice sounded behind her:

"Yes, it's frightful. Mamma says they are getting quite too inde-pendent. Cammini refuses to play for anything less than a thousand dollars, and they say he makes a hundred thousand a year. Just think of it! Papa says it's the income of two million."

Then Crevel's good-humored reply:

"Well, isn't it worth it?"

Miss Tellon turned away in disgust. Perhaps they were right, but why should she be reminded of it at the moment? She looked at Cammini. A thousand dollars a night! A hundred thousand a year! Why, he was a man of wealth, like her father. No doubt his daughter, if he should have any, would be forced into a marriage of conve-nience just as she, Veronica Tellon, was. Either that or a miserable fortune hunter. Was there no poetry or love left in the world?

When Cammini drew his bow across the strings again, the music had lost all magic for her. Throughout the evening she was moody and restless; she even allowed herself to be openly rude to Albert Crevel; and when the guests were gone she sought her room only to lie awake until dawn.

The middle of the following afternoon found her in the library read-ing a novel. She had reached page one hundred and seventy-three, where the hero first tells the heroine that he already has a wife, and she was therefore deeply absorbed in the story, when she suddenly became aware that something was annoying her. She frowned and tried to read on, but the annoyance deepened. What could it be? She looked up and opened her ears, and recognized the disturbing sound.

"Who is that at the piano?" she demanded in a tone of irritation, turning to her mother's secretary at a desk.

"Man tuning it," replied that lady, who was a Woman's Rights advocate and therefore would not add, "Miss Tellon," as a respectful secretary should.

Veronica returned to her book, but found it impossible to go on.

The monotonously repeated notes, cccc, eeee, gggg, jangled in her ears. Then the thought of the piano brought Cammini to her mind, Cammini brought the night before, and that brought Albert Crevel. And the thought of Albert Crevel, and others associated with him, had made her miserable the past six months—a crescendo of suffering. She arose suddenly with an impatient gesture, threw down her book and strolled aimlessly into the drawing room.

The piano-tuner did not even turn as she entered; probably he did not hear her. He had removed the top of the instrument and was busy banging keys and doing something with a wrench inside. Miss Tellon, impelled by a foolish and perverse felling of anger, approached and addressed him sharply:

"Is it necessary to make so much noise?"

He turned in surprise and looked at her.

"Sure. Awful, ain't it?" he said cheerfully, and went to work again.

Completely disarmed, Miss Tellon stood and watched him for some time in silence. Then she sat down on a chair and continued to watch him. He was a rather good-looking young man with wavy blond hair, laughing blue eyes and a boyish face. She couldn't tell much about his mouth because it was screwed to one side with intentness as he listened to the noises he was producing, but she saw that his lips were full of color, as was indeed his whole face. She smiled as the thought struck her that he was just such a person as the philosopher had in mind when he called man "the animal with red cheeks."

She amused herself with speculations concerning him. Was he married? Probably not. On second thought, certainly not. How old was he? Um—between twenty-five and twenty-six. What nationality was he? German-Swedish or Swedish-American or German. What was his home like? But here she failed utterly. She tried to picture a flat, but she knew very little about them; she had never been in one. She was trying to decide whether or not his father and mother were living when she suddenly became aware that he had stopped banging the keys and was putting on the top. That finished, he gathered his tools together and stuffed them in a little black leather case and picked up his hat.

Miss Tellon spoke abruptly:

"Would you mind telling me your name?"

He turned in surprise, and after a moment answered simply:

"Carlsen. George Carlsen."

"Oh," said Veronica. Then, "You are a Swede, I suppose."

"Yes," smiled the young man, with his blue eyes on her.

"You must excuse me," observed Miss Tellon with a touch of confusion, "but I was wondering about you."

"Oh, I see," said Mr. Carlsen. And seeming to regard this remark as an invitation to remain, he put down his leather case and seated himself on the piano bench.

"I'm always glad to talk to the ladies," he observed amiably.

Miss Tellon managed not to smile.

"It is a very estimable quality in a gentleman," she said.

"Sure. And valuable, too, in my line. They all like it, especially the married ones. Lord, how they sit and toss it out! The young ones too sometimes."

"It must be very interesting."

"That depends. It is once in a while, like with you, for instance. I could listen to you all day. When you came in the room I said to myself, 'Open your eyes, Georgie.' But I made a bet with myself you wouldn't say a word. You notice I didn't wait for a second invitation."

This time Miss Tellon could not repress the smile.

"You are very flattering," she said, vastly amused.

"Not yet," denied Mr. Carlsen emphatically, crossing his legs and leaning back against the piano. "That's what they all say when they know they've got the looks. I read somewhere that a woman is always picking on her strongest point just to call attention to it. Ten to one you're saying something mean about your hair every five minutes just because you know it's beautiful. I never saw such beautiful hair."

"Really—" began Miss Tellon, feeling that this was about enough; but he ruthlessly interrupted her.

"Come off now, you know it is. Looks just like some great actress—I forget her name—saw her in the movies the other night. Most beautiful actress on the stage. That's where you ought to be."

"What—?"

"On the stage. Sure you ought. You know, that's a thing I can't understand. Here you are, taking orders from somebody not a bit better than you are, waiting on table or combing hair or whatever you do, making maybe ten or twelve dollars a week, and you might just as well be a Sarah Bernhardt or an Eva Tanguay. They both started in the chorus. Where's the sense in it? Anybody could see that you're the kind that's got it in you. I saw it the first minute. As soon as you come in the door I said to myself, 'Take a peek, Georgie.' On the square."

Miss Tellon, at the same moment that she understood his audacity, felt greatly relieved. It was not that she, a princess, was pleased at being mistaken for a servant; she merely felt that what had been an inexcusable disregard of her dignity was become a legitimate amusement. What tremendous fun! She tried to bring a silly smile to her lips; she conceived that under such circumstances a maidservant would always wear a silly smile—of encouragement.

"By the way," Mr. Carlsen was saying, and his tone seemed to indicate that the time had come for serious business, "you haven't told me your name."

"No, I haven't," she replied stupidly.

"Well—" he observed meaningly.

"Jennie Bellay," said Veronica, her invention failing her, and reflecting that it wouldn't do Jennie any harm.

"Ah, Bellay!" said Mr. Carlsen as though he had been expecting that all along. "Pretty name. You don't mind if I call you Jennie, do you?"

"Well—you see, I don't know you—"

"That's all right. What's the use of being unfriendly? I like that name, Jennie. I suppose you go out sometimes of evenings?"

"Sometimes—yes."

"Ever go to the shows?"

"Why—yes."

Miss Tellon felt that she was playing her part miserably, but she managed to preserve the silly smile.

"They've got on a beauty down at the Stuyvesant now," went on Mr. Carlsen with increasing enthusiasm. "I don't suppose you'd care to see it?"

"Why—I don't know—"

"We could go down any night this week—any night you're off. What do you say we go?"

"But why do you want me to go?"

"Because I like you," said Mr. Carlsen promptly. "You ought to know that—how could I help it? I don't go around with my eyes shut. I'm not blind. I like you fine, and I want to like you better. Believe me, it won't be a hard job. When shall we go?"

"I'm not sure I can go," Veronica replied weakly.

"Oh, I guess you can. Why not? Shall I get tickets for Thursday night? I—"

He stopped abruptly, looking at her curiously as though he had just thought of something, then suddenly got up and stood by her chair, in front, quite close.

"Look here," he said, leaning down and speaking in a new tone, "don't you think I like you?"

"Why—I don't know—" stammered Veronica.

"Well I do, and I'll prove it," he replied gaily.

And the next thing Miss Tellon knew an arm was passed around her neck and a pair of firm lips were planted on hers. Mr. Carlsen was no bungler. He did the thing expertly, firmly and thoroughly. There was no roughness in it, but nevertheless his encircling arm held her as in a vise. This exhibition of the oldest art in the world lasted while a watch would tick off five seconds.

"When shall we—" he began to murmur in her ear. But she,

feeling herself partially released, sprang to her feet and stood trembling violently, with her face a flaming red all over.

"Oh—" she gasped, "I—you—you—"

Then a shadow caught her eyes, and she glanced at the door in time to see Albert Crevel enter. Carlsen, seeing her look, turned.

Mr. Crevel, dressed irreproachably in a dark walking-coat and gray trousers, advanced toward them with the easy familiarity of one at home.

Veronica heard his greeting but was unable to reply, and she saw him standing before her with a puzzled smile on his lips.

"What—" he began, looking at Carlsen.

Veronica made a great effort.

"It is just—just the piano-tuner."

She added turning to the other:

"You have finished, I believe?"

Mr. Carlsen was already picking up his hat and leather case. Whether he realized his horrible mistake is an open question; he may or may not have become aware that he had kissed a princess. Certain it is that he retained all his presence of mind, for as he straightened himself and turned after picking up his hat he sent a deliberate wink, superbly executed, straight at Miss Tellon.

"Good afternoon," he said pleasantly, and departed.

They watched him to the door. Then they turned to look at each other. Veronica's face was still a little flushed, but she had regained control of herself.

"Well!" said Crevel with emphasis. "What's all this? What's the matter?"

"Nothing," she replied coolly, setting herself on the piano bench.

"But you were positively flustered," he insisted. "What did he do? Was he impudent?"

She smiled faintly.

"Oh, no. We disagreed, that was all."

"Ah! I see."

He remained standing for a moment, looking at her, then sat down on the chair she had left shortly before. There was an uncomfortable silence. Veronica kept her eyes turned from him; a thousand mad thoughts were rushing through her brain, all the more confused because of her burning lips. She wanted to rub them with her handkerchief, but somehow could not. She was aware that Crevel was looking at her, and she felt a strain, a high tension, in the atmosphere.

Suddenly she turned and met his gaze.

"Albert," she said, "I can't marry you."

It was impulse that spoke, but as she heard the words coming from her mouth she experienced a feeling of divine relief. Then unbounded wonder. Where had she found the strength to utter them? For many months she had been trying to say just those five words; what drove them forth now? The kiss of a piano-tuner? Well, why not? Let us be thankful for anything that brings freedom with it! As for Crevel, of course he was shocked, astounded; he would refuse to believe her. She didn't know him very well, but she rather expected an explosion.

But he said absolutely nothing; he made no sound or movement, but merely sat and looked at her, though his eyes narrowed a little. It was she who was amazed. Hadn't he heard her? Surely he had. And finally he spoke.

"I've been waiting for you to say that for six months," he said calmly.

Astonishment—!

"But you took long enough to get to it," he went on, seeing that she was speechless. "Only two weeks before the wedding. That makes it inconvenient."

"You expected it!" gasped Veronica.

"Of course."

"But why—I can't believe—"

"My dear Veronica, I'm no fool. You have never wanted to marry me. And I knew you had the courage to say so, so it was merely a matter of time. But, by Jove, I've been frightened lately. I was afraid you were going to wait till we were actually at the altar—I was, really. That would have been awful. For of course we would have had to call it off."

Veronica was too amazed to speak.

"But why—" she stammered.

"Well?"

"Aren't you going—to insist on it?"

"On what?"

"On my marrying you."

"Good heavens, no!"

He smiled at her. His sincerity was unmistakable. She couldn't understand it. But what was it she couldn't understand? Oh, yes. She put the question:

"Then why didn't you—call it off—yourself?"

It was Crevel's turn to hesitate and search for words. He seemed suddenly stricken with a terrible embarrassment. The smile left his lips.

"I don't think I can tell you that," he said finally.

"Why not?"

"Well, I will." He took a breath. "You will probably laugh, but I can stand it."

Another breath.

"Because I love you."

Then he went on hurriedly, "You won't understand, but I'll try to explain. I've thought you knew all along, the past month or so. I do love you. The funny part of it is, I know just when it began, the very day and hour. It was when I first saw that you didn't want to marry me, one day last July at Newport."

Veronica glanced at him. She remembered that day very well, but she hadn't supposed he did. This began to sound interesting.

"I couldn't believe it at first," he went on, "that I loved you. It seemed so absurd. I'd known you nearly all my life—that is, I'd been

acquainted with you. You know how it was: they had it all fixed up
for us to marry each other a long time ago. Then after I came of age I
kept putting it off. I didn't know you very well, and I didn't like you.
Neither did you like me, though I didn't know it then. Finally I had
to give in and I asked you to marry me. That was the tenth of last
December."

He paused. Veronica nodded, and he went on:

"So we were engaged. I thought about it as little as possible, and I
saw you only when I had to, to keep up appearances. I began to think
I hated you and I regarded it as a weakness, because I knew we were
doing only what others do in our set. And besides, you—well, you—"

"I know," said Veronica shortly. "I was sentimental. You needn't
remind me of it."

"Then came that day at Newport. I was positively amazed to find
that you hated me too. Conceit, I suppose, but you cured it. And it
changed me entirely—I mean it changed you. You didn't seem to be
the same person. In a single hour, in one minute, I think, my hate
was changed to love. I laughed at myself, I cursed myself, I went out
on DuMont's yacht with the Halloway crowd. I did everything, but
the result was that when I saw you again I loved you more than ever."

Veronica stirred uneasily. Her eyes were on the floor.

"So you see what a fix I was in," Crevel continued. "As a matter of
fact, I had some pretty bad times with myself. But I finally decided
to leave it up to you. Several times I resolved to tell you—to try to
show you—but every time you did or said something that sent me
back to cover. It's an impossible thing to tell a girl you love her after
you're engaged if you haven't told her before. So I decided that if you
went through with it perhaps it would be all right in the end. But I
knew all the time that sooner or later you'd call it off. And you see,"
he finished, "I was right."

"It may be," Veronica said in a low tone, as if to herself, in answer
to her thoughts, "that you are merely—clever."

"No. Because I am not asking you for anything. You must not

misunderstand *that*. You must believe in my frankness, for I admit I am not giving up hope either. You have had no reason for disliking me except that you were engaged to me. Now, thank heaven, it's all over, and I can take my chance."

"Your chance—?"

"Of making you love me. I don't want to marry you now. That's past and forgotten. Thank God, you had the courage to do it! *I* couldn't; I wanted you too much for that. Listen: You will understand—you will feel it better if you do something. Give me back my ring."

As she heard the word Veronica glanced involuntarily at the solitaire diamond on the third finger of her left hand. Then, with a hasty, impulsive movement, she drew it off. There she stopped, and gazed at it as it lay in her palm, a symbol of misery and suffering, never to end. And now, merely by stretching out her hand, she could be rid of it forever.

She glanced at Crevel, a fugitive, wild glance, then down again at the ring.

"I think I must be crazy," she said slowly. "I don't want to give it to you."

"But you must. Of course it doesn't mean anything, but still you must give it to me. You will feel better then."

"I know." She paused. "But I don't want to."

He merely held out his hand. She did not move. He waited a moment, then rose to his feet and stood before her and spoke in a tone of impatience.

"This is absurd. We are acting like children. Come, give it to me." Still she did not move.

"Look here, Veronica," he said, and his voice began to tremble a little. "You don't by any chance imagine you love me, do you?"

"No," she replied, without looking up.

"Do you hate me?"

"No."

"Do you want to marry me?"

"No. I don't know."

"*Do* you?" He demanded. "Look at me."

She raised her eyes as far as his chin.

"Honestly, I don't know," she said almost pathetically. "I thought I hated you, but now it all seems to be changed." She appeared to recover herself a little. "The truth is I haven't the slightest idea whether I want to marry you or not. Not the slightest idea."

Crevel sat down, then got up. Suddenly he took a determined step forward.

"Look here," he said in a new tone, "there's a way of finding out. It won't hurt you, at least."

And the next thing Victoria knew an arm was passed around her neck and a pair of firm lips was planted on hers. Mr. Crevel also was no bungler. He did the thing expertly, firmly and thoroughly. There was no roughness in it, but nevertheless, his encircling arm held her as in a vise. This exhibition of the oldest art in the world lasted while a watch would tick off five seconds.

He released her and stepped back, his face pale as death.

"Now," he said, "you will know—if you hate me—"

She did not speak, but she saw a quivering movement pass over her body from head to foot. Something fell from her hand and rolled on the floor, but neither of them moved. Then suddenly a tiny spot of color appeared on her cheeks and spread slowly, like the birth of a summer's dawn, until her whole face and neck were suffused with a rosy flaming blush. More slowly still she raised her eyes to his.

It was half an hour later that they found the ring. They found it on the floor under the piano bench.

ASK THE EGYPTIANS

—⁓—

This intriguing story is one of Rex Stout's few stories to feature hints of the supernatural. In it, a poor golfer rises to stardom under the inspiration of a beloved dog. The story appeared in March 1916 in Golfers Magazine, *which began serializing* The Last Drive *four months later.*

"**D**ormie," said Tom Innes cheerfully, standing on the thirteenth tee. He took his driver from the caddie, addressed the ball with a professional waggle, and with a clean, well-timed swing sent it soaring through the air over the brook a hundred and seventy yards away.

"Nice drive."

This came from his opponent, Mr. Aloysius Jellie, who had in turn taken his driver in hand. In place of the other's athletic build and graceful, easy motion, Mr. Jellie was the possessor of an angular, every-which-way figure and his movements were awkward and inelegant. His lips tightened grimly as he waved the wooden club back and forth over the ball. A sudden jerk of his body, a mighty swish, and the ball hopped crazily from the tee and trickled over the turf some sixty yards away.

"Topped it," observed Mr. Innes sympathetically. "Too bad." But the last two words were drowned by another sound, a yelp of mingled pain and dismay that came from the third spectator of Mr. Jellie's foozle.

Caddies, being dumb by tradition as well as from self-interest, are not counted. The yelp issued from the throat of a dog, a white, middle-sized dog of heterogeneous pedigree who had sat on his haunches regarding Mr. Jellie with anxious eyes as he addressed the ball. As the ball hopped from the tee the dog had commenced to whine, and when the profound ineptitude of the shot became apparent, the whine increased to a long-drawn-out, unearthly howl.

Mr. Jellie did not reply to his opponent's sympathetic remark, nor did the howl appear to either surprise or bother him.

"Come on, Nibbie," he said without turning his head, and off he went towards the ball, with the dog trotting along at his heels and the caddie bringing up the rear.

"Brassie," said Mr. Jellie grimly, stopping beside the ball and holding out his hand.

The caddie hesitated. "Bad lie, sir. I think an iron—"

"Brassie," repeated Mr. Jellie, "I want to reach the green."

Then as the caddie pulled the brassie from the bag his employer suddenly changed his mind.

"Alright, midiron," he agreed.

A moment later the iron head whistled through the air, the ball rose high—too high—and dropped in the middle of the brook.

"Too much turf, sir," observed the caddie.

Again Mr. Jellie did not reply, and again he started off with the dog at his heels. Arrived at the brook, he stood on the bank and pointed at the spot where the ball had seemed to drop.

"Get it, Nibbie," he commanded.

The dog looked up at his master with an expression of amazed reproach. "Good heavens," his eyes seemed to say, "didn't you get over this?" Then he scurried down the bank, nosed about among the bushes at the water's edge, and presently set up a plaintive whine. Mr. Jellie took his niblick from the caddie and scrambled down. There the ball lay, buried in the weeds. The next few seconds were full of action. Mr. Jellie swung savagely with the niblick once, twice, three times; the caddie held his hand tightly over his mouth; the dog let loose a series of fearful howls. Finally the ball, gouged from its nesting-place, came to rest at the top of the further bank.

From there it was an easy mashie approach to the green, on which Mr. Innes's ball was already lying eight feet from the pin. Mr. Jellie holed out in two putts, and his opponent did the same.

"Eight," said Mr. Jellie.

"Four," said Mr. Innes.

"That's the match," the other returned. "Better than I did with Tom Hudson yesterday. He ended it on the twelfth green. Come on, Nibbie."

Fifteen minutes later, as the two golfers passed down the piazza of the Grassview Country Club house on their way to the nineteenth hole, Mr. Jellie called out to Mac Donaldson, the club professional, who was loitering about:

"Oh, Mac! Give Mr. Innes a box of balls and charge it to me."

Which explains why so poor a golfer as Aloysius Jellie never experienced any difficulty in getting a match. There was every reason why he should have been the most unpopular member of the Grassview Country Club. His average score for the eighteen holes was 121; he had once made a 98 and had framed the score card and hung it in the room which he kept at the club house the year round. He cut up turf frightfully; he was a strong man and his divots always flew so far away that no caddie could ever find them again. He refused to play in foursomes, and he was outspoken in his criticism of a bad shot, whenever and by whomsoever made.

Worst of all, he was the owner of Nibbie. Where the dog got the name of Nibbie was Mr. Jellie's secret, but it was openly asserted by other members of the club that it was a nickname, or term of endearment, derived from "niblick." Whoever took Mr. Jellie on for a match was forced to deduct beforehand a considerable amount of the pleasure and profit of the encounter by discounting the presence of Nibbie. He was always at his master's heels, and he was the only serious critic of his master's play. If Mr. Jellie topped his drive or missed a two-footer Nibbie howled his disapproval and dismay. A long iron or brassie over a hazard, or a soaring recovery from a sandpit, or the holing of a 30 foot putt, was the signal for joyous barks and caperings. But he was always careful to indulge in none of these noisy demonstrations while his master's opponent was addressing the ball; he appeared to know the etiquette as well as the science of the game. It was wonderful the way his actions and feelings responded to the movements of the little white sphere.

"That dog," said Mac Donaldson, the club pro, one day, "is Scotch. I don't know what kinds of a dog it is, but it's Scotch for sure. I never saw such an understanding of the game in any animal whatever, unless it was Tom Ferguson's cow who lay down on Sandy MacRae's ball so he couldn't find it, and Tom won the hole. It's a great dog, and I could name some humans he could give lessons to."

But it is certain that the other club members would never have stood for the ubiquitous Nibbie, with his eternal howlings and barkings, if they had not been so desirous to avoid offending Mr. Jellie; for Mr. Jellie, score 121, was always willing to play anyone on even terms for a box of balls or a set of clubs or a ten spot. He never won. The numbers of balls and mashies and drivers and putters he paid for every month was appalling. But he always refused to take a handicap.

"I am a strong and fairly intelligent man," he would say, "and I ought to be able to play golf as well as anyone. I refuse to baby myself with a handicap. Make it a ball a hole."

Then he would make the first in 9, and would probably be 61 at the turn. He usually took his defeats gracefully, but now and then after an unusually bad round he would become morose and refuse absolutely to utter a word. He was also known to lose his temper occasionally; once he had taken his bag of clubs and thrown them into the lake—the water hazard on the eleventh hole—and was prevented just in time from throwing his caddie in after them. It was truly pitiful, the earnest and determined manner in which he strove day after day to improve his game, and the sustained horror of his score.

Then came Nibbie's tragic end. Late one Saturday afternoon in May, there was gathered at the nineteenth hole a representative group of the members of the Grassview Country Club. Marsfield, the Egyptologist, was there, with his soft beard and sleepy, studious eyes; Innes and Fraser, lawyers; Huntington, Princeton professor; and several New York bankers and business men. They had just come in from the links; the day was hot and dry and they were emptying many tall glasses in which the cracked ice clinked.

They were talking, of course, of Scores and Reasons Why, otherwise known as Alibis. Fraser was explaining that the bite of a mosquito while he was addressing the ball had cost him the fourteenth hole and probably the match (though he had finished four down); Marsfield, the Egyptologist, was telling of a 20 foot putt that went absolutely in the hole and then bounced out again; Innes was making sarcastic and pointed remarks concerning the incredible luck of Huntington, who had beaten him 2 and 1.

"Ah," exclaimed Marsfield suddenly, interrupting himself, "here comes Rogers. Lucky dog! He got Jellie today. He was out Wednesday too and had him then."

"A bit thick, I call it," observed Penfield, who had once spent a month in England.

"He takes poor old Jellie for too much of a good thing," put in Huntington, glancing at the two men as they approached down the corridor.

"But I say, look at Jellie's face," went on Penfield. "Must be one of his bad days. Just look at him."

It was indeed evident from the expression on Mr. Jellie's face that he was far from happy. His eyes were drawn half shut, as if in pain, his lips were quivering with emotion and his face was very white. Mr. Rogers, his companion, appeared on the contrary to be making an attempt to conceal some secret inner pleasure. A scarcely repressed smile twisted his lips and a twinkle of delight shone from his eyes. As he reached the corner where the others were seated he greeted them with familiar heartiness and beckoned to the waiter for a glass of something. Mr. Jellie sank into a chair with the briefest of nods in reply to the others' greetings, thrust his hands deep in his pockets and gazed straight ahead at nothing with his eyes still half closed as though to shut out some painful sight.

It was Huntington who noticed at once an unusual vacancy in the atmosphere. He turned to Rogers to ask:

"Where's Nibbie?"

Rogers grinned, glanced apprehensively at Mr. Jellie, and replied in one word:

"Dead."

There was a chorus of astonished inquiry.

"Yes, dead," Rogers reiterated.

"Dead as a dead dog. Jellie killed him."

"What!" There was unbelief in ten voices.

Another broke in, Mr. Jellie himself.

They all turned to him.

"I suppose you're glad of it," he observed in a voice of mingled grief and indignation. "Well I'm not. I didn't mean to do it. It was at the tenth hole. Rogers had me four down. Nibbie—" Mr. Jellie hesitated and gulped a little—"Nibbie had been very demonstrative all the way. I was 64 at the turn. I'd made a lot of rotten shots, and Nibbie was right after me all the time. You know how he feels—how he felt when I made a bad shot. Well, on the tenth I got a beauty from the tee, right down the aisle about 220 yards. On the second I took a brassie and carried the brook. It sure was a fine shot, I'll leave it to Rogers."

Mr. Rogers nodded in confirmation. "I always have to play short there myself," he confessed.

"But Nibbie must have thought I didn't carry it," Mr. Jellie went on. "He must have thought I made the brook. Anyway, he evidenced disapproval. It made me mad, that's all there is to it. He'd been howling at me all day for my rotten shots, which he had a right to do, but that was the best brassie I've had for a month, and when he set up that yelp I turned before I thought and threw the club at him. Of course I didn't mean to hit him, or at least didn't mean to hurt him—"

Mr. Jellie paused to control the tremble in his voice.

"It must have caught him right in the temple," he finished.

It is not surprising that this recital of Nibbie's death caused no demonstration of grief on the part of those who heard it. Call it heartlessness if you will; the reply is that these men were golfers with golfers' nerves and that Nibbie had more than once made them miss a stroke. They did not even feign regret. They grinned openly; their remarks were for the most part facetious and satirical; one or two were openly exultant. There were ironic expressions of sympathy and advice.

"One trouble is," observed Rogers to the grief-stricken Jellie, "that now you'll have no way of knowing when you make a bad shot."

"And probably," added Huntington, "your game will suffer in consequence."

"Why not have the body stuffed and set it up on wheels?" suggested another. "The caddie could pull it around for you."

"Or have the hide cured and have a caddie bag made of it."

"Or use the hide for leather grips on your clubs."

"Anyway, you're safe for awhile," put in Marshfield, the Orientalist. "According to the old Egyptians, a dog's soul roams the earth for three moons after his death. For that long, at least, Nibbie will be with you in spirit if not in body."

Mr. Jellie got up abruptly and removed his hands from his pockets.

"You fellows think you're funny," he said quietly, looking from one to the other, " but it's no joke to me. Nibbie was the best friend I've ever had. He always found my ball in the rough, and he was a good sound critic."

"He was sound alright," observed Tom Innes, "if you mean noisy."

"Oh, I know he was a nuisance to the rest of you," Mr. Jellie agreed. "I don't blame you any, but I can't sit here and have a good time with Nibbie dead. I'm going up to my room."

And he did so.

He remained in his room all evening without eating any dinner. He was in fact a very unhappy man. A bachelor without home ties, the possessor of an inherited fortune and therefore spared the worries of the business of making a living, golf had for three years been the absorbing interest of his life. And what, he asked himself, what would golf be without Nibbie? What—for instance—what if he did carry the bunker from the eighth tee? There would be no joyful bark from Nibbie to acclaim the performance. What if a thousand things? Nibbie was gone.

His thoughts were dreary and melancholy as he crept between the sheets, and it was an hour before he slept.

Perhaps it was during that hour that a certain fantastic idea first entered his brain. He had thought during the evening of many ways of paying tribute to Nibbie's memory. He would give up golf. He would ask the club governors for permission to bury his dead at some appropriate spot on the links, say under the first tee. He would have the body stuffed and set up in his room. But finally he rejected all these plans in favor of one that had been suggested in a spirit of jocosity by someone downstairs. The more he considered it the better he liked it as a fitting and poetic method of expressing his sentiment for poor dead Nibbie.

About noon of the following Monday accordingly, Mr. Jellie took a train to Jersey City, accompanied by two men carrying a large wooden box with rope handles. At the Jersey terminus they took a taxi and were driven to a remote part of the town where the streets were dirty, the dwellings poor and dingy, and the atmosphere tainted with the smoke odors of numerous factories.

Before a door of one of the latter, marked "Office of the Darnton Tanning Company," the taxi halted and Mr. Jellie sprang out, followed by the two men with the wooden box. Five minutes later they were ushered, box and all, into the office of the president of the company. This was a dapper little man with eyeglasses and an engaging smile who got up from his chair to greet Mr. Jellie with outstretched hand in an enthusiastic welcome.

"Ah, Jellie, my boy," said he, "what a surprise! Glad to see you again."

The visitor returned the greeting, then turned to the two men, who had deposited the box in the middle of the floor, gave them each a five dollar bill and dismissed them.

"It's been four years since we've met," observed the president when they were alone.

"All of that," agreed Mr. Jellie, and there followed thirty minutes of reminiscences. After which Mr. Jellie came to the point of his visit. He first asked for a hammer, and when it arrived he removed the lid of the wooden box, disclosing to the other's astonished view the carcass of a white dog.

"There he is, Bill," said Mr. Jellie sadly.

"But what—what is it?" gasped Bill.

"Nibbie," replied Mr. Jellie. "My dog Nibbie. He died—he was killed Saturday on the links. I tell you what, Bill, he was an intelligent dog. He knew more about golf than I do. I want to pay proper respect to his memory. What I want to know is this, could you have the body skinned and cure the hide?"

"Why—I suppose so—"

"Then do so as a favor to me. I want the hide made as soft as possible. I want to use it for a particular purpose. I know it will be a lot of trouble, but I'll pay well for it. You'll do it, won't you, Bill?"

It appeared that Bill would. The details were discussed and it was decided that after being skinned Nibbie's body should be sent to a nearby crematory. Then Bill wanted his old friend Jellie to go home with him to dinner, but Jellie managed somehow to get out of that, and by four o'clock he was again on a train headed for the Jersey hills and the Grassview Country Club.

He played no golf that week. He had decided that so much was due to the memory of Nibbie. Those of the others who managed to get out for a day on the links tormented him without mercy, and when the Saturday weekend crowd arrived poor Jellie was forced to take to his room. Through the window he could see the smooth turf stretching away through the hills and woods, with here and there a spot of lighter hue that marked the putting greens, and he heard continually the sweet, seductive sound of the impact of wood on gutta percha. But he gritted his teeth and stuck to his decision, even throughout Sunday, when the putts trickle from dawn to dark and the tees grow hot.

Tuesday morning a package arrived from Jersey City. Mr. Jellie opened it in feverish haste, and there in his hand lay the skin of poor Nibbie, dark, wrinkled, hairless, certainly unrecognizable. But it seemed to the bereft master that the thing was alive; he fancied that he felt in its soft texture a spirit, a sentient thrill, and he remembered what Marsfield had said of the old Egyptian belief concerning the soul of a dog.

He took the skin down to the club professional, together with his bag of clubs, and said:

"Mac, here's a new kind of leather I got from a friend of mine. I think it ought to make a good grip. I've got eleven clubs here altogether. Do you think there's enough in this piece to make grips for all of them?"

The Scotchman took the skin and measured it, then made some calculations on a piece of paper.

"Plenty, Mr. Jellie," he replied. "What kind of leather is it?"

"Why—why—" Mr. Jellie stammered. "It's a sort of Egyptian

leather," he said finally. "I'd like to have the clubs tomorrow morning if possible."

The following day was Wednesday. Mr. Jellie was up early, as usual. After breakfast he went for a stroll in the woods back of the club house, but he was uncomfortable. He hadn't swung at a ball for ten days, and his hands itched. Any golfer can sympathize with him; who has not experienced that irresistible yearning to feel the ping of the wood, the sturdy impact of the iron? Mr. Jellie returned to the club house, and there, on the piazza, saw Monty Fraser gazing around him on every side as though in search of something.

"Ah, how are you, Jellie," exclaimed Fraser, his face suddenly brightening. "Thought I wouldn't go in to the office today and ran over for a little fun. But I couldn't find—"

He stopped suddenly, his face falling.

"But I forgot," he continued. "You're in mourning and won't play."

"No; that's all over," returned Mr. Jellie, eagerly.

"Then are you on for a match?"

"Just waiting for one."

Whereupon Fraser repaired to the locker room and Mr. Jellie went upstairs to don their fighting clothes. On his way back down the latter stopped to get his clubs from the professional. They were all ready, with pieces of poor Nibbie's skin wrapped neatly around the shafts.

"That's good leather, all right," remarked Mac.

"Want to put anything up?" asked Fraser as the other joined him at the caddie house.

"Sure. Anything," responded Mr. Jellie.

"Box of balls?"

"Sure."

"All right," the other agreed; "but really, Jellie, you've got to take a handicap. It's absurd. I go around in 85 to 90 and you average 115 or more. Take at least a stroke a hole. That'll make the match interesting."

"No, I won't," said Mr. Jellie, stubbornly.

And he wouldn't, though Fraser argued with him clear to the tee. They tossed a coin and Fraser won the honor. He was a good driver, and he got a ball 220 yards down the center. Mr. Jellie teed up and took his driver from the caddie.

It is amazing the number of extraneous and impertinent thoughts that can occupy a man's mind when he is trying to hit a golf ball. Though skies tumble and the earth shakes on its foundations he is supposed to keep his eye and mind directed on the ball and nothing but the ball; but such is the perversity and levity of the human brain that at the most critical instant it is apt to be concerning itself with mere trifles, such as the latest quotation on C., A. & Q. or the price of your wife's last hat. Mr. Jellie found himself considering the curious feel of the new grip on his driver. An inexplicable sensation seemed to communicate itself from the shaft into every part of his body, even to the tips of his toes; a sense of confidence, elation, mastery. Always before, when preparing to make a shot, he had been nervous, stiff, uncomfortable, and painfully doubtful of his ability to hit the ball at all; now he felt as though he could walk up carelessly and knock the thing a million miles.

"It's because I haven't played for so long," he was saying to himself. "It's because—*but I must keep my eye on the ball*—I haven't played—*but I must*—for so long—"

He swung savagely. To Fraser's eye it appeared to be the same old Jellie swing, stiff, ungraceful, jerky, ill-timed; and his astonishment was therefore the greater when he saw the ball sailing true and straight far down the course. Midway in its flight it appeared to gain new momentum, lifting gently upward, and in direction it was absolutely dead.

"Some drive," said Fraser, encouragingly, as the two men started down the fairway.

"Yes," agreed Mr. Jellie, who was intensely surprised. But what he was surprised at was the fact that he was not surprised. It was unquestionably the longest and straightest drive he had ever made. Two weeks ago that shot would have left him electrified with astonishment, and now he actually seemed inclined to take it as a matter of course.

"Well," he thought, "it's been ten days since I've played. Wait till I flub a couple."

The first hole at Grassview is 475 yards. The fairway is narrow, with hazards on one side and out of bounds on the other, and just in front of the green is a deep sand pit. On his second Fraser took a driving mashie and played a little short of the sand pit. Mr. Jellie, who had outdriven him by thirty yards, used a brassie and carried over the hazard to the green.

"By Jove, you're putting it up to me," said Fraser, in some surprise.

Mr. Jellie nodded. His face was a little flushed. Never before had he been on that green in two; more often he had made the sand pit on his third or fourth. He felt vaguely that something was the matter, and the curious thing about it was that he experienced no surprise. He had taken the brassie for the purpose of making the green, and as he addressed the ball he had felt absurdly confident that it would go there.

Fraser, who had played short, had only an easy mashie pitch left. He played it perfectly; the ball dropped on the edge of the green, rolled over the smooth turf straight for the pin and stopped six inches away, dead for a four. Mr. Jellie was twenty feet from the hole. He took his putter from the caddie, walked up to the ball and tapped it. It started straight, seemed to waver for an instant, then went on and dropped in the cup with a gentle thud.

"Three," said Mr. Jellie in a voice that trembled.

"Your hole," observed Fraser. "Good Lord, Jellie, what's the matter with you? Two under par! Some three! I got one under myself."

"Oh, I've sunk twenty-footers before," replied Mr. Jellie, with an effort at calmness. But the flush on his face deepened and there was a queer look in his eye.

On the second, a hole for a long and short shot, they got good drives and were on in two. Fraser's putt was strong by four feet, but he holed it coming back. Jellie's thirty-footer hung on the lip of the cup. It was a half in four.

The third is 320 yards. Mr. Jellie, retaining the honor, made his first poor shot from the tee. It was a long ball, but a bad slice carried it into the rough, in the midst of thick underbrush. "Ah," Fraser smiled to himself, "old Jellie's getting back on his game;" and, swinging easily, he got a straight one well out of trouble.

Mr. Jellie, kicking through the underbrush with his caddie, suffered from mingled emotions. Was it possible that he was going to return so soon to his eights and nines? This slice looked like it. At length the ball was found, buried in deep grass, with bushes and trees on every side; it was all but unplayable. One hundred yards away the green glimmered in the sunshine.

"Better play off to one side and make sure of getting out," counseled Fraser.

Without replying, Mr. Jellie took his niblick and planted his feet firmly in the grass. His eyes glittered and his jaw was clamped tight. The heavy iron swung back and came down with tremendous force, plowing through the grass and weeds like a young hurricane. Up came the ball, literally torn out by the brutal force of the blow, up through the underbrush it sailed, up over the tops of the trees, farther, still farther, and dropped squarely in the middle of the green a hundred yards away.

"My God!" said Fraser.

"Nice recovery, sir," said the caddie, in a tone of awe.

Mr. Jellie was smiling, but his face was pale and his hands trembled. He knew very well that he had made a wonderful shot. But what was this strange feeling that was growing stronger within him every minute, this feeling of absolute assurance that he could make a hundred such shots if necessary? He tried to reply to his companion's appreciative remarks, but his voice wouldn't work. He made his way out of the underbrush like a man dazed.

Fraser approached nicely and took two putts, but Mr. Jellie, whose ball was stopped eight feet from the pin, holed out for a three. The fourth, a little over 500 yards, was halved in five. By this time Fraser was beginning to wobble a little, unnerved by pure astonishment. Was this Jellie, the dub, the duffer, the clod? Was this thing possible? Can eyes be believed? Aloysius Jellie one under 4s! No wonder Fraser was upset with amazement.

The fifth is a short hole over a lake. Mr. Jellie stood on the tee, mashie in hand. He remembered how many hundreds of balls he had caused to hop feebly over the grass and dribble into that lake. Again his jaw set tight. Would the marvel continue? It did. He swung his mashie. The ball rose true and fair over the water and dropped on the green. Fraser, completely unnerved, got too far under his ball. It barely cleared the hazard, falling far short, and he lost the hole.

At the turn Mr. Jellie was six up. The cards were as follows:

    Jellie . . . . 3 4 3 5 3 3 5 4 4—34
    Fraser . . . . 4 4 4 5 4 6 5 7 7—46

From there on it was a farce. Mr. Jellie, it is true, appeared to be laboring under a great strain. His face was pale as death and his hands trembled nervously as he reached for his driver or knelt to tee up his ball. But his shots went straight and far, and his putts found the cup. He made a recovery from a sand pit on the eleventh that was only less marvelous than the one from the underbrush on the third. Fraser was shot to pieces, and the match ended on the eleventh green.

"I'm going to play it out," said Mr. Jellie in a husky voice, "and see if I can break 70."

Fraser could only stare at him speechlessly.

"All right," he managed finally to utter.

Very few men find in a lifetime the ineffable sweetness, the poignant, intense delight that the following days held for Mr. Aloysius

Jellie. For one awful, sleepless night he feared a fluke. He had made a 69. Great gods, could it have been a fluke? He sweated and tossed and slept not. As soon as dawn broke he took his clubs and flew to the first tee. A 240-yard drive, straight as an arrow—ah, thank heaven!

He made the first nine holes in 36, and, drunk with happiness, returned to the club house for breakfast.

Tom Innes arrived on the nine o'clock train, and Mr. Jellie took him out and beat him 6 and 5 in the morning and 8 and 7 in the afternoon. On the following day Silas Penfield was the victim, also for two matches. By that time Mac Donaldson had heard of the miracle that was taking place on the fashionable links of the Grassview Country Club, and Friday morning he took Mr. Jellie on for a match, and was badly beaten.

On Saturday nothing was heard at Grassview but talk of Jellie. His caddie had acquired an air of insolent arrogance. Mac Donaldson spoke of him in low, mysterious tones. But for the most part there was doubt, especially on the part of those men who had been winning innumerable boxes of balls from him for the past three years with ridiculous ease.

"Yes," said Marsfield, the Egyptologist, employing a formula of golf wit that is older than St. Andrews; "yes, Jellie might make a 69—for nine holes."

"I'll tell you what I'll do," retorted Mr. Jellie, turning on him. "I'll take you and Rogers and Huntington and play your best ball for five hundred dollars a side."

There ensued a clamor of discussion. Fraser took Marsfield to one side and advised him strongly to "stay off." Rogers was scornful, but cautious. Huntington, a good sport, decided it by declaring that it would be worth the price to see old Jellie do it.

Old Jellie did it, but not without a tussle. News of the match had spread over the links and through the club house, and by the time they reached the turn they were trailed by a gallery of some fifty persons. Mr. Jellie gave them all they were looking for. He went around 3 under par and won by 4 and 3. They forced him to make a speech in the dining room that evening, and in a toast he was referred to as "our next club champion."

And this Aloysius Jellie, who had been the sucker, the easy thing, the object of much amused contempt, became the glory and pride of Grassview. The months of June and July were one continuous succession of triumphs. Middleton, who had met Francis Ouimet in the semi-finals at Ekwanok the year before, was the only member of the club who dared to play him on even terms, and Middleton suffered ignominious defeat. The greatest day of all occurred in mid-July. Tom McNamara and Mike Brady had appeared at Grassview on a visit to their old friend Donaldson, and about the first thing Mac had spoken of was Jellie and his miraculous reversal of form. The two visitors expressed a desire to see the marvel in action.

And Mr. Jellie took on McNamara, Brady and Donaldson and beat them one up, playing their best ball.

He played exhibition matches with various visiting amateurs and pros, and suffered no defeats. On July 28 he won the New Jersey, and on July 12 the Metropolitan amateur championship. He lowered the course records from one to four strokes at Englewood, Baltusrol, Garden City, Wykagyl, Piping Rock and Upper Montclair. The whole golfing world was ablaze with his fame, and countless duffers tried to imitate his ungainly, bizarre swing, with disastrous results. The newspapers ran columns about him, and the sport writers unanimously predicted that with Jellie to lead the attack the next American assault on Vardon, Taylor and Braid would bring England's cup across the water. There was printed again and again the amusing tale of the dog Nibbie, and the story of his untimely death.

Mr. Jellie himself was far from forgetting Nibbie. Often, when at Grassview, he would stand for some time in his room gazing at a small bronze urn which occupied the place of honor on the mantel. It was inscribed:

Herein Repose the Ashes of
NIBBIE,
Faithful Companion and Critic of
Aloysius Jellie.
He Died on the 17th Day of May, 19—,
A Martyr to
The Angry Passion of His Master.

Mr. Jellie would stand and gaze at this urn, not in sorrowful memory of the past, but in perplexed and painful consideration of the present. Mr. Jellie was not a superstitious man. But what had happened could be accounted for only by admitting the supernatural, and one miracle is as likely to happen as another. Was it Aloysius Jellie who had astounded the golfing world by averaging under 4s for 342 consecutive holes? Or was it in fact, in some mysterious manner—was it Nibbie?

But it was another query, a corollary of this, that caused the frequent frown of worried perplexity on Mr. Jellie's brow. Finally, one evening in early August, he got Marsfield, the Orientalist, into a corner and asked him point-blank:

"How long does a dog's soul stay on earth?"

The other gazed at him in astonishment.

"Why, bless me," he responded, "I didn't know a dog had any soul."

"Of course not, of course not," Mr. Jellie agreed hastily. "What I mean is, I remember once you spoke about some ancient belief—"

"Did I? Perhaps so. There are many interesting ancient ceremonies and beliefs connected with the canine family. The Moslems, like the old Hebrews, hold them to be unclean. They were worshipped by the Asgans, and the Egyptians honored them. The latter held a belief that the soul of a dog remains on earth after death, either to console or torment his master, according to the treatment he received in life."

"Yes, that's it," said Mr. Jellie, eagerly. "And how long does—did—how long did they think the soul stayed around?"

"Three moons. That is equivalent to three months, or more accurately, eighty-eight days in our calendar." After a moment's pause Marsfield added: "Still thinking of the lost Nibbie, eh, Jellie? By Jove, old man, I should think the past two months would have driven him out of your mind."

"No, I haven't forgotten him," replied the other, thoughtfully. Then he shook himself. "Much obliged, Marsfield. Come on, let's join the others."

Late that evening, in his room, Mr. Jellie took a piece of paper and made a calculation. It appeared simple enough, though cryptic, consisting merely of a sum of four figures:

$$
\begin{array}{r}
14 \\
30 \\
31 \\
\underline{13} \\
88
\end{array}
$$

He sat gazing at the figures on the paper until the minutes dragged into hours.

Ever since Mr. Jellie's startling leap into the sphere of the masters all Grassview, members, caddies and pros, had been looking forward to an event which was now drawing near. It was discussed in the locker room, the caddie house, the library and the nineteenth hole. The opinion in all these places was the same, though expressed differently. In the caddie house: "Gee, Mr. Jellie kin lick them guys with nothin' but a putter." In the library: "Jellie'll win sure. Hurrah for Jellie!"

The approaching event was the annual tournament for the amateur golf championship of the United States, to be held on the Baltusrol links, August 8 to 13.

But though the opinion at Grassview was unanimous, else-where it was divided. The papers of the Middle West said that Chick Evans was due to win the great prize that should have been his long before. Down East could see no one but Ouimet. In the Metropolitan district some picked Travers, saying that despite Jel-lie's brilliancy he would probably falter under the gruelling strain of the National; but others, who had seen Jellie in action, favored his chances.

Two or three days before the tournament was to begin a delega-tion of Grassview members called Mr. Jellie into council to register a solemn protest.

"Mr. Jellie," said Clifford Huntington—he always called him sim-ply Jellie, but this was a grave occasion—"Mr. Jellie, we have heard that you do not intend going to Baltusrol to familiarize yourself with the course by practise before the tournament. Without any desire to appear presumptuous, we must say that we question the wisdom of this. No champion thinks it beneath his dignity to study the ground on which he is to fight his battles. Mr. Evans arrived at Baltusrol yes-terday. Mr. Travers and Mr. Ouimet will be there today. The per-petual honor and glory of yourself and Grassview are at stake. Mr. Jellie, we beg you to reconsider your decision."

The speaker sat down amid applause, and Aloysius Jellie arose.

"Mr. Huntington and the rest of you fellows," he said, "I appreci-ate your interest and kindness. But I see no necessity of reconsider-ing my decision. I don't need any practise."

And with those sublime words he sat down again, while cries arose on every side:

"But, Jellie, it's absurd!"

"They all do it!"

"Man, we want you to win this championship !"

"For the Lord's sake, Jellie—"

And Tom Innes put in:

"You know, you've only played Baltusrol once."

"Yes," replied Jellie calmly, "and I broke the course record by three strokes."

So they gave it up, but there were shakings of the head and doleful mutterings. Later in the day Monty Fraser approached him and said anxiously:

"You know, Jellie, old man, I don't want to seem officious about this, but we've got eight thousand dollars up on you. You really think you'll win, don't you?"

Jellie looked at him a moment and replied:

"Ask the Egyptians."

Then he strode off.

"Now what the devil—" muttered Fraser, gazing after him in bewilderment.

"'Ask the Egyptians'! I've half a mind to hedge."

On the morning of August 8 the golfing world gathered at Baltusrol. It was a busy and animated scene. Buses, taxis, and private cars were constantly arriving from all directions, especially from that of the Short Hills railway station. The broad piazza of the club house, overlooking the 18th green, was crowded with men and women of all ages and appearances, walking, talking and drinking, and there were even more on the lawns. Tents had been improvised to cater to the wants of the overflow of visitors. Gay expectancy was the keynote. Here and there you would see a face, usually with a permanent coat of tan, which wore the set, tense expression of a busy lawyer in his office or a statesman considering some delicate and difficult complication. That would be one of the contestants—one of the master golfers.

At five minutes past eight the first pair started off on the qualifying round. All day the wood and iron heads whistled and the putts rolled. The links, a bright green paradise in the Jersey hills, with clusters of trees here and there and occasionally a glimmering ribbon of water, stretched forth a lovely panorama for the eye. Some noticed and praised it, but for the most part the thousands of visitors were too busy following and applauding their chosen idols to pay any attention to the beauties of nature.

The best five scores of the qualifying round of 36 holes were as follows:

Jellie . . . . 70 - 71—141
Evans . . . . 72 - 76—148
Marston . . . . 75 - 73—148
Lewis . . . . 78 - 71—149
Gardner . . . . 73 - 77—150

That evening a crowd of Grassview members remained at Baltusrol for dinner. Aloysius Jellie occupied the seat of honor at their table, and his slouching form was the focus on which all eyes were centered. He had won the gold medal for the qualifying round by playing 36 holes 7 under par—an unprecedented score. At that pace there was no man in the world who could even make it interesting for him. The draw had come out as evenly as could be expected from that haphazard proceeding. Chick Evans, Gardner and Marston were among the lower sixteen; Travers, Ouimet and Jellie in the upper.

"Your man hasn't a chance to reach the finals," said a Mr. Higginbotham of Upper Montclair, stopping beside the Grassview table. He was glad to get away from there immediately after.

Jellie came through his first two matches with flying colors. To be sure, his opponents were not in his class—young Anderson of Clinton Valley and McBride of Oakdale. They were smothered.

For his third match he drew Ouimet, and the match drew the gallery. The great conqueror of Ray and Vardon had not been playing up to his best form in the tournament, but his prestige is great, and that, linked with the notoriety of his opponent, drew two thousand spectators. They saw some masterly golf, but the match was a farce. At the end of the first nine holes Jellie, out in 36, was 4 up, and he finally won 6 and 5. In the meantime. Jerry Travers had beaten John

Anderson, and it was Jellie against Travers in the semifinals, with Bob Gardner and Chick Evans in the other half.

"Only two more to beat, old man," said Tom Innes that night to the hope of Grassview.

Mr. Jellie nodded, but did not reply. It did indeed appear, as the sport writers had predicted, that the strain of the great tournament was telling on him. His face was drawn a little and his eyes had the reddish hollow look of a man who is not getting enough sleep. He was getting morose, too, and touchy. That same evening at Grassview, when Huntington had asked him why he didn't try the jerk stroke on full mashies, he had responded in ironic terms more heated than elegant.

"It's getting old Jellie's goat," declared Monty Fraser, anxiously. "We must make him go to bed early tonight."

The following day was one that Jerry Travers and four thousand spectators will never forget.

Travers and Jellie teed off at nine o'clock, and the gallery followed. Jellie, who appeared haggard and nervous, was expected by everyone to crack. As he took the driver from the caddie and addressed the ball the trembling of his hands could be perceived by those fifty feet away.

"It's a shame to take the money," whispered Grantland Rice to a friend. "Why, the man's a nervous wreck."

And yet the nervous wreck won the first hole, a par 5, with a 3. Travers, who had been on his game all week, merely smiled. The second was halved in 4. The third, a short hole at Baltusrol.

Jellie won by sinking a 30-footer for a two. Again Travers smiled. But when Jellie reached the green on the fourth in 2, a long tricky hole with an immense sand pit just in front of the green, an amazed murmur went up from the great gallery, and Travers was observed to bestow a thoughtful and serious look on his opponent.

From there on it was a heart-breaking, merciless struggle between perfection and transcendence. Never before had Travers, the king of match play, gotten balls so straight and far with the wood, never had he laid his irons to the pin with such deadly accuracy, and he putted as only Travers can putt. How he was beaten on that day he cannot yet understand. Jellie was unsteady as a sapling in a storm. He sliced continually and forced himself to play many shots from hazards and the rough. It was these incredible recoveries that caused the great throng of spectators to gasp amazedly and stare at one another in speechless wonder, then to burst out into a roar of applause that shook the Jersey hills.

The match ended on the 29th green. Travers played the first 18 holes in 69, Jellie in 67. Their scores for the 29 holes were 109 and 114.

It was the golf of supermen, unbelievable, miraculous, staggering. And the strain told. Travers was hardly able to stand as he grasped his conqueror's hand for the congratulations of a gentleman; the lines on his face made it look old and a smile would not come though he tried for it. Then Jellie was caught up in triumph on the shoulders of Tom Innes and Monty Fraser and, followed by the cheering, happy, worn-out throng of spectators, they started for the club house. Huntington, running along to relieve Fraser or Innes should they tire, shouted in Jellie's ear:

"Evans beat Gardner, but he'll be pie for you tomorrow! We knew you could do it, Jellie, old man! Wow! Old Jellie! Wow-ee!"

They jollified for an hour at the club house, then tore their hero from the arms of the admiring throng and bustled him into an automobile. It was nearing dusk when they reached Grassview.

"Now," said Huntington, "we'll have a good dinner and then take Jellie up and put him to bed. He still has Evans to beat, though if he plays as he did today that'll be easy enough. Only one more, Jellie, old man, and for God's sake get some sleep. You look pretty bad. Tomorrow at this time you'll be amateur golf champion of the United States."

So after dinner they escorted him to his room and left him there, with a last reminder that they would leave at half past seven in the morning for Baltusrol and the final victory.

The first thing Mr. Jellie did when they had gone was to lock the door. Then he walked to the window and raised it and stood looking out on the night. Unseeingly for a long time he gazed at the stars—perhaps Sirius was among them. Then he turned from the window and went over and sat down on the edge of the bed. In the glare of the electric light the appearance of his face was enough to warrant the solicitous advice of his friends. It was sunken and haggard, and pale as death.

His hands fumbled nervously with the white counterpane. The grim light of mingled fear and despair was in his eyes.

"Eighty-eight," he said aloud involuntarily, as a thought forced itself into speech.

He got up and went to his desk and began scribbling mechanically on a sheet of paper, like a man in a trance. He covered the sheet on both sides, doing over and over again the sum:

$$
\begin{array}{r}
14 \\
30 \\
31 \\
\underline{13} \\
88
\end{array}
$$

He reached over and tore a sheet off his desk calendar, disclosing to view the date of the morrow: "Saturday, August 13." In the blank space left above the date for memoranda there was a large cross scratched in red ink. He sat and gazed at it for a long time, while the minutes stretched into hours, with the hopeless eye of a man doomed. The night grew cold, and all sounds about the club house ceased, and still he sat gazing at that date on his calendar.

Long after the clock in the hall below had struck one, he pulled himself out of his chair and walked over to the mantel, where reposed a bronze urn bearing an engraved inscription. Mechanically he read its words, over and over again. A gleam of hope appeared in his eye, but swiftly died out, to give way to an expression of increased despair.

"Nibbie," he groaned, stretching out his hands to the urn, "O, Nibbie, why didn't I kill you just one day later?"

He tottered across the room and threw himself face down on the bed.

At dawn he arose and dashed cold water over his face. There was a new air of determination about him now, the air of a man resolved to know the worst; his movements were abrupt and decisive, as though he were pressed for time, he took his bag of clubs and quietly left the room, closing the door gently behind him. All was still in the club house. He tiptoed stealthily down the stairs, through the halls and over the piazza to the lawn.

The East's first delicate blush appeared on the horizon as he reached the tee; the magic air of the early morning, moistened by the dew, filled his lungs. He took the driver from the bag and teed up a ball. Trembling fearfully he gripped the shaft and took his stance. He tried to analyze his feelings, to discover if that wonderful sensation of confidence and mastery which had suddenly come upon him three months before had as suddenly left, but all within him was chaos.

He swung at the ball.

It dribbled off the tee and rolled thirty yards away. He picked up his bag and started after it. This time he used his brassie and missed it altogether. He tried a driving mashie, and pulled into a hazard. Doggedly, grimly, he took up his bag and followed it. He made the first hole in eleven.

The details are painful; let us avoid them. At a quarter to six Mr. Jellie holed out on the ninth green, and; adding up his score with trembling hand, found that he was 76 at the turn. There was an insane light in his eyes and he was muttering aloud to himself, but his actions seemed to be under perfect control. He filled his bag full of stones, strapped the clubs in tightly, walked to the lake on the eleventh hole and threw it in. He saw with satisfaction that it sank at once. He hastened back to the club house, and saw with relief that none of the members were down yet. A porter who was sweeping out the library greeted him respectfully as he passed, but Mr. Jellie made no response. He went up to his room, packed a travelling bag, and was down again in five minutes. The walk to the railroad station is a mile and a half, and it took him only a little over a quarter of an hour. The whistle of an approaching train was heard as he entered the station. He crossed over to the ticket office and demanded:

"Give me a ticket for Mexico or South America."

"We don't keep 'em," the agent said. "You can get one in Philadelphia."

"Alright," said Mr. Jellie, "give me a ticket to Philadelphia."

"That's your train coming in now," said the clerk as he shoved the pasteboard under the wicket.

Mr. Jellie hurried to the platform. The train was nearly empty. He found a seat in the corner at a distance from the other passengers, sat down and pulled his hat over his eyes. A moment later the train started.

Five thousand people waited at Baltusrol for three hours on the morning of August 13. But he whom they expected never came, nor was he found, though the search was frantic. And thus for the first and only time in history the amateur golf championship of the United States was won by default.

In a little town down South, on the banks of the Mississippi—he didn't get as far as Mexico—Aloysius Jellie is leading a lonely and monotonous existence. He is in communication with his friends in the East and may return to New York some day, though he refuses to answer certain queries which they make in every letter. Sometimes he plays checkers with the storekeeper, and he is quite an expert.

He can't bear the sight of a dog.

THIS IS MY WIFE

—⁓—

This romance story marks Stout's only appearance in Snappy Stories, *a twice-monthly "Magazine of Entertaining Fiction" that catered to the women's market.*

The first thing you would notice about the room was the light—dazzling, glaring, bold; a perfect riot of light, whitish yellow, that came from four immense chandeliers in the ceiling and innumerable electric lamps on the marble pillars, attached to the walls, on the tables, everywhere. Then your ears would be assaulted, and you would hear the clinking of glasses, the muffled footsteps of waiters, the confusing hum of conversation from half a thousand tongues, and mingled with all this the sound of music, now suppressed, now insistent, that came from the orchestra on the rear of the raised platform at one side. And finally you would glance at the platform and observe the two figures, a man and a woman, who appeared there, in the spotlight.

The man, fair-haired, sallow-faced, bright-eyed, of medium height, was dressed in correct evening white and black, save for a bit of red that peeped out from one edge of his waistcoat; the other, more girl than woman, was a pretty, saucy little thing with black hair and eyes that sparkled. Her costume apparently consisted of about twenty yards of diaphanous material, pink in color, draped around her form and caught somewhere with a pin.

While the orchestra played, these two danced, slowly and rather gracefully at first, then with increasing abandon and violence, ending with a series of dizzy gyrations that caused the twenty yards of pink to float wildly in the air. Suddenly they halted; the girl placed her locked hands on the back of the man's neck, and he began to whirl. Her feet left the floor; still he went around, faster and faster, while the orchestra played at a frenzied speed, with cymbals crashing and drum rattling. The thing ended with a sudden tremendous burst of violence, an orgy of sound and movement; and the audience of diners interrupted their meal long enough to applaud enthusiastically.

The dancers, who had left the platform, paused at the rear.

"Shall we take it?" asked the girl.

"No, what's the use?" replied the other, mopping the perspiration from his face and hands. "Come and have a drink."

They moved off to one of the tables against the wall, one of the few unoccupied in the immense room, and beckoned a waiter.

"You were up too close again," said the man abruptly, after he had given the order.

The girl looked at him. Seen thus closely, she appeared to be more of a woman than a girl. The eyes that had sparkled for the audience looked tired and old, and there were two little puffs of flesh beneath the corners of her mouth. Nevertheless, she was pretty.

"I was no closer than last night," she replied.

"I can't help that. You were too close. You nearly pushed me over."

"Well, it's not my fault if I'm not tall enough. Wait till something happens and then talk."

"That's easy enough to say," retorted the man, pulling out his handkerchief to wipe off the perspiration that was beginning to appear again on his sallow face. "But it's hard enough without somebody trying to pull you over. One flop, and, bingo! goes our sixty per. You ought to be more careful."

"Aw, cut it," said the girl indifferently. "Gee, I'm thirsty! Where's the waiter? Oh, hello, Dibby!"

This last was addressed to a fat, jolly-looking young man who was sauntering toward their table.

"Hello!" The newcomer nodded, seating himself. "How's things, Bronson? I say, Claire, I just met the new soprano. She's on next. Not bad-looking. What are you drinking?"

Then, as the waiter appeared with the order, the fat man burst into laughter and winked at the girl. "Lemon juice and fizz. Bad for the stomach," he said gravely. "But you ought to cut the green stuff, Claire. On the level, I mean it. Waiter, bring me some Dubonnet and sherry. Are you really off, Bronson?"

The other merely nodded, sipping his lemon and seltzer.

"What about the new soprano? What's the matter with Mawsey?" asked Claire.

"Canned," replied the fat man gaily. "Last night. Thank the Lord! Say, she was good, just like a counterfeit V. No? Rotten!"

"What's the new one like?"

"Don't know. Haven't heard her perform. She's on next. Tall and queenly. Where's the waiter? I'm thirsty as the devil. No wonder—been drinking too much today. By the way, you should have been with us this afternoon, Bronson. Where were you?"

"I don't know. Uptown," replied the sallow-faced man.

"He went for a walk in the park," put in Claire, and her eyes sparkled at the fat man.

"So I did," Bronson asserted carefully.

"As for me, I slept till two o'clock," Claire continued. "Wow, but I was tired! We had a little supper last night, and I went to bed at half-past three. We kept Harry awake, and he threw his shoes at us, and one hit me on the side and made a blue spot as big as your hand. Really, you should have been there, Dibby. We had a swell time. Old

Rumford brought six bottles of champagne, and May dropped one on the fire-escape—"

"'Sh," interrupted the fat man. "Break off, Claire, and give me the fate of the fizz later. Here comes the new one. Let's see if she's got anything."

They turned to look at the stage as the orchestra began the introduction to a popular song. The young woman who appeared on the platform was visibly ill at ease. Her cheeks were flushed, and her fingers were pressed nervously against the skirt of her black, clinging gown; her shoulders and arms were bare and startlingly white, and her golden hair assumed a striking luminosity in the glare of the spotlight. It was an effective picture, and a slight ripple of applause ran over the immense room.

She began to sing. It was easy enough to see that she was new to the cabaret. She made no flowing gestures, she did not roll her eyes, she did not even clasp her hands over her heart when she sang of love; she merely stood still and sang, in a tender and sweet voice, two verses and two choruses of a silly song. Once, toward the end of the second verse, she faltered and nearly stopped, with an appearance of sudden agitations; but she avoided catastrophe. It was probably her physical attractiveness that earned the burst of applause that followed—whereupon she repeated the chorus and retired with a little smile and a bow.

"Not so rotten," said the fat man graciously, turning to his companions at the table. "A little bit of the pose à la country lyceum, but all she needs is some action. Did you see her stumble when some guy winked at her or something? She'll get over that. Lord, when I think of Mawsey! Take it from me, old Snyder knew what she was here for. That kind don't get away with it for nothing. Was you here, Bronson, the night she—what's the matter, man? You're white as a ghost! What's the matter?"

Bronson's sallow countenance had lost every vestige of color, and he was gazing at the empty platform with a vacant, dull state that was almost terrifying.

"What's the matter?" Claire and the fat man repeated together in surprise.

Bronson drew himself together with an apparent effort, shifting his gaze uncertainly, while a sudden flow of color came to his cheeks.

"I don't know," he stammered finally. "Something funny—I guess it's my stomach—I don't feel well. Very sudden. I—I'll be back soon."

And he rose abruptly, with a nod, and began to make his way through the maze of tables and chairs to a café for men at the other end. When he had reached it he found a chair in a secluded corner and sank down, burying his face in his hands. Soon he lifted his head, and for a long time he sat looking at nothing with strained, suffering eyes. Now and then he would sigh deeply, and his chin would sink slowly on his chest; then he would pull himself up with a start and resume his vacant stare. He seemed half dazed.

"I wonder," he murmured aloud, suddenly, "if Dibby has taken her out. I suppose he has."

He stood up to look through the glass partition over the heads of the diners in the main room. His eyes sought the table he had left half an hour before: it was empty. Evidently Claire and the fat man had gone off together. Bronson reentered the room and made his way down the aisles. As he passed he heard whispers on either side: "That's him. That's the dancer." He did not stop till he had reached the left of the platform, at the rear, where several small tables were gathered together in a group.

At one of these tables, over against the wall, a young woman with golden hair and bare arms and shoulders was sitting alone, with her chin resting on her hands and her eyes downcast. It was the new soprano.

For a long minute Bronson stood looking at her in silence, while the color came and went in his sallow face. Then suddenly he shook himself, took a quick step forward, and touched her on the arm.

"Rina," he said, in a strange, suppressed voice.

She started and looked up, and as she caught sight of him an expression of amazed recognition came into her eyes.

"Harry!" she exclaimed in so loud a tone that those at near-by tables glanced over curiously.

"Yes; it is I." Bronson paused a moment, then, moving slowly and deliberately, seated himself at the other side of the little table and crossed his arms on the cloth. "Quite a surprise, isn't it? It was for me, a little while ago, when I saw you come on the platform."

"It is—yes," stammered the young woman, looking from one side to the other to avoid meeting his eyes. She seemed terribly embarrassed. "I didn't know you were in New York," she observed lamely.

The corners of Bronson's mouth were twisted into something like a smile. "No," he said slowly; "I suppose you didn't. You wouldn't, you know. But that isn't—that doesn't matter." He broke off and gazed at her for a moment in silence, then said abruptly:

"What are you doing here?"

"Why"—she gave a little uneasy laugh—"you see—working."

"When did you leave Granton?"

"A month ago."

"Have you been here ever since?"

"Yes."

"Singing?"

"Trying to. This is my first job."

"Where's Guilford?"

"I don't know. He is—He is—"

The answer wouldn't come. Bronson waited a moment, then continued abruptly:

"Didn't you marry him?"

There was another pause, longer than before. The young woman sat motionless, with her eyes on the table, giving no sign that she had heard. Bronson was fingering a napkin nervously; his face was very white. He called a waiter and ordered some Scotch, telling him to hurry, then turned to the young woman and repeated his question in a voice that trembled.

"Didn't you marry him?"

Another pause; then suddenly she looked up and met his eyes for the first time. Her face, too, was white.

"No," she said slowly and distinctly; "I didn't. He—he jilted me."

Bronson straightened up with a movement of surprise, then the twisted smile appeared again on his lips.

"What?" he said. "What? You don't mean—"

"Yes; I mean just that." She leaned forward. "Harry, I want to tell you—"

"Wait a minute, Rina. Where the deuce—oh, there he is! . . . Here, waiter! Yes; that's right. No, leave the bottle here."

He tipped the bottle till his glass was three-fourths full of amber liquid, then lifted it and drained it to the bottom, while a slight shiver passed over him. Almost immediately the color came to his cheeks. He turned to the young woman.

"Now go on, Rina. You say you didn't marry him?"

"No, I didn't. And I'm glad, Harry, I'm glad. No, wait till I tell you. I never liked him—really. I've wanted to tell you so. It was because he was rich, and I'd always been so poor, and you were poor, and I hated Granton—I've wanted to tell you—"

Her tongue was loosened now; the words would not come fast enough. She leaned forward, looking into Bronson's eyes, and spoke rapidly, disconnectedly, as one who feels the pressure of time.

"I was selfish and mean, but you don't know what those things—money, and living in New York, and all that—are to a girl. That night, the night you left—it will be a year tomorrow—I cried myself to sleep. I didn't lie when I said I—cared for you. No, I didn't, Harry. If you had only stayed!

"But you went away—I didn't know where—and then he—he began—I don't know, but after a while he went away, back home, to New York. I didn't care. I wanted you. I didn't know where you were.

I stood it in Granton as long as I could, and then I ran away and came here. There! I wanted to tell you, and ask you—to forgive me."

She halted. Bronson did not speak. Instead, he filled his glass again with whiskey, and emptied it. When he looked up the crooked smile on his face was more pronounced than before; it was almost a distortion. And when he spoke it was to ask a question in a curious tone of detachment:

"When did Guilford leave?"

"Why, in August, I think. Yes. But, Harry, listen—"

"Have you seen him since?"

"Yes." A look of annoyance and distaste flashed into her eyes. "I saw him tonight."

"Tonight!"

"Yes. Here. In this room. He was sitting at a table on the other side; I saw him while I was singing. He saw me, too, and sent me this."

She handed a little white card across the table. He took it and read:

MR. WILLIAM LEE GUILFORD

Below this was written in pencil:

Will you go to supper with me?
W. L. G.

Bronson gazed at the writing in silence for a minute, then looked up at her with his crooked smile.

"Well," he said, "I suppose you're going."

The girl did not reply. Instead she took the card and tore it into bits, making a little heap on the plate in front of her. "Harry," she said in a tone that was almost a whisper. And as he remained silent she repeated: "Harry. Harry, I never want to see him again. Don't you know—what I've told you?"

"Yes, I know," he replied bitterly. Then, smiling: "That was what you said a year ago, wasn't it, Rina? And Guilford—damn him! But there, you'd better accept. I suppose he's still here. Call the waiter and send him over. Good advice from an old friend."

And Bronson did what all smokers do when they are trying to appear calm. He took a cigarette from a packet and lit it with trembling fingers.

"But, Harry, I don't want to see him. I don't, really. I want you. I—I was so *glad* to see you!"

"Thanks. But that doesn't alter the advice."

"Harry!"

"No, it doesn't. I mean it."

"Harry, don't you know—can't you see—"

"Listen here, Rina," he interrupted her, his eyes narrowing. "Now, this is straight. You told me once before that I was the only one. Cut out the imagination. Quit kidding yourself."

"But I'm not—"

"Yes, you are. It's the same thing over again. And—well, it don't go."

She began to protest, murmuring rapidly little broken bits of sentences that seemed meaningless, while he shook his head slowly from side to side, always with the twisted smile on this lips. And suddenly, looking into his eyes, she seemed for the first time to become aware of their hardness, their sinister coldness, and she stopped abruptly, with a quick, sharp breath, like one who passes from a warm house into a winter night.

"Oh!" she said slowly, painfully. "Then—I see—it is you—you do not care—"

Her eyes fell, and she began pushing the bits of paper about in the plate with nervous fingers. Then she looked up again into his eyes, with an expression of appeal, of misery and regret.

"Oh, Harry," she cried in a whisper. "I—I thought—if you still loved me—"

And as they sat looking at each other, the smile faded from Bronson's face and his eyes filled with hunger—poignant, actual hunger, like the eyes of a staring animal.

"Rina," he said huskily.

She shook her head, unable to speak.

"Yes, yes, yes," he whispered fiercely. "I love you, Rina. I won't have you think I don't. You don't know what you've done. I love you, I love you, I love you. . . ."

He repeated the phrase over and over. Then suddenly he jerked himself up and passed his hand over his forehead, like a man awakening from sleep. He continued more calmly:

"But I don't think you ever loved me. No, I don't. I don't think you ever loved anyone. I'm wiser than I was a year ago, Rina. There are all kinds of girls—women—and I've met a few of them. You'd be surprised how much I've learned on Broadway in one year.

"I'm not the same man you used to know in Granton. I've changed. I've been drinking pretty hard, for instance. It was my own fault, but I was trying to forget you. I never will. Do you remember that the last night, the night you sent me away, you had on a yellow dress with white on it, and yellow shoes? Whenever I see a woman in a yellow dress I want to run and tear it off her. Once when I had been drinking—but that doesn't matter. I can't think of anyone but you.

"I'm working here, you know, at the cabaret. I'm a dancer. Do you remember how I used to talk in Granton—my high ambitions, my confidence, my—my decency? Do you remember the first time you told me you loved me? I'll never forget that. We were on the porch—on the steps—and it was moonlight. Your mother had just gone in, and we could hear her walking around inside. I didn't notice it then, but later, in my memory, I heard her footsteps, like in a dream, only much plainer. You wouldn't let me kiss you, but I didn't care.

"And the days that followed! The most wonderful days, so happy! Oh, I thought you loved me, Rina! Why shouldn't I?

"And then Guilford came.

"At first I was merely uneasy, then I was wretched, tormented with jealousy. I wanted to kill him! I would lie in bed all night, awake, feeling my fingers around his throat. I dreamed of his gasps, his death-rattle—I could hear it! I knew from the first that life held nothing more for me, that I was doomed.

"I came away. I tried to forget—I've tried every way possible—and I can't do it. But I'm getting—philosophical. Call it drunk if you want to. Another year, and I'll be all in. And listen, Rina, and for God's sake do what I tell you! Go back to Granton. New York is no place—"

He stopped abruptly. A waiter had approached and was handing Rina a card. She read it at a glance, then turned:

"Tell him no," she said distinctly.

The waiter bowed with a little knowing smile and turned to go. But he found his way blocked by a tall, blond man in evening dress. At sight of him the waiter halted with an appearance of embarrassment.

"The lady said to tell you no," he stammered.

"That's all right," the blond man replied, pushing his way forward. "I'll speak to her myself. Hello, Rina," he added, stopping beside her chair and looking down at her.

Bronson turned pale as he rose to his feet. Rina also half arose, then sank back into her chair. A tiny gleam of white showed above her lip as her teeth closed tightly over it. Bronson was glaring at the blond man. She took in her breath sharply as she saw the look in his eyes, and opened her mouth to speak before he could act. But another voice broke the silence.

"I beg your pardon; I thought you were alone," said the blond man, in a smooth, easy voice. "I got impatient waiting for an answer to my invitation, so I followed the waiter. By Jove, it's good to see you again! Nearly a year, isn't it? Aren't you going to say hello, Rina?"

He put out his hand and laid it on her white arm.

But Bronson's eyes, narrowed to thin slits, were gleaming out of his pale face like points of lightning, and the gloss of his black coat shimmered in the dazzling light as a shiver of emotion shook his frame. Rina rose hastily to her feet, half upsetting her chair, and put out her hand as though to hold him back. Then she turned to the blond man.

"Mr. Guilford," she said in a voice that was distinct in spite of its tremor, "let me introduce you to my husband, Mr. Bronson. You met him once or twice a year ago, in Granton."

The blond man stared for a moment in surprise, plainly disconcerted. But he quickly recovered.

"You don't say!" he exclaimed pleasantly. "Really? Allow me to congratulate you—both of you. Yes, I remember you now, Mr. Bronson."

And he held out his hands, one to each of them. They stared at him without moving. Then something—perhaps the expression of Rina's eyes—caused the color to come into his face with a sudden rush, and he dropped his hands.

"Really!" he repeated, with a foolish, uncomfortable smile. And he turned without another word and went away.

Rina watched his back move down the aisle. Then:

"Harry," she stammered, "Harry—you see—"

She stopped abruptly, caught by the expression of his face. He was grinning, actually grinning, with his mouth twisted to one side and the muscles of his cheeks distorted. And as she looked, amazed, he suddenly burst into laughter—sharp, ringing laughter that drew the attention of twenty tables. He said nothing; he did not move or shake his shoulders; he merely stood still and laughed like a crazy man, while the diners turned around in their chairs to look at him in amused wonder, and Rina stood silent, speechless.

But suddenly he stopped, as his gaze was caught by something at the rear of the platform, which he faced, behind Rina.

"Ah," he cried, "there she is now! Dibby! Claire! Come here!"

Rina turned in time to see the approach of a little, black-haired creature by the side of a fat, jolly-looking young man. They had on their wraps, having evidently come from the street.

"Here, Claire," Bronson was saying. "Here, I want to introduce you to Rina Warner, an old friend of mine."

And as Claire approached he took her hand and bowed deeply.

"Rina," he said, "this is Claire, my wife. We were married a month ago."

Then he began to laugh again.

SECOND EDITION

—⁓—

This story about a broken engagement and a more promising marriage appeared in Young's Magazine.

Harry Sackerville was only thirty-six then, but he had already built the railroad to China and handled the Algerian situation for the French government, for which he received the Cross of the Legion of Honor. He was not yet vulgarly famous, but his name was known in high places, and it was said that London was about to retain him to clear things up in Persia; but the plan fell through. When he returned from Africa he found, to his astonishment, that New York had decided he was a great man. He was dined by the Lotos Club, and the magazines and newspapers begged for articles and interviews on everything from Kabyles to Roquefort cheese. It was one of those little tricks fortune is so fond of playing.

After a month of New York, having taken too large a dose of teas and dinners and motor rides, Sackerville was unspeakably bored. Then he received a request for an interview from someone in the State Department at Washington. At the end of three days he was back in the metropolis, more restless than before. The evening of his return he dined with some friends at a downtown club; the company was congenial, the wines were good and Sackerville drank more than was necessary. The next morning he woke up with a headache.

"I'm sick of this place anyway," he said to himself, yawning at the window.

He dressed, breakfasted, packed his bag and caught the ten o'clock train for Utica.

He was turning back to an early page in his book of life. It was in Utica that he had spent his first seventeen years in the world, for the most part an orphan and penniless. In all the nineteen years since he had left, the day after his graduation from high school, he had not been back; he had not found time, and, besides, his memories of youth were not cheerful. One in particular—that of Melissa Hayes, with her red hair and white skin and large blue eyes. She had been in his class.

What a curious mechanism is the human heart! Violent emotions may fill it, break it, and in a short time depart, leaving no trace of their passage; while some youthful impression, hardly noticed at the time, may find its place in a little corner and then, as the years pass, gradually and silently steal its way to the center.

Sackerville could remember now that he had admired Melissa Hayes nineteen years before, but he had no recollection of any eager passion for her. One night, however, asleep in the Chinese wilderness, he had dreamed of her red hair on his face and the thought of her had held him ever since. In the desert, in the midst of rough engineering camps, at moments of peril, amid the comforts of a Paris or Berlin hotel, he had thought of her; not always—for he was an enormously active man—but often. There had been at least one girl—the daughter of the French consul at Cairo—whom he would have married but for the memory of Melissa Hayes. And other women, too—but he did not care to think of them.

So he was going to Utica to visit his boyhood friend, Andrew Beach, with whom he had corresponded at intervals. He pulled a letter out of his coat pocket as he leaned back in the chair of the pullman. It was on a business letterhead: "Andrew Beach, Fancy Groceries, Wholesale and Retail." He smiled. Queer how men could bury themselves under bags of potatoes in a little upstate town and get happiness out of it! Old Andy, too. *Was* he happy? Sackerville wondered.

Then he thought of Melissa Hayes and admitted to himself that it was her red hair which was taking him back to Utica. It was absurd, of course; probably she didn't live there anymore and certainly she was married. He told himself that the image in his heart was not Melissa Hayes at all; it was a memory, an abstract desire, an ideal. It could make no difference if he saw her and spoke to her—the disturbing image would remain in his heart to tantalize him forever; but he wanted to see her—

And it was of her he thought as the train flew swiftly along the bank of the Hudson. He leaned back in his chair with an unopened book on his knees, gazing through the window at the curving outline of the hills across the river. He found himself getting impatient the other side of Albany; then, as he neared his destination, he was taken with a curious reluctance, almost a timidity. He was sorry he had come. But when the train stopped he leaped to the platform, summoned a cab and gave the address on Andrew Beach's letterhead.

Ten minutes later he was shaking hands with Andy in a little office with the word "Private" on the door. After the first greetings the two men stood looking at each other in silence for some time.

"You've changed a lot, old man," said Sackerville. Indeed, it was difficult to believe that this little fat, bustling grocer, already half bald, was his old boyhood friend. There was nothing to go by, no feature he could place—but yes, the eyes. They had the same sly, twinkling expression he remembered so well. Come to think of it, this was just the sort of man one would have expected Andy Beach to grow into. No doubt he was adept at the tricks of the trade.

"Yes, I'm doing fine," the grocer was saying. "Three floors here and a warehouse over on Fillmore Street; you know, opposite old Pat's livery stable. I've got the biggest wholesale business in the city. Show you my plant in the morning—" he glanced at his watch—"too late now. We'll go home and have some dinner. Mrs. Beach will sure be glad to see you. Got your bag?"

"Yes, but I'll send it down to the hotel," said Sackerville.

But Andrew Beach wouldn't hear of that. Let his friend Harry stay at a hotel? He should say not! His wife would never forgive him! He gave some orders to subordinates in the office, linked his arm in Sackerville's and led him out to the curb where a motor-car was waiting with a chauffeur on the seat.

"Ah!" said Sackerville.

"Yes," said the grocer, motioning him to get in. "Some car, eh? Good as any in town. I work hard, and I believe in getting what I can out of life. The best is none too good for me when I can afford it."

As the car sped through the darkening streets he continued his chatter.

"I see you've been doing big things," he observed, "in Africa and places. There was a whole page about you in the *Herald* a week ago Sunday; I suppose you saw it. My wife read it aloud to me. Well, I'm glad— See there? Old Snyder's drugstore. Yep; still there. Things still look familiar, don't they? It don't seem possible you've been gone twenty years. There's old Carroll's church, but he's dead; remember how we used to pester him? By the way, you've got here just in time for *the event*, so don't be surprised if you find things every which way you know, Melissa's going to be married next week."

Sackerville sat up. "Melissa?"

"Yes. My daughter. I've spoke about her in my letters, I suppose. Always called her Melly, but she won't stand for it anymore now she's engaged. All right, so I say Melissa. She's a fine girl."

"Melissa!" Sackerville repeated stupidly.

"Yep. Named after her mother—Melissa Hayes—she was in our class—remember the tall girl with red hair and big blue eyes? Of course, I wrote you about it. I married her about a year after you left."

"No, I never knew it," said Sackerville after I pause. "But I—I remember her."

"Sure you do. I must have written you about it, but it was a long time ago. She's been a good wife, Harry, except for a few queer notions. She's society. And then— Here, see that big house on the corner? No, the one with the closed porch. That's Dan Harrison's— remember Dan? He's in real estate. Very successful. We'll drop in on him tonight. Here we are! Yep, this belongs to yours truly. Got a hundred feet both ways—garage in the rear. Good Lord! I ought to have telephoned Melissa! She'll give me the dickens."

As Sackerville got out of the car and ascended the steps of the broad, deep porch, he felt ironically amused at himself. He had sought the ideal of his heart and found the wife of a provincial grocer! *Tant pis!* No one but a fool would have expected anything better. He was sentimental enough to feel a repugnance about crossing the threshold; he did not want to meet her. Certainly it would not be his Melissa, whose face had haunted him in the desert and wild places of the earth.

"Sit down—in there—make yourself at home—back in a minute," Andrew Beach was saying as he disappeared down the hall.

Sackerville entered a large modern parlor and seated himself on a covered divan in the recess of a double window. Looking around, he told himself that the room was not half bad; there was even evidence of taste. The furniture was all in dark tapestry, except a table and chair of kioto wood near the fireplace; the walls were dark gray, and there were few pictures. At one end was a pianola with a cabinet of rolls. The whole was bathed in the soft light of an electric pedestal lamp in a corner; and Sackerville was idly taking in these details and commending them when he heard steps in the hall. He told himself that it would be the grocer's wife, and he braced himself. The steps approached the door—

"My God!" cried Sackerville aloud, springing to his feet.

"Oh!" came a startled voice. "I beg your pardon—I didn't know there was anyone—"

It was Melissa—Melissa of the wilderness! He could not understand it, and he stood staring stupidly as she entered the room with a quick, unconscious grace and crossed to the table. He felt stunned and silly. There she was, tall, slender, youthful, with her large soft eyes relieving the fire of the splendid hair, and her skin like frozen snow. She took a book from the table and turned to leave. She neared the door.

"Oh, here you are!" came the voice of Andrew Beach. "Sackerville!" The grocer entered the room, followed by a large tall woman with flushed face and shining eyes. "Harry, this is my wife and my daughter Melly—all right, Melissa then. Two of 'em. First and second edition. What do you think? Looks just the same, don't he? He's a great man, daughter, but don't be afraid of him. Yes, you've heard us speak of Harry Sackerville. Remember the piece in the *Herald* a week ago? Come on, Harry, if you want to wash up; dinner's about ready. I'll show you your room."

Upstairs the astonished Sackerville moved about in a daze as he washed his hands and face and changed his linen, while his host sat on the bed and chattered. He had seen her, he was to dine with her—that was as far as his thoughts could get. She existed. She was here. What supernatural luck! He felt a glow in his breast.

"You'll have to excuse the women," Andrew Beach was saying. "They'll probably eat and run. Busier than two hens the week before Easter. This wedding business is awful. Lord, it's funny to think of Melly getting married. Only yesterday—"

Sackerville dropped the soap on the floor.

"—she was a kid on my knee. It's a bad thing, Harry, when your children grow up. Though Melly—Melissa's all I've got. There's bound to be things you don't like, and you wonder if they'll be happy. Take this man going to marry Melissa; I suppose he'll do, but I don't like him. Railroad man—owns the lines both ways up the valley—I guess he's about the richest young man in town, but Lord, it won't make Melissa happy just to be able to take free rides on a railroad. It's her mother's doing. Society bug. Says her daughter will be the most prominent matron in the city. I don't like it. Who wants to be a prominent matron? It ain't wise."

This chatter carried them to the dining-room, and there Andrew Beach subsided suddenly and completely to give his wife a chance. Mrs. Beach talked rather slowly in order to make sure of her pronunciation. Her accent was very refined. She opened with a discussion of school reminiscences with Sackerville, then spoke at some length of the pleasure it gave one to entertain so distinguished a guest at one's own table in an informal manner. She gushed. This lasted till the roast, when she began talking of her home, having been started by a compliment from Sackerville. It was such a satisfaction to one to surround one's self with artistic things. Thanks to Andrew's commercial success—she smiled approvingly at her husband—she had been able to gratify her tastes. Also, she had raised her family to a position at the very top of society, and the hour of her greatest triumph was at hand. No doubt Andrew had informed Mr. Sackerille of the approaching marriage of her daughter to Mr. John Gowanton.

The distinguished guest admitted that he had been so informed.

"The most eligible gentleman in the city," said Mrs. Beach emphatically.

Her husband muttered something that sounded suspiciously like, "Damphool."

"What did you say, Andrew?" she demanded.

"Nothing," replied Mr. Beach hastily, conveying some meat to his mouth.

At that moment Sackerville did something he had been trying to do since the beginning of dinner. He met the eyes of Melissa Beach—and they twinkled. Unconsciously he returned her glance with the frank familiarity of an intimate friend, so clearly and obviously was she the Melissa of his heart, whose image had been with him many years; and she flushed and looked away. He watched the delicate color tint her white skin and found a place for it in his memory; and when, in a few moments, her eyes stole back, he was still gazing at her, and the flush deepened. He had no sense of his own rudeness; he was merely seeing in reality what had so often charmed his heavy-lidded eyes in the lonely nights.

"Really, the best family in the city—" Mrs. Beach was saying.

That night Sackerville lay awake to think. Not despairing thoughts, though it would seem that he had found the object of his dreams only to lose it. He was a man who had fought with mountains and deserts and gangs of lazy criminal men and sneaky little diplomats; and ordinary foes, such as social conventions and ambitious matrons and best families, held no terrors for him. On the whole, his thoughts were optimistic and happy.

"I wonder what kind of fellow this Gowanton is," he said to his pillow, and turned over and went to sleep.

The next day, Sunday, he and his old friend Andrew sat on the porch and talked over old times while the mother and daughter went to church. In the afternoon they motored into the country. Sackerville sat in front beside the grocer, who drove, while the tonneau was occupied by Mrs. Beach, Melissa and Melissa's fiancé.

Mr. Gowanton was a fat, red-faced young man without any neck, very jolly and talkative. He laughed continually, with or without reason, in a high thin falsetto, and his conversation consisted entirely of personal recollections of the most irrelevant nature.

"Regular fool. Sorry he got Melly," said Andrew Beach in a hoarse aside to his friend.

Sackerville nodded, smiling.

When they got back from the ride Gowanton stayed to dine with the family, as a matter of course. At the table his jollity was more in evidence than ever, until, by a chance remark of his host's, he discovered that Sackerville was the man who built the Tsing-Tso Railroad.

Then he began talking construction and equipment, and displayed an insight and knowledge of the subject really surprising in a country capitalist. Sackerville warmed and by degrees allowed himself to be drawn into a recital of his varied adventures.

"Great stuff," said Gowanton, chewing, "but it won't pay dividends."

"Military road," observed the grocer sententiously.

"No doubt it's exciting," put in Mrs. Beach, "but it is so unsettling. One must have a home and a position in society. Going all over the world like that—no permanence—"

"Sort of superior vagabondange?" smiled Sackerville, who had been trying for an hour to meet Melissa's eyes. "Yes, of course, such a life has its disadvantages. A man gets so he lives mostly in his dreams, as far as sentiment is concerned. Like a friend of mine, an army officer in India. He had a dream one night, sort of an apparition. It was the face of a girl, very beautiful, as he described her to me once, and he kept seeing that face for years. It took him entirely and he got superstitious about it. He fancied himself in love with her; he could not believe it was only a vision, and he would have nothing to do with any woman. For ten years he remained faithful to that shadow of a dream. Then he went home to England on leave, and he met her at a dinner in London—the eyes, the hair, the face, the voice, everything the same. She was married to another man."

"Oh, how awful!" cried Melissa.

"Of course, being an officer and a gentleman, he could say nothing," commented Mrs. Beach.

"What did he do?" demanded the grocer.

"He killed the husband and took her out to India," said Sackerville calmly.

And he looked into Melissa's eyes, to find them startled and a little skeptical but filled with a strange friendliness.

That night he lay awake again, thinking, and slept with a smile.

The next morning he was up early, but he appeared to have

nothing in particular to do, for he accepted the grocer's invitation to go downtown with him and look over the store and warehouse.

"We'll come home for lunch," said Andrew Beach. "This afternoon I have to go to the church and practice giving my daughter to that Gowanton. Rehearse a wedding! Tomfoolery! Well, it'll all be over tomorrow noon. She'll be married then. Crazy to leave your old daddy, are you, Melly? Come on, Harry, the car's waiting."

But when he had spent three hours gazing at rows of boxes of tomatoes, sardines, soup, cheese, and a thousand other things, and the time came to go to lunch, Sackerville said he would prefer to remain downtown. Nor would he meet his host later at the church, where the wedding was to be rehearsed.

"Don't blame you," said Andrew Beach. "Damn nonsense. Wish you'd let me leave the car for you."

Sackerville declined this offer again and set off afoot. All afternoon he roamed over the city alone, searching landmarks of his youth; and now and then he would meet a face that lookd familiar and yet strange, awakening a memory that had lain dormant for many years. He found nothing that attracted or moved him, and his thoughts were really of Melissa, who was to be married to John Gowanton at noon of the following day. He still felt the strangeness of having seen her and spoken to her in her youth and fresh beauty, just as she had so often appeared to his fancy; there seemed to be something fantastic about it. How beautiful she was! What unbelievable luck!

"If I had been four days later—" he thought, and grew pale.

It was an aimless afternoon, except for one errand which he performed at the city hall about four o'clock, in a dingy little room with a sign: "Marriage Licenses," over the door. Sackerville walked to the desk and asked for a license for the marriage of Henry Sackerville and Melissa Beach.

"What!" said the astonished clerk, a sharp-nosed young man who knew things. 'Why, Miss Beach is to be married—"

"Listen," Sackerville interrupted. "This is a joke. I'm going to play a joke on Gowanton. I ask for the license. It's your business to make it out."

With a meaning look at the sharp-nosed young man he pushed a ten-dollar bill across the counter, and five minutes later departed with the license in his pocket.

That evening at the dinner table the talk was all of the wedding. They discussed the rehearsal, which Mrs. Beach declared had gone off beautifully. Even Dan Harrison, the best man—by the way, Sackerville would remember Dan Harrison as an old classmate—even he had seemed for once to lose some of his awkwardness. If only it went as well tomorrow!

"I hope John behaves himself tonight and retires early," said Mrs. Beach. "He is so—so *popular*. Melissa, you must go to bed right after dinner and get some rest. I'm sure I don't know how we've stood it all. Did you see Mrs. Carroll's gift, Mr. Sackerville? So tasteful and rich! You should be a very happy woman, Melissa, so many friends—"

The end of dinner stopped her. The men went out on the porch to smoke their cigars, and for once Andrew Beach was silent, as befitted a man who was to lose his only daughter on the morrow. It was barely nine o'clock when Sackerville arose to go to his room, saying that his long walk had made him sleepy.

"I'm going to turn in, too," said Andrew Beach, following him. "I hope I can sleep."

"If only she's happy—" said the grocer, parting from his guest at the head of the stairs.

But Sackerville did not go to bed when he entered his room. Instead, he sat down on a chair near the window and lit another cigar. It was a long black cigar and took some time to smoke, but when it was finished he lit another. Though the window was open, few sounds entered in that quiet residential district. Now and then an automobile passed, and occasionally the jangle of a streetcar could be heard at a distance. Sackerville kept looking at his watch, and when it said eleven o'clock he arose, threw away his third cigar, went to the door of his room and opened it.

The hall was quite dark, but he knew his position. At the further end, some distance away, was the room of the grocer and his wife, who, he hoped, were both sound asleep. In the other direction, across the hall, was another door; he stepped forward, groping along the wall—it ought to be about here—ah! He raised his hand and tapped softly on the panel. After a pause he tapped again, a little louder.

A slight movement, a barely audible rustle, sounded within the room, then footsteps. A voice came:

"Is it you, Mother?"

"No. It is I—Sackerville."

There was a startled exclamation quickly suppressed, and the door opened a little.

"What—what is it?" came a voice through the crack.

"I want to talk to you. I knew you would be awake. Will you come downstairs?"

"Oh—why—I—I can't!"

"You must. Only a minute. I will be in the library."

Without waiting for a reply, Sackerville turned and groped his way back through the hall to the stairs. He tiptoed silently down to the library, where he switched on the electric pedestal lamp, then went to the windows and drew the shades. He sat down on a chair, then got up again and began pacing silently up and down; he could hear his watch ticking in his pocket. He had a curious feeling, not exactly impatience; the minutes seemed to hang in the silent air. Then, hearing a noise at the door, he turned quickly.

"Ah," he said, "I knew you would come."

Melissa looked at him from the door. She wore a house-dress of pale green, caught at the throat with a silk cord and a girdle at the waist; and the soft dull glow of her hair seemed to melt into the dim light so that her face was a spot of intense whiteness in a somber frame. She was more beautiful than any vision could have been.

"And how—how did you know that?" she asked, between a whisper and a murmur.

Sackerville smiled. "Curiosity will do anything," he said. "Won't you come in so I can close the door? We mustn't wake anyone."

"But I am not sure I want to come in."

"Yes, you do. Come."

And as she took a step forward he went to the door and closed it noiselessly, then took her hand and led her to the divan in the windows.

"This is—I was never so imprudent in my life," said Melissa. "What is it? What's the matter with me? What do you want?"

"Just to talk with you." Sackerville sat down beside her. "You are to be married tomorrow, so I won't have another chance. I suppose this strikes you as—well—a little unconventional?"

"A little," said Melissa with a smile. She looked at him. "Yes, it was curiosity. And you—you just wanted to see if I would come. Wasn't that it? Well, I did, and now—"

She started to rise.

"No. Wait. I want to ask you a question first. Are you in love with Gowanton?"

Melissa sat down again, with a little startled exclamation, and turned eyes of amazement on him. It was an absurd, incredible question from a man she had barely met, a stranger; she must protest, she must assert her dignity. . . . But his eyes were on hers, and they were certainly not impertinent. . . .

"I am going to marry him," was what she said.

"I know. That would be enough for most men, but not for me. Of course, you don't love him. You are being married off, that's all. That's why I think I have a right— Do you remember the story I told last night of my friend the army officer? Well, that was me. It is your face that has haunted me for ten years. Only I didn't know you were quite so beautiful. I'm not making love to you, I'm just telling you the facts. And since it will be too late tomorrow, won't you do this for me? Won't you talk with me frankly and honestly, like old friends, just for five minutes?"

"But this—no—I can't believe—" said Melissa breathlessly.

"You must. You're only a girl; you haven't realized some things, their seriousness. I know you don't love Gowanton. Of course, you don't love me either; but I love you and I want you. As far as your promise is concerned, I don't give a hang for it; that's up to your mother. She's arranged it; let her get out of it. It amounts to this, do you care for Gowanton more than you do for me? Of course, I'm a stranger; you don't know me; but do you know him any better, really? Do you care for him even a little bit? Tell me."

There was no reply. Melissa sat looking straight ahead, with her fingers playing nervously with the silken cord at her throat. Suddenly her head fell forward and she covered her face with her hands. There was a long silence. Sackerville could see her white neck curving under the pale green of her dress, and her great mass of hair like a cushion on her lap. The ticking of the clock could be heard from the hall, through the closed door. He sat without moving, waiting, for a long time; then he put out his hand and touched her shoulder. She shivered all over and sprang to her feet.

"That was exactly what was the matter with me," she said slowly, in a trembling voice. "That was why—but I didn't know it till tonight. And now it is too late."

She glided to the door and opened it.

"No," she said without turning her head, "no, I don't love him."

She disappeared in the darkness

Here is a scene of activity; seven or eight servants running around, preparing everything from a hot iron to a wedding breakfast; six bridesmaids dodging in and out of every conceivable sort of errands, or none at all; Mrs. Beach holding on to her daughter by a long something and yelling frantically for pins; Andrew Beach roaming around the halls in a cloud of cigar smoke swearing under his breath and looking at his watch every two minutes. And it still lacked an hour and a quarter till noon, which was the time set for the wedding at the church twelve blocks away.

Andrew Beach was just seating himself on the porch in the vain hope of escaping from the turmoil for a few minutes when his friend Sackerville appeared from somewhere and said calmly:

"I've just telephoned Gowanton that you want to speak to him. He's coming right over. It would be best to take him up to my room, out of the way."

"What are you talking about?" demanded the grocer, leaping to his feet. "Are you crazy, too? *I* don't want to see Gowanton. What's he coming here for?"

"No, but I do," replied Sackerville. "Take it easy, Andy. I'll explain to you shortly. There's something I want to say to you and Gowanton together. He'll probably come in his car; he ought to be here— There he comes now!"

A big gray limousine had appeared down the street, and soon it drew up at the front curb to deposit Mr. John Gowanton, redder than ever, on the brick walk. He looked stiffer than usual, too, but that was merely the effect of his very new clothes.

"What is it, what is it?" he puffed, ascending the porch. "Good morning, Mr. Beach, Mr. Sackerville. Is there anything the matter— Melissa—"

Andrew Beach was flustered himself, but he managed to follow Sackerville's instructions and lead the way upstairs to the guest-room. They met three or four servants and a bridesmaid or two in the halls, but no one noticed the bridegroom's presence. Sackerville placed chairs for Mr. Beach and Mr. Gowanton, then seated himself on the edge of the bed.

"But what is it? What's the matter?" repeated Gowanton, who was beginning to be alarmed by all this mystery. He looked at Beach, who in turn looked at Sackerville; and Sackerville got up from the bed and walked to the window, where he stood with his back to the others looking out on the lawn with its great shade trees, while Gowanton kept saying over and over, "What's the matter, Mr. Beach? What is it?" And the grocer shook his head confusedly, wondering what on earth his guest was up to.

"Look here," said Sackerville, turning suddenly, "I've been hesitating. I've thought perhaps—but it has to be done this way."

He went over and stood in front of Gowanton, close to his chair.

"I sent for you," he said in a sharper tone. "Beach had nothing to do with it. I sent for you to tell you that you can't marry Melissa."

The grocer's cigar dropped to the floor. There was a swift silence, then Gowanton's falsetto laugh sounded nervously in the room.

"Oh—I see—a joke," he stammered. "Ha, ha! I—pretty good!"

"No," said Sackerville, sharper still. "It's no joke." He turned to the grocer. "You must forgive me for this, Andy; I think you will. As for you, Gowanton, I don't care to make any apologies or explanations. I don't criticize you. I will even admit that you have as much right to happiness as I have. But I happen to be stronger—so much the worse for you. You can't marry Melissa Beach, because I'm going to marry her myself."

"By——" cried the grocer, starting up.

Gowanton was on his feet, too, but he was too astounded to speak. What can you say to a madman? Who ever heard of anyone going up to a bridegroom on his wedding morning and telling him he is going to take his bride away from him? It isn't done, that's all. Stupefied, Gowanton grew red and pale by turns as he stood and gazed at Sackerville with his mouth open.

"Why—" he stammered, why—you must be crazy—"

"No." Sackerville smiled. "I don't wonder you're surprised. No doubt it's a bit stiff. If I may say so, I am treating you as well as I possibly can. I could—I am pretty sure I could—have run off with her last night, but that wouldn't have been fair to her or you either. I was talking to her in the library. She doesn't love you, Gowanton, and she doesn't want to marry you. She isn't even willing to marry you. Why, she'd even prefer me. So you can't have her."

It was at this point that Andrew Beach stepped softly to the door and turned the key in the lock. Why? Probably he didn't know himself. He merely felt that it would be best to have the door locked, so he locked it. Then he turned with his back against it and stood looking at the two men facing each other in the middle of the room.

"So," Gowanton was saying, "you've been talking to her."

"Yes. Last night."

"And you knew—you knew—"

"Yes, I knew."

"Then—" Gowanton paused, and his eyes slowly left Sackerville and went to Andrew Beach at the door.

"I am sorry," he said to the grocer, "to have to call your guest a cad in your own house."

Then his eyes came back.

"You are a cad, Mr. Sackerville," he said calmly.

But Sackerville never budged. "No doubt," he said drily. "I don't measure a man by his manners, Gowanton. Anyway, you're wrong. I have a thousand claims here to your one. She is mine, really mine, but you wouldn't understand if I tried to explain. She is mine, but I'm going to give you a chance."

He turned.

"Andy, will you send for your daughter? And ask her which of us—Gowanton or me—she would rather marry."

"No, he won't!" cried Gowanton suddenly, spring to the door. "It's absurd! Why, it's absurd! Mr. Beach—"

"Don't let him out, Andy," said Sackerville.

"But it's ridiculous, I tell you! I won't stand for it! Why, you—"

"Wait a minute, Mr. Gowanton." Andrew Beach raised his voice for the first time. "You have reminded me that this is my house. I'm going to do what Sackerville asks. I've known him longer than you have, and I think—anyway, he's right. Melly ought to have a chance, and I'm going to give her one. You wait—"

He unlocked the door, poked his head out and called to a servant in the hall. Then he closed the door again and turned to the two men.

"We haven't much time," he observed, glancing at his watch. "It's twenty after eleven. We were to leave for the church at a quarter to twelve. The only thing is, if Melissa—"

A knock sounded. A voice came:

"Daddy!"

The grocer opened the door, and Melissa entered. He stepped forward to take her hand, then sprang back so suddenly that he nearly lost his balance as another figure, that of his wife, advanced across the threshold.

The mother and daughter stood, one a little in front of the other, stopped short by the appearance of three men where they had expected to find one or, at the most, two. But Mrs. Beach soon found her voice.

"John!" she cried, looking at Gowanton in amazement. "What in the name of goodness are you doing here?"

The bridegroom scowled. Andrew Beach proved his bravery by coming forward and opening his mouth to explain; but Sackerville, knowing that to be both useless and dangerous, put his hand on his friend's arm and said something in a low tone, and Andrew Beach nodded and turned to his daughter.

"Melly," he said, "come here."

She obeyed wonderingly. All in white, enveloped in lace and satin, she looked so fresh and lovely that she seemed to belong to a different world from those common-looking men in their black and gray. She went to her father's side, glancing first at Gowanton, then at Sackerville.

"Listen, Melly," said the grocer, patting her hand, "I want to ask you something I should have asked you a long time ago. I've been a bad father; but it's not too late. Tell me the truth—remember, the truth—do you want to marry John Gowanton?"

"*Good heavens!*"

It was Mrs. Beach's voice.

"Are you crazy, Andrew? I knew it was something—when I saw John here—I knew it—"

But her husband silenced her for once. You would never have supposed that authority to be concealed in the little grocer's breast unless you had heard him in a business crisis.

"Not another word from *you!*" he commanded.

Then he turned to his daughter.

"Do you want to marry John Gowanton?" he repeated.

But though Melissa had had a moment to recover from her astonishment she could only stammer:

"Why, I am—yes—that is—"

"No, don't be frightened," said the grocer. "Tell me the truth; do you want to marry him?"

Melissa looked at her father, at Sackerville, at her mother, and finally at Gowanton. She looked at him a long time, directly in his face, as if she were seeing him for the first time. And then her eyes dropped, and she saw her bridal dress with its folds of white, and her face suddenly grew pale with resolution.

"No," she said, in a low, distinct voice. "No, I don't want to marry him."

A sharp cry came from her mother:

"Melissa!"

"Let her alone," said the grocer. "You've done enough as it is. Thank God, it's not too late. Mr. Gowanton—you've heard—I'm sorry—"

If Gowanton's face had been red before, it was purple now with emotion. It could be seen that he was hard put to maintain his role of gentleman. He looked very much as though he wanted to hit somebody.

"You mean—" he stammered violently and could get no farther.

"Yes," said Andrew Beach. "I'm sorry."

Gowanton choked. He glared at Sackerville a moment, then he

turned and bowed formally to Melissa; then he went to the door, wheeled and bowed to Mrs. Beach. The next moment he was gone— gone in a rush down the stairs and through the hall to where his big gray limousine waited at the curb.

"And now," said Mrs. Beach in tense tones of fury, "now, Andrew Beach, perhaps you'll explain—"

"You bet I'll explain," said the grocer grimly. "But first, I know you've been to a lot of trouble for this wedding, and there's a church full of people down the street waiting for us. It's been a big expense, too, and I don't like to throw away money. Gowanton's gone, thank God, but we'll give Melly a chance to dig up another bridegroom."

He turned to Sackerville.

"Just ask her, Harry. Ask her yes or no. No pushing. Only, if she wants to and you want to, I'll get a car to take you to the church and we'll have some fun with society."

He looked steadily at Sackerville for a moment, patted Melissa on the shoulder, then went and took his wife by the arm and led her into the hall, closing the door behind them.

There was silence in the room—absolute silence, save for the soft rustling of the wind in the trees, through the open window. And the breeze entered, and there was a faint movement among the folds of lace on the bridal dress. . . . Sackerville saw it. . . .

Suddenly he spoke.

"Gowanton's gone," he said. "So there's no hurry now. I don't know what I've done, Melissa, and I don't care. When a man wants something as I want you he will do anything. I want you to marry me now, but I'll wait if you say so. You must decide. They are waiting for us."

He took a step toward her. She looked up and met his eyes questioningly.

"I have loved you ten years," he said. "I have waited that long. I will love you all my life. Melissa— Will you—"

And then, still with her eyes on his, she nodded.

He was close to her now, and he bent his head and touched his lips to her hair, the hair that he had felt on his face one night in the wilderness.

"I never thought—" he said, "I never dreamed—"

But that could not have been strictly true. There was that license in his pocket!

IT HAPPENED LAST NIGHT

—꩜—

This story appeared in The Black Cat *in January 1917; it was reprinted in* The Canadian Magazine *in 1936. John McAleer knew of the 1936 publication but not that the story had first appeared nineteen years earlier. Discussing the story in his biography of Rex Stout, McAleer describes it as a "slick romance" that "reads like apprentice work." In this, McAleer was prescient: it* was *apprentice work, in the same sense that all of Stout's early stories were. In any event, the story presents itself as a rather typical Stout romance, but closes with an unexpected twist—and not the expected sort of unexpected twist.*

I knew that she was inaccessible to me. When I first found the thought of her whirling about in my mind, the sensible thing would have been to go to the corner café for a drink and drown the fancy like a man. She belonged to another world, and anything I might do would be like a dog baying at the moon. I knew that; but I entertained the thought and caressed it, encouraged it. I was intoxicated.

I had seen her once or twice before, but from that afternoon on Fifth Avenue dated my obsession. I had come downtown in the subway and stopped off at Forty-second Street on some errand or other, when suddenly she swept into sight. I already knew her by name and reputation, much as you know a famous prima donna or a royal princess. I stopped and stared like a fool, and then, half-unconsciously, drawn by an irresistible attraction, turned and followed her. She was dressed fashionably, but in faultless taste; her large dark eyes looked out from under the modish rim of a Doquet straw and her pale oval countenance and curved red lips, contradicting each other, imparted a piquant distinction to her appearance. Men turned to look at her. Knowing that I was making a fool of myself, I nevertheless followed her up the avenue. Every now and then she stopped to look at a window display while I stood a few yards away gazing at her from the corner of my eye. It was a senseless performance; I certainly had no thought of accosting her on the street, but I was impelled by an overpowering fascination.

After that the thought of her was constantly in my mind. Wherever I found myself, at the office in the morning, at home at night, on the subway, there was always before me that pale oval face with the red lips, to my torment. I dreamed of our meeting, of addressing her, of those red lips smiling at me in welcome, of the friendly pressure of her hand, and I thought of what I should say and how she would answer me. I composed a thousand speeches and turned each one over and over in my brain to perfect it and make it worthy of her. I was mad.

All that, knowing she was inaccessible, immeasurably above me. Humble as I was and of the poorest connections, the conventional channels were closed to me with insurmountable barriers. But I could not forget her. Heaven knows I tried; but in the end I gave it up, and one evening, gritting my teeth, I said to myself, as I was going home on the elevated:

"Very well, I'll meet her, somehow, and take my chance. Anything will be better than this ceaseless yearning."

My heart felt lighter after this resolution, but by the time I got home I was lost in contemplation of a hundred wild schemes that darted into my mind; so much so that I forgot to kiss my wife as I entered the flat. We had been married only about a year and honeymoon days had scarcely waned. Five minutes later, as I sat in the front room reading the paper, I suddenly remembered and jumped up and hurried to the kitchen, uneasy. My wife stood stirring something on the stove and I stopped and kissed her on the cheek before I noticed that anything was wrong.

She turned around quickly, and I saw tears in her eyes.

In the scene that followed, I was certainly not myself. It was not only that I had forgotten the kiss that evening. My wife had said not a word during the previous weeks about my preoccupation and brooding, but I learned now that nothing had escaped her notice. She accused me of neglecting her, of ceasing to love her, of being indifferent to her. I confess I acted a perfect ass. I should have told her everything, and she, sensible little woman that she is, would have seen the thing as I did and have done all in her power to help me out of my trouble. But the vanity and stupidity of man are boundless. I hesitated and evaded.

"It's only business, dear," I declared. "I'm worried, that's all."

As a matter of fact, things were very well at the office; but it could not be denied that I was worried. In the end, it was patched over somehow, though that was the most uncomfortable dinner since our marriage.

In the days that followed, I continued revolving in my mind schemes for meeting her—wild, impossible schemes—conceiving and rejecting them in endless succession. Nothing else seemed to matter but her, only her! If I could only speak to her! Only hear her voice and see her smile! Only hear the words that I imagined on her lips! One morning, at my desk in the office, I sat with these thoughts in my brain—they were never absent—quite unconsciously writing her name, over and over, on a sheet of paper, until it was filled. I was lost in my dreams, when suddenly I heard a voice at my elbow:

"What's that for?"

I looked up to find my partner, Harris, gazing in bewilderment at her name scribbled all over the paper. I jerked myself up in my chair and hastily turned the sheet upside down, while I felt the blood rush into my face or out of it, I don't know which.

"What's that for?" he repeated.

Then he saw the expression on my face and his look of puzzlement changed slowly to one of incredulous understanding as he stood and stared at me. I said nothing and he stared in silence for a long while.

"You're a damned fool," he said at length, calmly.

"It can be," I retorted and seizing my hat, I jumped up and left the office.

I wandered about the streets for hours, and though I had several appointments for that day I kept none of them. I was wandering in the light of a glorious vision and was blinded by it. Of course Harris was right: I was a damned fool. But I couldn't help it. I walked at random, not knowing or caring where I went, with her face always before me.

Suddenly I saw her.

It was on Broadway, somewhere in the Thirties, about five o'clock in the afternoon. She was walking uptown, unhurried, with an assured, leisurely step that was, in fact, deceiving; for when I turned and followed her I found that she carried herself along faster than one would think. I threw caution to the winds and marched along almost at her heels. A happy chance came presently to my assistance, or I believe I should have been ass enough to accost her on the street and thereby have utterly ruined myself in her sight.

Luckily my timidity held me back until she had reached Forty-second Street; there she turned west and a few steps from Seventh Avenue entered the lobby of the Stuyvesant Theatre. I was close behind her as she approached the box office; I looked over her shoulder as she purchased two tickets in the orchestra for the performance of "Peaches and Cream" that night, and noted the numbers on the coupons.

At that moment came my inspiration. I waited till she had disappeared again into the street, then approached the ticket seller.

"One for tonight, orchestra."

He turned to glance over the rack, pulled out a coupon and started to put it in an envelope. Meanwhile, I was studying the chart of the theatre under the slab of glass on the ledge.

"What row is it?" I inquired.

"Fourth. Aisle."

"Got anything in the eleventh, near the centre?"

He nodded, after consulting the rack.

"Right here. Fine seat." He pointed to the location on the chart. We were getting hot.

"I'd prefer the other side, if possible."

He frowned impatiently and mumbled something I didn't catch as he turned again to the rack. Out came another coupon; a quick glance showed me its number. A moment later, I had parted company with a two dollar bill and was emerging into the street with a ticket that called for the seat adjoining those purchased by her.

I didn't go back to the office that evening; I wouldn't even have gone home to dinner but for the necessity of changing my clothes. I forget what lie I told my wife, but it couldn't have been a very good one, for my mind was entirely occupied with the question whether or not to wear a dress suit. I knew that the audience at the Stuyvesant was usually about half and half, and I finally decided on my new grey business sack, for I had no desire to appear in false colors. Anyway, hired dress suits are generally of antiquated model, and I knew her eye would detect it at a glance, accustomed as she was to such things. I wished to give myself every advantage possible.

I had a hard time deciding just what to write, and the idea came to me that it would be better to go down to the office first and use the typewriter; but in the end I went out to a stationary and cigar store for a newspaper wrapper with mucilage on the end and used that. Before I finally copied it, as plainly and neatly as possible, I tried fifty different ways of saying what I wanted to in the fewest words, and even then I wasn't satisfied with it.

I was in an agony of suspense, and not disposed to sit around and talk with my wife till time to go, I went out for a walk. Then the thought struck me that something might happen on the subway to delay me, so I rushed to the station and took the first train downtown. I reached the theatre a little after seven and stood in the lobby till the doors opened. I was the first one seated.

Then I encountered my only difficulty. She had bought two tickets, adjoining mine on the left, but which one would she occupy? It was an even chance that she would occupy the seat next to mine. I felt certain that her companion would be some relative or woman friend, since she had bought the tickets herself. So I took the program from the arm of the seat next to mine and opened it at a page near the back, for I didn't want her to see it before the show began, and I knew that during the first or second intermission she would look through the whole program. They always do. So I pasted the newspaper wrapper on which I had written my appeal in a page near the back. The brown paper stood out conspicuously against the white. I closed the program and replaced it with a feeling that if the thing didn't work it wouldn't be my fault. I had done my best.

I tried to amuse myself by watching the theatre fill up, but I was horribly restless and turned around constantly to see if she were coming. At last she would know my name! At last she would speak to me! For I assured myself that she couldn't be so heartless as to ignore me. She couldn't! As the time passed my restlessness increased to a torment of suspense.

A minute or two before curtain time she arrived. I was watching the aisle to the right, but she came unexpectedly down the other side and was already pushing her way past the row of knees to her seat before I saw her. My heart leaped with joy as I saw that she was in front; she would sit next to me, as I had hoped! Behind was her companion, a pleasant-faced lady of fifty-five or so, no doubt her mother, or possibly an aunt.

They had barely time to get seated and take off their wraps before the house darkened and the curtain rose. Out of the corner of my eye I could see her profile, delicate in its severity, and the soft rounded contour of neck and shoulders, her dark fine hair contrasting startlingly with the whiteness of her skin. I haven't the remotest idea about the first act. I scarcely breathed—so close to her, almost touching her! There in front of us her breath was mingling with mine! And soon she would read my name. She would speak to me. I was a-quiver with excitement and hope. Would they never get through that foolishness on stage?

Then the curtain, applause, and the house was light again. She spoke to her companion; they discussed the performers. I was in a fever of impatience. They talked for so long that I feared the second act would begin before they finished. Finally she began turning the leaves of her program. She read, "What the Man Will Wear," "The Golfer," and "Here and There." She skimmed over the advertisements, turning the pages more rapidly. I could feel myself trembling in my seat, and suddenly I was aware that she had reached it. She was reading the slip of paper I had pasted in her program. I bit my lips to keep myself steady. She read it a second time, a third. I felt, rather than saw, her swift glance. There was a silence, a rather long silence, and then her voice came:

"Really, this is rather clever."

I turned. Yes, she was speaking to me! I swallowed hard and tired to answer, but couldn't She saw, and smiled—a divine smile!

She spoke again:

"You wrote this? You put this here?"

I nodded, and stammered, "Yes. I did. Forgive me, but it was the only way." Suddenly my voice came, and I continued swiftly: "No doubt you think it bold and in bad taste, but I have been trying for months to think of some way of meeting you. To one in my humble position the conventional channels were closed. I knew no one that could or would introduce me. I thought of calling on you, but of course you wouldn't have seen me, and you would have been right. So I did this. It was the only way I could think of. I beg you not to be offended."

I stopped, wondering if I had said too much or not enough. But I could see she was smiling; at least she wasn't angry. She read the slip over again. I heard her murmur, "How amusing." No, she wasn't angry. Suddenly she turned to me:

"Really, I think you deserve—well, we'll see. You deserve respect for your originality at least. Let's see; tomorrow's Thursday. Will you call in the morning at ten—between ten and eleven? Wait—" she smiled—"take this and use it as your card when you come." She tore out the slip I had pasted in her program and handed it to me.

I tried to stammer my thanks; she waved them away smilingly and turned to speak to her companion, who had been regarding us in wondering curiosity. The lights began to go out for the second act. My heart was so full of elation I couldn't sit through such a banal performance; besides, would it not be more delicate not to remain? She might feel obliged to converse with me; might think I expected it; it would be presumptuous. And I wanted to get away to think it over.

I took my hat and coat and edged my way to the aisle. In the outer lobby I put on my coat and hat, took the slip of brown paper, read it over once more and folded it; but before placing it in my pocket, I gaily carried it to my lips. The doorman, standing nearby, stared at me in amazement. Perhaps he would have been still more amazed if he had know what was written on it:

> "*The man sitting on your right is Abe Goldstein, of Harris and Goldstein. They are a new firm without much capital, but they have an original and artistic line with the punch. He only asks a chance to show you.*"

And that was the way I became acquainted with Sadie Levine, buyer of ladies' suits for the most exclusive house on Fifth Avenue. Usually it takes years to get an account like that. It happened last night. I called on her this morning and sold her a bill of fourteen different numbers, three of each, for a total of $1,760.50. How's that for a first order?

OLD FOOLS AND YOUNG

—⚇—

Stout's longest and last piece for Young's Magazine *was this novelette. It appeared in the April 1918 issue, but must have been written more than a year earlier, as Stout had been busy collaborating with his brother Robert in promoting a school banking system, the Educational Thrift Service, since the end of 1916. This farewell appearance marks the only time that one of Stout's early stories for* Young's *was promoted on the cover: "OLD FOOLS AND YOUNG – Complete Novelette by REX T. STOUT"*

Before the large granite pillars flanking the entrance to Rose-lawn—one of those showy country estates that turn the east bank of the Hudson into an unbroken series of formal parks and flower gardens—a high-powered Shinton roadster came to an abrupt stop early one July morning. At the wheel was a man of middle age, not more than a year or two either side of forty; he was the sole occupant of the car. The perplexed and somewhat resentful expression of his pleasing, still youthful countenance showed that he had certainly not halted as a tribute to the surrounding landscape, though such a tribute would have been not undeserved. On one side green valleys and gently sloping hills, thickly wooded, rested and charmed the eye with their endless variety of form and color; on the other, gardens and terraced lawns led past the buildings of the estate to where a glimmer of the broad river shone through the foliage. The day promised to be hot, but just now a gentle, steady breeze was stirring freshness in the air.

The man in the car, having stopped, had taken a letter from his pocket and glanced through it. It read as follows:

Fred:

Morton Waring has just telephoned that Kate is ill, and I am going right over; so again I have to call on you to help me out.

Three girls are to arrive here today from New York, from that East Side Vacation Club, and now I can't be here to receive them. They would probably feel slighted with no one here except the servants; so won't you come over and do the honors? Just make them welcome and turn them loose; they can amuse themselves. That's a good brother; I know you'll do it.

I'll be back this evening or tomorrow.

I forget what train they're coming on; it's in my desk somewhere. I 'phoned, but you were out, so I'm sending this over by Simmons.

JANET

The man at the wheel refolded the letter with a grunt of irritation and returned it to his pocket.

"No, she doesn't even say what train," he observed glumly to the radiator. "Of course she wouldn't. Well, I'll have to find out."

He started the motor and turned into the driveway between the granite pillars. It led him deviously, around sweeping curves, to the carriage entrance of the house itself—a large rambling structure of gray stone and uncertain architecture, set in the centre of a century-old grove not more than a hundred yards from the bank of the river. A man came running up from the garage in the rear, touching his cap as he approached with a deferential,

"Good morning, Mr. Canby."

"Good morning, Simmons. Put her away," returned the other as he leaped out and mounted the steps of the piazza. At the door he was met by a red-faced middle-aged woman who greeted him with unfeigned relief and began to explain vociferously that her mistress had left so suddenly she didn't know what to think, and she had been so afraid Mr. Canby wouldn't come, and the young women expected from the city any minute—!

Without waiting for her to finish, Canby passed through to the front of the house and on upstairs to his sister's writing-room, where, after a ten-minute search, he finally found a typewritten letter containing the information that the Misses Rose Manganaro, Mildred Lavicci and Nella Somi would arrive Wednesday morning on the 10:50 local; also, Mrs. Janet Morton Haskins would please accept the profound thanks of the East Side Vacation Club for giving these working girls the opportunity of enjoying the myriad delights and advantages of country life for the two weeks they would be free from their toilsom labor in the cruel city. . . .

"This is what comes of having a widowed sister with contemplations on humanity," observed Canby, as he tossed the letter back in the drawer. 'Here's a nice job I've got. Pleasant task for an aged bachelor: playing croquet with Tired Working Girls! I'm not sure it's even decent. Lord, what names! Manganaro!—Lavicci!—Somi! They won't be able to speak English, their hands and feet will be in the way, and they'll have their pockets full of garlic to nibble between meals! Sis says she'll be back tonight or tomorrow, and maybe she will and maybe she won't. Oh Lord! Hanged if I'll go to the station, anyway; I'll send Simmons."

Downstairs, having summoned the chauffeur from the garage

and delivered his instructions, and having ascertained from the housekeeper that the rooms of the expected guests were in readiness, Canby deposited himself in a shady corner of the piazza with a morning newspaper, a box of cigarettes, a bottle, a siphon, and a glass. Soon he saw Simmons, in a new seven-passenger touring car, winding along the driveway on his way to the station, seven miles distant. Canby sighed and returned to his paper. He had had a match on for this morning with Garrett Linwood, a guest at his own country home, some fifteen miles to the northeast, and he had expected at about this hour to be standing on the sixth tee, driving across the brook. That's what comes of having a sister. . . .

Buried in the sporting page of his newspaper some forty-five minutes later, Canby came to with a start at the sound of the returning automobile whizzing along the driveway. Hastily tossing off his glass and throwing the paper aside, he reached the central arch of the main portico just as the car drew up at the foot of the steps.

The three young women from the East Side Vacation Club descended rather stiffly, with embarrassed movements. Canby glanced at them with idle curiosity and then spoke, welcoming them to Roselawn in the name of his sister, their hostess, and explaining her temporary absence. They mumbled something in reply, and Canby, somewhat embarrassed himself, was relieved to find the housekeeper at this elbow.

"Mrs. Garton will show you your rooms," he finished. "I trust you had a pleasant journey."

"I'm going back for the luggage, sir," came from Simmons.

Canby nodded; in his indifference he had forgotten all about it; but, come to think of it, of course even working girls would have luggage. Having followed the housekeeper with his eyes as she led the visitors into the house, he returned to his corner on the piazza and took up his newspaper; but by the time he had finished the financial page he was vaguely uneasy. As host *pro tem.*, he felt that he probably ought to do something; so a few minutes later, he started in search of Mrs. Garton. As he crossed the reception hall he heard footsteps above, and there, on the landing of the great staircase, stood his three guests, huddled together as if for protection and gazing down at him doubtfully.

"I was just looking for you," said Canby, trying to make his tone pleasant and fatherly. "Thought you might like to come out on the piazza—quite cool and cheerful. Later I'll take you over the gardens, when the sun isn't so hot."

There was a movement on the landing, and a "Thank you, sir," came down to him. He reflected with relief that they did appear to understand English, at least; and when they had descended the stairs he led the way outside.

There, after they had been distributed among the comfortable wicker chairs and he had rung for a maid to bring cakes and lemonade, he took the trouble to look at them. The two nearest him were easily classified as Italian peasant girls, with their dark skin and hair and eyes, rather coarse features and large hands and feet. They wore brightly colored dresses and one had a large yellow imitation rose in her hair. The third was more difficult; in fact, the longer Canby looked at her the more difficult she became. Her soft brown hair, combed back from her forehead, revealed a well-formed brow, smooth and white; her features were regular and her skin of a delicate velvety texture; and the hand that rested on the arm of the chair was small and exquisite in shape. She wore a laundered dress of light tan with a black velvet bow at the throat, and the low collar permitted a view of a dainty neck between the softly curving shoulders. Nineteen, she may have been, or twenty, and was of that delightful size and figure that makes any other woman always seem either too large or too small.

Canby took in these details, or most of them, gazing at her with something like astonishment. Curious his eye hadn't picked her out from the others as they got out of the car; but, after all, there was nothing noticeable about her, nothing startling. That was just it; it was only after you noticed her that you saw her. There was something decidedly attractive and appealing about the little red mouth, with the sensitive lips neither closed nor parted; and the total effect of her attitude and expression was of quiet, well-bred modesty as she sat there, all unconscious of Canby's stare.

He turned to the girl nearest him:

"I know what your names are," he said with an apologetic smile, "but I don't know how they're distributed."

Her black eyes, honest and patient, returned his look.

"Mine is Rose Manganaro," she replied. "This," she indicated to the girl next to her, "is Mildred Lavicci. And Miss Somi—Nella Somi."

So her name was Nella Somi. That might be anything. He wished that she would turn her head so he could see her eyes. He ventured some trivial question, but it was Rose Manganaro who answered, and a conversation was started. She spoke of the hot city they had left behind, and the ride up the Hudson, and the beautiful homes they had passed on the way from the station. Then cakes and lemonade arrived, and Canby amused himself by watching their white teeth as they bit into the yellow squares. Nella Somi, he remarked, took no cake, but merely sipped her lemonade. After that their tongues were loosened and the two Italian girls talked freely and unaffectedly. Mildred had noticed some men playing golf on the way from the station, and Canby described the game in detail for their benefit.

Thus the time passed somehow until luncheon, and after that they returned to the piazza. Canby had promised himself that, as soon as he had sat at the table with them, he would leave them to their own resources and drive back to Greenhedge for the match with his friend Linwood, who was waiting for him; but, now that the time had come, he didn't go. The desultory conversation of that morning was resumed, and the afternoon dragged away. Nella Somi spoke hardly at all, but the others made up for it. Finally, the shadows began to lengthen and a cooling breeze arose from the direction of the river. Rose Manganaro spoke of the gardens.

"I'll show you around if you want," offered Canby. "Not so hot now."

"Oh, we wouldn't trouble you, sir," replied Rose, getting up from her chair, "we can go alone, if it's all right. Are you coming, Mildred? Nella?"

Mildred was already on her feet, but Nella Somi declared that she was too comfortable to move. Canby at once decided to stay where he was, but rose politely as the two girls passed in front of him on their way to the steps. A minute later they had disappeared around the bend of the garden path. When Canby sat down again he moved over to the chair left vacant next to Nella Somi.

"You don't care for flowers?" he ventured after a little.

"Oh yes, I love them," she replied quickly, "but it's so hot, and I'm so tired."

"In an hour it will be cool; we're quite close to the river here, you know. In the evenings, on the water, it's really chilly."

"In a boat, you mean."

"Yes; especially in a swift one."

Suddenly she turned her eyes on him, and he saw them for the first time.

It took his breath. He had expected them to be brown, from the darkness of her hair, and their clear vivid blue almost startled him. The lashes, heavy and drooping, were even darker than her hair, and the effect was striking and strangely beautiful. If she had purposely kept them from him throughout the afternoon she appeared now to have changed her mind, for she returned his gaze frankly and artlessly, to the point of disconcerting him. The vivid blue eyes held curiosity.

"You don't do anything, do you?" she observed finally.

"Do anything?" he repeated.

"Work, I mean."

"Oh! No." He forbore smiling. "That is, no regular work. I have an office in New York, but I'm very seldom there."

"How funny! I have to work so hard and you do nothing at all." There was no resentment in her tone; her interest in the question seemed purely academic.

"Your hard work doesn't seem to leave much impression," returned Canby.

She calmly noted his gaze resting on her pretty white hands.

"I wouldn't let it," she replied with a smile. "Anyway, it isn't that kind. I sort candies, and I wear gloves." She twisted about in her chair the better to face him, with a quick graceful movement of her supple young body. The blue eyes were half closed as if in speculation. "To think of a big ugly man like you with nothing to do, and me working all day long," she continued. "I could be so pretty if I had time for things!"

"I'm not sure it would be safe for you to be much prettier," returned Canby with a laugh. To himself he added, "Or possible either." He went on aloud: "But am I so ugly as all that?"

The blue eyes flashed a smile, then were serious:

"All men are ugly," she declared daintily; "it's a part of them. They're clumsy and not nice to look at. If only there were something else to marry!"

"Are you thinking of marriage?"

"Oh, yes; Tony, Rose's brother. But I haven't promised yet, and I don't think I will. He's very nice, but so—so ugly." She paused a moment. "There were a lot of men on the train this morning and they were frightful."

"Did they annoy you?" demanded Canby in the tone of a protector.

"No; they never do. Of course, they often speak to me, on the street too, but that's all."

"What do you mean?"

"I look as if I didn't understand them and say something in Italian or French. They always look frightened and go away. Americans are so afraid of a foreign tongue."

"You speak Italian and French?"

"Yes. My mother was French; she was born in Paris. But, my goodness!"—she laughed a little for the first time, a low soft ripple of sound that enchanted the ear—"I tell all about myself, don't I? *Parlons un peu à votre sujet, monsieur.*"

Canby protested that the topic would be unutterably dull, and a moment later found himself somehow involved in a discussion of neckties, how started he could not have told. It appeared that Nella Somi favored black and gray, because none of the gayer colors went well with the coarse complexion of the male; and she particularly disliked such shades as orange and green. Canby remembered that a green four-in-hand was at the moment around his neck, and he felt uncomfortable. They talked on various subjects, and finally arrived at tennis. Miss Somi had spent her two preceding vacations at a girls' colony on Long Island, where they had played daily, and Canby proposed a set.

He found racquets and balls, and sport shoes of his sister's for Miss Somi, and together they walked to the courts, at the foot of the north terrace near the lake. Canby was so interested in watching his opponent that he forgot everything else until he heard her call, "Fifty-love," and then he set to it in earnest; and though he lost the game he succeeded in carrying it to deuce. After that he stopped trying.

The girl's movements, incredibly quick and graceful, charmed him by their appeal to his feeling for the beautiful; she was Diana and the racquet was her bow. The red lips parted and the white teeth flashed as she called the score; her flushed cheeks made her more lovely than ever; and once, at the net, in the middle of the fourth game, her blue eyes sparkled directly into his, and he stood there stupidly as the ball whizzed past his shoulder.

The girl tossed her racquet on the ground.

"You're not trying, and I won't play any more," she declared. "I'm tired, anyway. I wonder where Rose and Mildred are."

He picked up the racquet and followed her to the piazza, where they found the others returned from the garden. It was nearly dinnertime, and they entered the house. Half an hour later at the table, Canby found that Miss Somi's loquacity had entirely disappeared. She did not look directly at him once during the meal.

The conversation turned for the most part on flowers, for Rose and Mildred were full of enthusiasm over the gardens. Such wonderful blossoms and so many they had never seen before! One of the gardeners had kindly told them the names of the plants. His name was Jensen, and they thought him a very nice man. Tomorrow he was going to show them how the water was forced into the fountain, and some Italian bulbs he had in the greenhouses.

After dinner Canby proposed an alternative: would they go motoring, or take a walk down by the river? Miss Somi professed indifference; the others, after a sustained discussion in their native tongue, declared for the river. Before they started, Canby telephoned to the Waring home, and was told that Mrs. Waring was much better and that his sister would return home that evening. Then, after sending a maid for wraps for the girls, for it was nighttime now and quite cool, Canby led the way along one of the broad paths leading to the rear of the park. Miss Somi was beside him, and Rose and Mildred, chattering in Italian, were at their heels.

There was a bright full moon and the stars were thick in the heavens; so that, though it was quite dark in the shadows of the grove, when they emerged on to the riverbank there was a shimmering track of light on the rippling water and a silvery radiance was everywhere. The bluffs of the opposite shore rose black and indistinct, and had the appearance of being at a great distance in the soft mysterious light; and the noises of the night, the cry of an owl somewhere in the trees, the chug of a motor boat far up the river, and, more faintly, the lapping of the water on the bank, came to them with the evening breeze, and when they spoke their voices were lowered as if in fear of disturbing the fairy scene. They wandered a space along the bank, speaking a little, and then, reaching the boathouse, Canby proposed a row. Out on the water it was quite cool and the girls drew their wraps about their shoulders. Canby pulled across to the opposite shore and a half mile or so upstream, then crossed back over and floated down with the current.

"It was such a nice ride!" declared Mildred Lavicci a little shyly, as they landed at the boathouse.

Rose agreed, and added something about Mr. Canby being so kind, not a bit like a rich man. Nella Somi said nothing.

They strolled slowly back up the bank, the bright moonlight throwing their grotesque shadows across the water's edge. From the direction of the house came the sound of a motor car on the driveway.

"That's my sister, Mrs. Haskins," Canby informed Nella Somi at his side. "If she wants to know how I've substituted in her absence, I hope you'll give a good account of me. Remember, I let you beat me at tennis!"

"Yes, but I could have won anyway," retorted the girl with a little defiant toss of the head. "I didn't half try, you know."

The other two had moved on ahead and had now stopped to wait for them at the beginning of the path leading into the park. When Canby and Miss Somi came up they stood there a time looking out over the water. Then Rose and Mildred turned into the path, and the others slowly followed at a distance.

All at once, just before they reached the enveloping shadow of the trees, Canby was aware of a sudden startled movement from the girl at his side. Then she stood stiff, as though paralyzed, with her gaze fastened on the ground ten feet ahead; and, following the direction of her eyes, Canby saw a large black water-snake basking in the moonlight with its beady eyes glittering like diamonds.

"No danger," he reassured her, "it's just a—"

At that moment the snake moved swiftly toward them, and he was interrupted by a cry of fear from the girl. She turned, and he saw her eyes filled with terror, and, the next thing he knew, his arms were around her protectingly, while she clung to him closely, like a frightened child.

"Where is it, where is it?" she cried, while he soothed her:

"Really, it won't hurt you; really, it's quite harmless! It's only—"

There were footsteps on the gravel walk, and a voice suddenly sounded:

"Well, Fred!"

Canby looked up and saw his sister standing there, regarding the chivalrous scene with an expression decidedly ironic. Feeling rather foolish, he loosened his arms, and Miss Somi swiftly drew away.

"Hello, Janet!" he returned calmly. "Back already? This is Miss Nella Somi. We just saw a snake."

II

Later that night Canby motored back to Greenhedge, his own estate, fifteen miles distant, where he found his friend Garrett Linwood mixing gin fizzes in pairs to while the hours away during the absence of his host. Linwood was a retired broker and capitalist, a widower a little over fifty, with an immense fortune and one aim left in life: to go around the Wanakahnda course in less than eighty. That was why he was at Greenhedge now; the Wanakahnda Country Club was distant only a ten-minute drive. He met Canby with the information that he had that day got a four on the long ninth and a three on the seventeenth.

The next morning they played the postponed match; then, leaving Linwood at the links, Canby jumped into his roadster and half an hour later, at Roselawn, announced to his surprised sister that he had come for lunch. He spent the afternoon on the tennis court with Miss Nella Somi of the East Side Vacation Club; he had the firm intention of inviting himself to dinner, but changed his mind when he learned that several guests were expected from neighboring estates.

During the week that followed Garrett Linwood was considerably mystified by the peculiar conduct of his friend Canby. That gentleman became suddenly most unreliable; he would disappear unexpectedly and turn up again several hours later without any explanation; he actually seemed to have taken a dislike to golf! Linwood couldn't understand it.

As a matter of fact, Canby didn't understand it himself. In his reflections, of which there were many during this eventful week, he hotly denied the possibility of his becoming enamored, at the age of forty-one years, of a nineteen-year-old child. So he called her: child. He played tennis with her, he took her motoring and motor-boating, he sat with her for hours at a time in the gardens or on the piazza of Roselawn, listening to her prattle and looking at her. Mostly he looked at her; the delight of it was never-ending, for her beauty was of the kind that could withstand long inspection and the fierce rays of the sun and the flushed cheeks of exertion; and not only withstand these things, but profit by them. He enjoyed hearing her talk almost as much as looking at her; her queer turns of expression, her simple, frank philosophy of the working-girl, her innocent delight in the luxuries of wealth as exhibited at Roselawn, even her occasional moody silences, when nothing would get a word from her.

There were occasional broad lapses from what Canby's world considered good form, but they merely served to amuse him and attract him the more by their piquancy, especially as there was never any touch of vulgarity in anything she did; her gestures, her tones, her dress—none was ever in the slightest degree offensive. She seemed of different mould from the Italian peasant girls.

One night, without being questioned, she spoke of her parentage. Her mother had been a French actress; her father, a Hungarian office-holder. Both had been dead some years, and Nella, left practically penniless, had come to America at the age of fourteen; so far as she knew she had not a relative in the world. Her father she remembered scarcely at all, but her mother had been very beautiful.

The attitude—or attitudes, for there were many of them—which she assumed toward Canby interested and piqued him. She would ask him scores of questions on some subject—the theatre, for instance, or the great hotels of the world capitals—and hang with delightful breathless attention on his words, like a curious child; and the next moment she would snub him on no provocation whatever and subtly withdraw herself. She never alluded to the incident of the snake and the moment she had been held in his arms; neither did Canby, but it was often in his mind. They were together hours of every day; though when they went motoring or out on the river Canby would take the Italian girls along for the sake of appearances. Telling himself that it was absurd for a man of his age to use formal address with a young girl in her teens, he called her by her first name, and she made no objection. Thus the days flew by until only one remained of their two-weeks vacation.

"So you return to New York tomorrow," Canby was saying. It was an hour after lunch and they were together in the garden, strolling aimlessly about from one shady spot to another; the day was too hot for tennis. Over near the fountain, some distance away, Rose and Mildred were seated on a bench with their hostess, who was reading aloud from a novel.

The girl, who had been in one of her silent moods since luncheon, nodded without speaking. She was dressed in white from head to foot—linen dress and canvas shoes—and, bareheaded, carried a blue parasol. The blue eyes did not sparkle with their usual life; they were serious, even a little sombre, as she bent them on the path before her.

"I'm sorry you're going," Canby continued, "deeply sorry. I've enjoyed your visit immensely."

Still she was silent; but presently she sent him a quick glance, then looked away again before she spoke:

"You've been very kind to me—to all of us. And—something else. After the first day I thought you liked me; that is, I thought you were interested in me—that I—I pleased you. And I was a little—not afraid, but disturbed, because I know how rich men treat poor girls. So I want to thank you for not being—for being nice to me."

"Good heavens, you needn't thank me for not being a brute!" Canby exclaimed.

"I do, anyway." Suddenly she looked up at him and laughed. "You wouldn't have been much to blame—would you?—after the way I acted that night when I saw the snake."

"You were frightened," said Canby gruffly.

"Yes. Ugh, I hate them so, and fear them! But I really believe I threw my arms around you, didn't I?"

"You did."

"How funny! I never did that before to any man; but then, of course, you're so old."

"Of course," he agreed without enthusiasm.

"Well, it's all over now. Tomorrow I go back to that smelly flat and the sorting-room and standing up all day long and Mr. Horowitz who shouts at you. . . . But it's fun, anyway, to work. I really don't mind it, only it gets tiresome, and there are so many beautiful things you can't have."

"And to Tony," came from Canby.

"What—to Tony?"

"You go back to Tony."

"Oh!" She laughed and he caught a flash from her eyes. "I'd forgotten all about him. *Tant mieux!* But he'll begin to make love to me again, I suppose."

A little later they joined the others near the fountain, and were greeted with short nods, for page 280 of the novel had just been reached and things were exciting. Nella Somi sat down to listen, and Canby, feeling restless, wandered aimlessly about the paths. He had a project in mind and he was impatient to set it afoot.

He was not over-satisfied with himself. He had been astonished and enraged that morning to find three gray hairs in his head; and the discovery was singularly inopportune, inasmuch as his friend Garrett Linwood had been congratulating him only the evening before on the preservation of his youth. He reflected somewhat pityingly that Linwood himself was really getting quite old; a few years more now and he would be sixty. Three score! By comparison with that patriarchal figure he, Canby, was highly jejune. Something within him whispered, "Still youthful enough to be a fool, and too old to enjoy your folly."

He snorted impatiently. Who spoke of folly? Could ever man be too old to feel the charm of innocence and beauty and health and youth, when all were combined in one rare adorable creature? To contemplate folly as a result of that charm was another matter. Canby did not contemplate it.

Presently he wandered back to the house; and later, hours later it seemed to him, his sister and her guests, having finished the novel, followed him. Canby, in the library, heard them in the hall; he heard talking of packing and their footsteps as they began to mount the stairs. In a moment he was at the door of the library calling up:

"Janet! Will you come down here a minute?"

When his sister entered the library a few minutes later he closed the door behind her; then suddenly forgot how he had decided to begin.

"They go back tomorrow?" he said finally, jerking his head in the direction of the stairs.

His sister replied that her guests were to take the nine-thirty train the following morning.

"Miss Somi also?"

"Of course."

Canby cleared his throat. "I was wondering, Janie, if you hadn't noticed anything unusual about her."

"About Nella Somi?"

"Yes."

"I have." The woman of experience, veteran of a dozen society campaigns and a thousand skirmishes, turned a quizzical eye on her bachelor brother. "Nella is an extraordinarily clever girl; one of the cleverest girls, in fact, that I have ever seen."

"Oh, I don't mean that," Canby returned impatiently. "Of course she's clever; that is, she's not a fool. I mean, don't you think she's unusual?"

"Cleverness is unusual."

"But don't you think she's different, different from her cl— No, to the devil with class! But she strikes me as being intelligent and refined far beyond the ordinary girl, of any class whatever. Her out-look on life is sensible. Her mind is pure. She is attractive personally. She is neither impudent nor ignorant. She has the soul of an artist; she loves beautiful things without gushing over them. There's no silly sentiment about her. And she is brave; she's alone in the world, and she looks at life cheerfully."

"Well," replied Janet, seeing that he had finished, "granting that all you say is true, what of it?"

There was a silence, then Canby turned and spoke abruptly:

"Why don't you adopt her?"

It was plain that his sister had not expected this.

"Adopt her!" she repeated in astonishment.

"Yes. You're a widow, past forty, and you need someone; why not her? She'll give you a new interest in life. As for her, she deserves something better than to sort candy and marry an Italian laborer. She's too fine for that sort of thing. She would be a daughter to be proud of, with a little finishing. She would—"

He stopped short. His sister was laughing at him. There was real mirth in her laughter, too. He looked at her in amazement.

"What the deuce is so funny?" he demanded.

"Oh, my dear Fred!" The mirth subsided a little. "Men are really the stupidest creatures—that is, nice men like you. And yet, in this instance it is a little wonder." She was suddenly serious. "Nella Somi is really an incredibly clever girl. She has taken you in, my dear. Don't worry about her marrying any Italian laborer; she wasn't made for that. You think her sweet and guileless and innocent. She may be innocent enough, but she certainly isn't guileless. To put it vulgarly, she has dangled her bait before you—oh, with consummate art!— and you have swallowed it, hook and all."

"Bah!" exclaimed Canby. "You women—"

"Don't misunderstand me," Janet put in quickly. "I'm not condemning her. Under different circumstances I might be her friend, and admire her. I don't say she's bad. I do admire her. With good birth and a fortune she would be a remarkable woman; a valuable friend and a dangerous enemy. But—I don't fancy her as a daughter. Perhaps I should apologize for not warning you, but it amused me so to watch her, and her moves were so perfectly executed, I hadn't the heart; and besides, I really didn't fear, for you're an exceptional man. Anyway, now you know."

"But you don't really believe all that!" cried Canby. "Of Nella Somi?"

"My dear boy, it's true."

"Pardon me, it's absurd. Why, Janet, she's nothing but a child! You women, with your intuition and perspicuity, make me tired. It's absurd! Why, I could tell you—"

"You needn't tell me anything, Fred; I've seen it all. I haven't anything against her. But to adopt her—hardly!"

And though Canby continued his protests, his sister was firm. Finally, permitting himself some acutely caustic remarks concerning suspicious women and the habit of judging others by one's self, he perforce accepted her decision.

He was deeply annoyed, not so much by Janet's refusal to act— she had a right to do as she chose—as by her stubborn injustice. Had he not studied Nella Somi for two weeks—her simplicity of thought, her disinterestedness, her girlish friendship, her absolute avoidance

of the sort of feminine wiles he had grown to detest? He told himself that he understood his sister well enough; she had lived so long
in the atmosphere of artificiality, that she was unable to recognize
natural and divine charm, direct and unadorned, when she saw it.
So much the worse for her, he reflected scornfully. But what of his
generous intentions for Nella's future, thus so unexpectedly balked?

He went out and sat on the piazza with his feet on the rail—an
attitude which Janet detested. He hoped she would see him. For
more than two hours he sat there, and when Rose and Nella came
downstairs, having finished their packing, and were later joined by
Mildred and their hostess, he merely nodded without turning his
head. About ten minutes before dinnertime he suddenly leaped
to his feet, and, without paying attention to the others' inquiring
glances, he went to the garage, jumped into his roadster and was
off. He covered the fifteen miles to Greenhedge in a few seconds less
than a quarter of an hour, dined with his friend Linwood, and had an
extended talk with his housekeeper.

By eight o'clock he was back again at Roselawn. They were surprised to see him, and Janet had something to say about his running
off at dinnertime. All the reply her brother vouchsafed her was a
meaningless and rather impolite grunt. Without preamble, he asked
Nella Somi if she would go out on the river with him. The girl turned
to her hostess with a look of inquiry.

Janet glanced at her brother with an expression of mingled
amusement and disapproval, then turned to the girl and said drily:

"By all means go, my dear, if you wish."

It was a starry, moonless night, and the river was smooth as glass,
with no tide or wind to disturb its surface. In silence Canby and
Nella had walked side by side through the park, and neither spoke
as, reaching the boathouse, the skiff was untied and they shoved off.
Instead of pulling for midstream Canby allowed the craft to float idly
down with the current, now and then swinging her out a little to clear
some obstruction near the bank. The stars gave just sufficient light

for him to make out Nella's features as she sat motionless on the seat near the stern with a dark mantle around her shoulders, bareheaded.

"I suppose you're all packed ready to go," said Canby at last, breaking a long silence.

Nella nodded her head, then, reflecting that he might not see her in the darkness, pronounced the word, "Yes."

"The two weeks have gone swiftly," Canby resumed after a moment; "that is, swiftly for me. I have thought sometimes that you and Rose and Mildred found it rather tiresome with no young people around."

There was a short silence; then he was somewhat surprised to hear a gay little silvery laugh from her.

"Now you're looking for a compliment, Mr. Canby," she declared, with the laugh still in her voice. "All right, I don't mind. We haven't found it tiresome one minute, because you've been so good to us. We like old people."

"But you're glad to go back?"

"My goodness, no!" He had the impression of a flash from the blue eyes, though he could not have seen it in the darkness. "I guess you don't know much about girls, Mr. Canby, if you think there is anyone who would be glad to leave all this—" she waved her hand toward Roselawn—"for a—for down there. That wouldn't be natural. But—well, I don't cry about it. I've got to go, and I go, and I'll make the best of it. I believe Rose and Mildred mind it more than I do. *Ma petite, sois philosophe.* That's what my mother used to say. You see, I am."

A silence. Ahead there was a protuberance on the bank, and Canby pulled sharply on the starboard oar to clear it. They floated past.

"Would you like to stay?" asked Canby suddenly.

"Stay here?"

"Yes. Not at Roselawn. But I—For several days I've had an idea . . . Of course, you know I like you, Nella. In these two weeks I've grown fond of you; so, really, what I have to propose is more selfish than it is gener-ous, but I think of you too. You deserve something better than the life you have been forced into by circumstances. I wanted my sister to adopt you, but she had made plans that rendered it impossible. So I thought—I wonder if you'd care to come and live with me?"

Without giving her time to reply he went on hastily:

"I mean, of course, as my ward. I could be appointed your legal guardian. Later, if we thought it advisable, I could adopt you and give you my name—that is, I don't know if bachelors can have adopted daughters, though I don't see why not. I assure you I'm not a difficult fellow to get along with. . . ."

"But, Mr. Canby! Why do you want to do this for me?"

"I said I was fond of you," he returned gruffly.

'But I—I don't know what to say." She was sitting up very straight on the seat, rigid. "It is so—it's like a dream! A beautiful dream! You really like me so well? I'm not always a good girl, you know. Often I am—I am—*méchante*. And you want me to come and live with you always, and have nice things. Oh! I . . . I . . ."

"Well, what do you say?" His voice lacked a little of being steady.

For a moment there was no reply. Then all at once the boat rolled crazily to one side as she jumped from her seat and bounded amidships to where he sat at the oars; and before Canby quite knew what she was about she had dropped on her knees before him and put her hands on his shoulders, drawing him forward, and planted a vigorous kiss on his cheek.

"There!" she cried like a delighted child, and kissed the other cheek too.

III

Not counting Nella Somi, there were two people who met with surprises that night that made it memorable for them.

The first was Mrs. Janet Morton Haskins. Telling herself that she knew men, when she had seen her middle-aged brother attracted by

the girl from the East Side Vacation Club she refrained from inter-
fering by a single word or gesture; it would have only added fuel to
his ardor; and when he had returned after dinner for a *tête-à-tête*
row on the river her thoughts were cynical. Even good old Fred, it
seemed, was capable of things.

Thus far her reflections. Imagine, then, her stupefied indignation
when good old Fred returned at ten o'clock with the girl, helped her
into his roadster, went upstairs for her luggage and put that in also,
and then announced calmly:

"I'm taking Nella home with me. You wouldn't adopt her, so I will!"

Janet almost shrieked. She did, in fact, raise her voice; but, by the
time intelligible words came to her lips, the roadster had disappeared
down the driveway, so suddenly that for a full hour she succeeded in
persuading herself that it was only a bad dream. Out of justice to her
it should be added that when she awoke to the reality of it she didn't
even take the trouble to go to the telephone and call him up. Perhaps
she did know something about men, after all.

The second surprised individual was Mr. Garrett Linwood. Having temporarily given up gin fizzes for fear of their effect on his golf
score, he had taken a pitcher of lemonade and an interesting book
to the billiard room at Greenhedge, and had reached chapter XIV
a little before eleven o'clock, when he heard his host's automobile
outside. Chapter XIV being mostly description of scenery, which he
detested, he threw down the novel and strolled idly down the hall to
the door, and, arrived there, stopped short and opened and closed
his eyes two or three times as if to wake himself up. For this thing
that he saw surely could not be: Fred Canby crossing the threshold
with a dark-haired, blue-eyed girl by his side! Or was it a witch, or
a fairy? Linwood blinked harder, and he heard his friend address
someone as Nella and tell her that this was Mr. Linwood, his guest.

Linwood bowed mechanically, still wondering when he would
wake up, and stood by in stupor while he heard Canby send for his
housekeeper and say to her:

"This is Miss Somi, Mrs. Wheeler, the young lady I spoke about this evening. She is going to live with us. I suppose her room is ready? Then you will show her, please. I'll take you over your new home tomorrow, Nella. Bedtime now. I'll send your things up immediately. Good night."

Later, in the library, Linwood sat and listened to his friend's wondrous tale; and though he was a fairly skeptical man he did not smile overmuch during the recital. When it was over he said calmly:

"Canby, you're a fool!"

"I wasn't aware I had asked for your opinion," the other retorted.

"True enough; you didn't. But remember I'm as much beyond fifty as you are beyond forty, and besides, having had a wife of my own for a total of twenty-one years—bless her memory!—I've studied the creature on its native soil. Nothing against Miss—What's her name? Thanks!—Nothing against Miss Somi; I don't know her at all, and I don't intend to offer any advice or begin any argument. I merely make the observation: Canby, you're a fool; but the thing's done. You have sworn that you have no personal intentions in the matter, matrimonial or otherwise, and you're a sincere and honest man. May you never have any regrets; and that sentiment should be sanctified in burgundy."

Whereupon Canby rang a bell and the burgundy was brought.

The following morning, up early and out of doors, Canby found Linwood in a corner of the lawn near the garage lustily swinging his driver at a parachute ball. They had barely exchanged greetings when they heard footsteps and, glancing up, saw Nella Somi coming down the path. She was bareheaded, without a parasol, and the glow of health and youth was all about her like a radiance.

"Good morning!" Canby called, and she crossed over.

As she nodded to them on her approach, turning her vivid blue eyes from one to the other, Canby simply stood and looked at her as though there were nothing else in the world worth doing.

"Sleep well?" he asked.

She laughed a little. "To tell the truth, I did," she confessed. "*Comme une marmotte.* When I went to bed I was so excited I was sure I wouldn't sleep at all—and I don't know what happened!"

When they were alone again a little later Linwood looked at his host and said:

"By Jove, Canby, now I *know* you're a fool. A rare wind-flower. What does Pope say: 'Snatch a grace beyond the reach of art.' She has done so."

After breakfast Linwood went off to the golf links, and Canby showed Nella about her new home. Compared with magnificent Roselawn, Greenhedge was quite unpretentious. The house was of brick and stone, high and old-fashioned, set in the midst of a grove of ancient elms, with terraced lawns sloping toward a small pond on one side and the driveway and gardens on the other. Completely surrounding the whole was a broad and high hedge, trimmed square; in the rear, beside the garage, there were kennels with a dozen Irish wolf-dogs, and a disused tennis court lay between there and the house. Nella displayed an eager childish interest in everything; she patted the dogs and picked a bouquet in the garden, and it was decided that the tennis court should be put in commission without delay.

When they returned for a tour of the house they were joined by Mrs. Wheeler, and Canby observed that Nella was already in the good graces of the old housekeeper. Everything pleased her, giving Canby delight in her pleasure; and when they reached the room where the portraits of past Canbys were hung she examined each of them critically, listening meanwhile to the other's not too sympathetic remarks on the various virtues and vices of his ancestors. In the billiard room he taught her how to hold a cue and make a carrom; she was enchanted.

"By the way, about your own room," Canby observed as they wandered on to the piazza after lunch, "you may do as you please about it, you know. Those hangings have been up I don't know how long and will have to come down anyway; you shall have it decorated to suit yourself."

"You are too good to me, Mr. Canby," she replied simply.

They strolled out under the trees and sat down in a garden swing.

"I was talking to Mrs. Wheeler about it this morning," Canby resumed, "and we thought it would be a good idea to fit out that room next to yours as a dressing-room. They're connected, you know. There's so much extra space, we might as well make use of all we can."

"A dressing-room for me!" exclaimed Nella.

He nodded; and then, so quickly that he was scarcely aware it had begun before it was over, he felt warm arms about his neck and cool lips on his cheek, and he heard her voice in his ear:

"There, you're so good I couldn't help it!"

Canby looked into her blue eyes, feeling himself tremble as the blood raced through his veins. He had to control himself, and it required an effort, an effort so pronounced that his head swam. Decidedly, this was dangerous, and must be stopped.

"You mustn't do that, Nella," he said at last, managing a steady voice somehow.

The blue eyes opened a little in wonder.

"Why not?"

He discovered suddenly that he had no reply. To be sure, why not? He couldn't very well say to this girl: "Because you awake my passion." He had assumed toward her the attitude of guardian, of parent; what plausible objection, then, to a filial kiss? But what should he reply?

"Well, you are really somewhat of a young lady," he stammered finally.

"*Mais, mon Dieu*," she retorted, "I'm to live with you! And you're so old! And when I love anybody and they're nice to me, I kiss them!"

He found a mixture of bitter and sweet in that. He looked at her, and saw the feminine in her eyes, a fleeting first hint of the universal lure, the endless invitations; of course, he told himself, all unconscious. After all, she was nearly twenty. . . .

"Last night," Nella continued artlessly, "I was thinking of what good times we'll have, if you're really fond of me, like you said. I know—" she hesitated—"I know I'm awfully ignorant; like the other day when Mrs. Haskins introduced me to Mr. and Mrs. Lodge, and I shook hands with him, and he looked so funny, and you told me afterwards I shouldn't. There are lots of things like that I don't know, and I thought that of evenings we could come out here together or on the porch, and I'd sit on your lap while you told me all about such things. But if you don't want me to kiss you, I guess, you're not really so fond of me . . ."

"Good heavens!" Canby exploded. "Of course I want you to kiss me!"

"All right, then I will," she returned calmly. After a moment she added thoughtfully: "I think I know what the trouble was, Mr. Canby. You were afraid I'd expect you to kiss me back, and of course you don't like to kiss anybody; that's why you never got married. But I won't ask you to." An instant's pause, and her eyes danced roguishly. "Except on my birthday," she added. "Then you'll have to give me three kisses for a present. One here—" she tapped her right cheek with a dainty figure—"one here—" a tap on the other cheek—"and one here." And she pressed the tips of her fingers against her lips.

This was rather too much. Artless or no, it could not be expected of a man to sit cold against the fascination of it. Canby rose abruptly to his feet and proposed a drive. Instantly she was for it, and together they went to the garage and got out the roadster. He broke all the speed laws in Dutchess and Putnam counties that afternoon.

Returning about six o'clock, just thirty minutes before the Greenhedge dinner hour, as they turned the last corner of the driveway they caught sight of Garrett Linwood, back from the golf links, seated on a canvas chair in a shady corner of the lawn; and, standing in front of him, talking with considerable rapidity and animation, was a young man with wavy brown hair dressed in a suit of summer silk and swinging a heavy black walking-stick.

"Oh, somebody's here!" said Nella, touching Canby's arm.

Canby too had seen the young man.

"It's Tom," he replied. "Tom Linwood; Mr. Linwood's nephew. Probably run down from Newport to make a touch."

"A touch? What's that?"

"To ask for some money."

When, a minute later, they joined the two on the lawn, this surmise was at once corroborated by the young man himself. He greeted Canby respectfully and hastened to assure him that there was no occasion to fear the inconvenience of an unbidden guest, as he had merely come on a flying visit to his uncle on a pressing matter of personal finance.

"Always glad to see you, my boy," Canby declared, shaking hands. "As for your finances, let me give you a tip: show your uncle how to lower his golf score ten strokes, and you can have his entire fortune. . . . Nella, this is Mr. Tom Linwood. Miss Somi, my ward, Tom."

The young man turned his dark eyes on Nella for the first time, meeting her blue ones, vivid and startling under the heavy lashes. She half extended her hand, then, with a flush and a quick look at Canby, hastily dropped it. The young society man all at once lost his air of easy good manners; his gaze was developing into a stare.

"I'll just let Mrs. Wheeler know you're here," Canby was saying, as he started for the house.

"Wait a minute!" came from the elder Linwood. "Tom isn't going to stay."

"What! Of course he is."

"No." Linwood's voice had a touch of grimness. "He's going back to New York on the six-thirty-five, and he's going to be at his office tomorrow morning at nine. There's been enough of this Newport foolishness for one summer."

"What about it, Tom?" asked Canby, laughing. "You'll stay to dinner? There's a later train."

The young man glanced at this host, at his uncle, and back at Nella.

"Why yes, thanks; I'll stay if you don't mind," he replied.

On his way to the house, Canby debated in his mind what to do with Nella, feeling that it would be unfair to expect her to preside at her first dinner at Greenhedge with guests. However, since she had had the advantage of observing his sister in the performance of that duty for two weeks, he decided to risk it.

With a critical, though sympathetic, eye on her throughout dinner, he was amused and astonished to observe how thoroughly she had taken advantage of her opportunity at Roselawn, and that, too, without having had at the time any idea that she would so soon have use for that knowledge. The phrases that she used in indicating their seats to her guests were copied verbatim from Janet; when she served a ragout from casserole there was a reproduction of Janet's every moment. She *was* clever, Canby observed inwardly, amazed; though he was far from beginning to believe in what he considered his sister's spiteful estimate of her. The dinner, though informal, was a somewhat complicated affair for a nineteen-year-old girl who two weeks previously had been sorting candy in a Manhattan factory and living in an east-side tenement; but she reached the end with complete success, without a single false step.

Afterwards they went out to sit on the lawn, and, the two elder men engaging in a controversy on the war, young Linwood proposed a walk to Miss Somi. An hour later they returned, and, just before the time came for him to go to the station, whither his uncle was to drive him, the young man managed to get a word alone with Canby.

"Is it possible, sir, what Miss Somi tells me about herself—candy factory and all that rot?" he demanded. "I can't believe it."

Canby gave him an affirmative.

The youth whistled. "Well, believe me," he observed softly to himself as the other moved away, "Uncle Garry is dead right about Newport foolishness. Nothing to it; nobody up there can touch *her*. In the future my vacations are going to be spent on the classic east side of little old New York."

IV

For some time after that, Garrett Linwood made his daily pilgrimage to the Wanakahnda golf links alone. Canby's days were full, what with tennis with Nella, and motoring with Nella, and walking and talking with Nella, and improving Nella's mind, and trying not to make an old fool of himself with Nella.

The last became more difficult every hour, as her charm completely enveloped and permeated him. There was always a new gesture, a new expression, a new tone, to be watched for; of all the interests that he had ever had in life she became the strongest. He had many an argument with himself, but they ended always in the same decision: wait and see; which of course was no decision at all, and that was not like Fred Canby.

Linwood, sour widower of two-and-fifty, at first ignored the new member of the household more or less completely, contenting himself with courtesy; at length, however, he gave way before her gay good nature and the buoyant charm of her.

"By immortal time," he declared one evening to his host, "since you won't marry her, Canby, I'll swear I'm tempted myself!" He even went so far as to invite her to Wanakahnda for a day on the links and an initiation into the mysteries of the ancient game; but the look of thankful relief that appeared on his face when she declined sent her into peals of laughter.

Thus weeks passed.

One day Mrs. Wheeler, the housekeeper, came to Canby and asked when he was going to New York.

"I don't know, perhaps next week," he replied vaguely. "Why?"

"It ought to be soon," returned Mrs. Wheeler with emphasis. "It ain't my business, and she don't seem to mind, but I don't see how the poor dear does it. When I asked her she said she come up here expecting to stay only two weeks, and she didn't have any too much for that. Don't you tell her I said anything, but I'm sure I don't want to see the poor dear naked, and that's what—"

Canby stopped her.

"What in the world are you talking about?"

Mrs. Wheeler became suddenly brief:

"I'm talkin' about clothes."

"Good Lord!"

Canby leaped to his feet and started in search of Nella. In the past week he had begun to notice that she was wearing the same things rather often; but, never having been concerned in the condition of any woman's wardrobe, it simply hadn't occurred to him that he had any responsibility in the matter. Now he reproached himself; also, he should before this have arranged for his appointment as her legal guardian. There would be no difficulty about that; she was absolutely alone in the world, without any ties whatever.

Early the following morning they started for New York in the roadster. It was the last day of August, and the pulse of summer was beginning to wane; on the foliage were the first faint signs of the season's death; the air, though hot, was not oppressive, and when they got to the Albany road they found the breeze from the river cool and brisk. Nella was at the wheel; in the past two weeks she had become expert.

Canby took advantage of the occasion to tell her certain things that he thought she ought to know.

"I'm going to make application today for appointment as your legal guardian," he informed her as they rolled along at thirty miles an hour. "That means that I will be responsible for you just as a father would be. Before you agree to that you ought to know definitely what to expect. I have an income of something over twenty thousand a year. I own Greenhedge. There is no one else in the world dependent on me, and another thing I will do today is make you the sole beneficiary in my will—that is, you'll get everything when I die. I'm not a wealthy man as New York goes nowadays, but I have enough."

When they arrived in New York he explained his plans for the day; and in accordance with them, at Forty-second Street he transferred Nella to a taxi-cab and handed her a well-filled purse. He had sufficient confidence in her taste to feel no anxiety for the propriety of her purchases; and besides, any advice from him on the subject would be worse than useless. So he left her, after appointing a rendezvous with her at one o'clock.

Downtown, in the brokerage office in which he had an interest, on Cedar Street just off Broadway, his sudden appearance caused a degree of surprise. Matters of business kept him there for over an hour, after which he departed to keep an appointment arranged over the telephone with his attorney. More surprise here, profound and sustained, at his abrupt announcement of the acquisition of a ward; it ended with the lawyer's assurance that the legal phase of the transaction would present no difficulties whatever; he would enter the application that day, and in a week or so the thing would be done. Then the alteration of the will was attended to, and it was half an hour after noon when Canby found himself again on the street.

He crossed the sidewalk to the curb, opened the door of the roadster and was getting in when he heard his name called from behind:

"Mr. Canby! It's a wonder you wouldn't look at a fellow! When'd you come in?"

It was Tom Linwood, smiling as always, resplendent as to attire and assured as to countenance. They talked a little, the young man asking with mock solicitude concerning the state of his uncle's golf score.

"You see," he explained, "I'm naturally interested, because if he ever gets a seventy-nine he'll die of joy and I'll be a rich man. . . . By the way, how is Miss Somi?"

Canby replied that Miss Somi was very well, and thoughtlessly added that she was at the moment uptown shopping.

"No! Is she really?" Young Linwood's face brightened. "You don't happen to know just where she is, do you? Perhaps she'd take luncheon with me."

"I'm on my way to take her to lunch now," replied the guileless Canby.

"Yes? By Jove, that's fine! You don't mind if I come along?"

And almost before Canby knew how it happened they were seated side by side in the roadster on their way uptown.

They were at Sherry's a few minutes before one, and a little later Nella entered. Her face was flushed and her eyes were beaming with the unprecedented joy of the morning's experience; in three hours she had bought a thousand dollars' worth of clothes. Ineffable delight!

She came forward to greet Canby with so pervasive an air of happiness that for a moment he feared one of her demonstrations of fond gratitude there in the restaurant lobby. Then she caught sight of his companion.

"Oh! Mr. Linwood!" she said prettily.

The luncheon that Canby had looked forward to with so much pleasure proved rather an uncomfortable affair for him. In the first place, they had barely finished the clams when he began to reflect that Tom Linwood was an uncommonly handsome young man, and the trouble was that Nella seemed to have noticed it too; the Lord knows, she kept her eyes on him enough. And Tom, with incredible cunning, having discovered that Nella was under the spell of her first shopping orgy, began to describe in detail the frocks he had seen at Newport that summer. Fine masculine subject for conversation! But what really caused Canby discomfort was the sight of the youth in the brown eyes calling to that in the blue.

They had nearly finished when Canby, hearing a woman's voice pronounce his name, turned to find Mrs. Ponsonby-Atkins approaching with her daughter Marie. She stopped to talk and inquire about his sister, while Marie chatted with Tom Linwood; there was absolutely no help for it, and he finally introduced "Miss Somi, my ward." Good breeding held fast; Mrs. Ponsonby-Atkins never blinked an eyelash; but, as she moved away, her back seemed somehow to be saying in her own picturesque manner: "Fred Canby with a beautiful Latin princess for a ward! Where the devil did he get her?" Not that he was ashamed of Nella—far from it—but the encounter was inopportune and undesired.

And finally, out on the sidewalk, young Linwood calmly invited himself to Greenhedge for the coming week-end. He would arrive early Saturday afternoon, he declared, if it would be no inconvenience; and Canby, perforce, assured him it would not.

Alone again with Nella, bad humor was out of the question. He suggested a matinée. She clapped her hands in delight; so he telephoned to Greenhedge that they would not be home for dinner, and got tickets to something on Broadway. Her first visit to a theater other than movies. Nella was entranced; and Canby, with his eyes on her rather than on the stage, was entranced also. In the third act, when the heroine defied her wicked father, the brutal detective and the world in general, Canby felt Nella's little hand creeping into his; his fingers closed over the trembling captive and held it fast till the curtain fell. For that twenty minutes he scarcely breathed.

After it was over they started for home, stopping at a roadhouse not far beyond Yonkers for dinner. The night was cool and pleasant when they resumed their journey two hours later; a crescent moon hung in the clear sky with its attendant twinkling stars, and the smell of the harvest was in the air. Nella, tired out from her unusual day, let Canby have the wheel; she seemed thoughtful and talked scarcely at all.

Whey they arrived at Greenhedge, a little after ten, everything was quiet. The gardener had waited up to put the car away, and in the house they found Mrs. Wheeler, who replied to Canby's inquiry with the information that Mr. Linwood had gone to bed half an hour before. She added, turning to the girl:

"Your things came, Miss Nella."

"No! Really? So soon? Where are they?"

"Upstairs, in your room."

"Oh! Come, I must show you!"

She took Canby by the hand and half dragged him to the stairs. He protested that it was late, that she was tired and should rest, that it could wait till morning, but she wouldn't listen to him. At the door of her room, however, she suddenly halted.

"You stay here a minute," she commanded, and went in alone, leaving him there in the dark hall. He kicked his heels while the minute lengthened into five, ten; and finally he rapped on the door.

"All right, you may come," her voice sounded from within; and he turned the knob and entered.

The room was flooded with light, so that the contrast with the hall blinded him for a moment. Then he looked at Nella. She stood in the middle of the room with Circe's smile on her lips and a laughing light in her blue eyes. That was as far as Canby got in detail; he had an impression of a smart blue frock, entrancing little slippers and a drooping, lacy hat that framed her piquant face with loveliness. He looked, and caught his breath.

"Do you like me?" she demanded.

The poor man could only nod.

She pretended to pout. "I don't believe you at all. I'll try again. There's lots more." She turned to the bed, near which lay a great heap of boxes and bundles of all sizes and shapes. "I know what I'll do! Go out in the hall again."

He felt that he was making rather an ass of himself, but what could he do but obey? So out he went again into the dark hall, and re-entered at her call a few minutes later.

The blue frock and hat lay on the bed, discarded; and before him stood a vision in creamy white. She was bareheaded; her throat gleamed whiter than the filmy stuff that enveloped her, and her arms too as she swept him an old-fashioned curtsey and the flowing sleeves opened. Around the waist a heavy silken girdle drew in the folds to her slender form.

"*Mon peignoir*," she announced, observing the effect on him. "*Comment le trouvez-vous, monsieur?* Isn't it just lovely? Tell me, isn't it?"

"It—it's pretty nice," Canby stammered.

"But yes! And oh, everything is so nice! I never dreamed I would have a single one of these beautiful things, and now I have them all, and all because you are so kind to me—and I just *have* to kiss you!"

And once more he felt her arms about his neck and her lips on his cheek—both his cheeks. He stiffened and held himself rigid; when she drew away he remained so, holding himself together by a great effort. And he succeeded in mastering the impulse of desire, but as he stood there motionless, devouring her with his eyes, the thought that his abstinence was folly, his spartan control senseless and purposeless, seized him and overwhelmed him. Still he remained without moving, his muscles tense.

"Oh, now you're angry!" Nella was saying in pretty girlish despair. "I *do* want you to like me, you are so kind, and—See!" Her manner changed in a flash. "That's the way it ought to be, isn't it?" Up went her hands to her head, there was a quick movement, another, and the mass of dark brown hair tumbled about her shoulders and down her back, reaching to the waist; one thick wavy strand hung in front, in startling contrast to the white gown.

"There! Isn't it nice and long?"

Canby, mad with the beauty of her, took a step forward.

"Nella!" His tone was dry—he had to make it so; his face was pale. "Nella, do you love me?"

"Of course I do," she said simply.

"No, not like that." He moved forward quite close to her, his eyes on hers. There was a pause.

"I really believe you don't understand," he said abruptly. "I've got to explain. If it goes on like this you'll drive me crazy. You remember a long time ago I said I was fond of you? I am. I am fonder of you than I have even been of anyone in my life. So you see why I can't stand this sort of thing."

"But I'm fond of you too, and I like it!"

He groaned. "Yes, I know you are, but in a different way; at least, I think it's in a different way, and that's what I want to find out. You thought, Nella, that when I asked you to come and live with me—you thought that was what I wanted; but what I really wanted—though I wouldn't admit it to myself at the time—was to ask you to marry me."

"Oh! Why didn't you?"

"Yes, that was what I wanted," he went on, ignoring her question, "though I tried to deceive myself. This is what I get for trying to shut my eyes to the facts. But, good heavens—the thing was impossible! It is still impossible. I'm more than twice as old as you. You are not yet twenty; I am past forty. It would be unfair to you, terribly unfair. When you are thirty-eight I will be sixty. Oh, I've made all the combinations. But now—I don't know. Perhaps I owe myself a chance. I couldn't bear to take advantage of you, your innocence and youth, but after all, if I could make you happy, and the Lord knows I'd try—"

"But you *are* making me happy!"

"I know. I mean, if you could love me. Not as a grandfather, my dear child. Garry Linwood told me I was a fool, and I begin to respect his judgment. For, I suppose, you could never have the feeling for me that I want you to have, that I have for you. If you did, it couldn't last. I'm too old—hopelessly old."

"You are not!" cried the girl. "And I do love you!"

He was suddenly silent. He stood and looked at her, and all at once his face changed. All the determination of it, all the lines of resistance, were swept away by a fierce wave of emotion. He made a quick step forward and took her in his arms, but still holding her a little away from him. He was trembling from head to foot.

"Nella!" he said. His voice was husky. "Does this—do I frighten you?"

She shook her head, smiling at him as she declared calmly:

"Of course not!"

The next instant he crushed her in his arms, the last vestige of control vanished. Her own arms remained by her side, but for that matter she could not have moved them had she wished, so closely did he hold her. He kissed her hair, her cheeks, her throat, and then he found her lips. Her soft supple body next to his filled him with an indescribable warmth; his senses floated away in a whirl of tumultuous passion. Her lips were firm, yet yielding; there was no response in them, yet somehow they seemed to withhold nothing. He drew her closer, and felt the pressure against him in her effort to breathe.

The sweetness of her lips! Given or taken, the whole world was in them. He was drinking at the only fount that could quench his thirst, and he would not relinquish the draught. He neither knew nor cared how long he remained thus, straining her to him, for the force of all the weeks of repression surged into his arms and kept them round her. He could not even tell if she resisted, though that would not have mattered, for it was not tenderness that inspired this embrace.

"You are mine!" His tone was fiercely, savagely triumphant. "Mine, Nella!" Again he had her lips.

Then all at once the wave subsided as suddenly as it had come. He released her, almost pushing her from him in his revulsion. He turned his back and covered his face with his hands.

The girl's voice came:

"Oh, how tight you squeezed me! I could scarcely breathe!"

"Good heavens!" cried Canby, wheeling about. "And that's all you felt—" He checked himself and gathered his scattered senses. When he spoke again his voice was bitterly ironic. "And I wanted to be your guardian! Nella, I'm an old fool. Don't misunderstand me; I wouldn't insist on your love. My desire is to have you for my wife, on any terms; but I won't ask you, and that's all there is to it. Later, we'll see. Forget everything I've said. If I asked you now to marry me, you would?"

She seemed to hesitate.

"Yes, I would," she said at last.

"Very well. All the more reason why I shouldn't ask it—now. I've got to think the thing out. I see I haven't really thought about it; I've merely tried to make myself believe lies. It's all a question of your chance for happiness, and I swear I won't rob you of it. I'm tempted unspeakably. If we—if you find you can love me, we'll see. Good night, and forgive me."

He had reached the door when her voice came:

"Don't you want me to kiss you good night?"

"I do not!" he replied grimly; and the next instant the door closed after him.

V

If only Canby had possessed a sufficiently active sense of humor to see the comedy in the thing it would have saved him many a bad hour. Or, if he had been a reader of modern fiction he would have known that in the past ten years hundreds of wealthy, middle-aged bachelors have suffered untold miseries through their unhappy passion for their beautiful young wards, and he would have been much less disturbed by the appearance of youth upon the scene in the person of Tom Linwood; for he would have known beforehand that it was inevitable, and the very triteness of the situation would have soothed his pain a little.

But he possessed neither of these desirable advantages, and thus, when Tom Linwood came on Saturday for the weekend and began to appropriate Nella's waking hours with the calm assurance of arrogant youth, Canby felt the turning of the screw in no small degree. He reproached himself, was unutterably disgusted with himself, but all to no effect. He deliberately made opportunities for the two young people to be alone together and then berated himself for an ass. But he was determined to seize no unfair advantage on account of the position he held with regard to Nella; youth should have its chance with her.

At dinner Sunday evening he said to young Linwood:

"Why don't you stay up with us a while, Tom? You could go down of mornings on the seven-thirty-five and get back in the evening in time for dinner. It's only a two-hour run."

The alacrity with which this invitation was accepted was equalled by that with which Canby immediately regretted having extended it. He told himself that it was more than fairness demanded; but the thing was done.

He had the days with Nella, however, and they were full of joy for him. If young Linwood was making any impression on her heart it was not evidenced by any change in her attitude toward Canby or any lessening of her pleasure in his company. They played tennis and walked and rode together as formerly, and he read to her a good deal—this last to improve her mind, and she did not refrain from expressing her gratitude. They were in September now, and the countryside lay in peaceful exhaustion after the summer's heat.

The elder Linwood played golf, hanging on with grim tenacity to his resolution and purpose; but his reports from the links, though invariably optimistic, showed small progress. Canby was amused. Linwood had come up for the month of July, and here autumn was fast approaching without any sign of an intention to depart from Greenhedge. His own magnificent country estate on Long Island, not to mention a bungalow in the Adirondacks and a cottage at Bar Harbor, remained closed that he might pursue an elusive dream on the Wanakahnda golf links. Still he appeared to be growing a little discouraged, for his pilgrimages were becoming less frequent; he spent some of his days at Greenhedge now.

One evening Canby and Linwood sat on the lawn of the northern terrace smoking and talking; three of the Irish wolf-dogs lay at their feet, and a wooden table between their chairs held glasses and a bottle and a pail of cracked ice. Nella and Tom had gone off somewhere an hour before in Linwood's new Binot racer, which he had allowed his nephew to bring up from New York. The night was cloudless and cool, with the stars gleaming intermittently through the foliage of the trees as the breeze stirred the leaves above them.

"I'll probably run down Tuesday," Canby was replying to a question from the other. "Andrews has written me that it will be necessary to appear in court that day in regard to my appointment as Nella's guardian. I'll attend to the other matter then too. Much obliged for that tip on Copper United, Linwood; I've cleared thirty thousand."

The elder man waved the thanks aside. "Don't mention it. Didn't cost me anything, you know." After a moment's silence he added: "So you're going through with the guardian business?"

Canby, filling the glasses, nodded. "I am."

"Well," Linwood chuckled, "it'll probably be a short job. You may have your hands full for a while, but it won't last long. Why don't you marry her yourself, Canby, instead of flopping around like a sick fish?"

"Would it be fair to her?"

"Why not?"

"Don't be a donkey, Linwood; you know why not as well as I do. She's a mere girl, and I—well, I'm no unfledged nestling. As a matter of fact, she's consented to marry me. I refused. There's twenty-two years between us; it wouldn't be fair to her."

Linwood snorted. "What do you think a girl wants a husband for, anyway?" he demanded. "Do you still believe in the moonish ecstasy, the connubial coo-coo? Bah! Of course it's not surprising; you're a bachelor. I've had the advantage of experience. The call of youth is well enough as a pre-election platform, but it's an issue that soon dies. Fair to her! Her eyes are open, aren't they? You merely put it up to her, yes or no, and she can decide what she wants. And you refused!"

"But you don't understand," Canby protested. "Ordinarily I wouldn't hesitate, but you see I've done things for her, and merely out of gratitude—"

"Don't fool yourself," the other interrupted. "No woman worthwhile ever yet married any man out of gratitude. I may add that this little lady is distinctly worthwhile. If she takes you it's because she wants you, no matter what her reason."

Canby seemed to be impressed. He picked up his glass and drained it before replying.

"But isn't it true," he asked then, "that Nella would certainly be happier with—well, with Tom, for instance?"

"Oh, of course!" Linwood's tone was heavy with sarcasm. "Undoubtedly! So she would have the pleasure of running to me every Saturday to get enough to buy pork chops."

"Linwood, you're a depraved cynic."

"Canby, you're a doting driveler."

With that exchange of courtesies they left the topic and drifted back to the stock market. But Canby had in reality been impressed, as we always are by any argument that fits in with our desire. He reflected that Linwood had a good understanding of the world and the life that was lived in it, and that his judgment was probably sensible, as it was certainly to his liking.

After all, not to flatter himself, he was a decent sort of fellow; there was no assurance that Nella would do better, and she might conceivably do worse. The memory of her in his arms came to him, as it had many times before, and he felt his blood grow warm at the recollection of that incomparably blissful moment. The sense of the sanctity and innocence of her youth was still strong within him, however, and colored his thoughts; what he feared was to take advantage of her ignorance and purity, and he asked himself how she could possibly be expected to make a decision for herself when the real question was of necessity hidden from her. And possibly it was already too late. Was her heart still her own to give? Folly, idiotic folly, to have deliberately placed before her the fascination of Tom Linwood's youthful graces!

Most of these reflections came to him as he wandered alone in the garden, having left Linwood to take the dogs back to their kennels; and the fear of young Linwood's rivalry was immediately suggested by the sound of the returning Binot racer on the driveway.

Canby sat on the bench in a secluded corner of the garden and dug about in his brain for a decision. Surely he had given youth a fair chance and an able representative. If the joy of having her was still possible, why not seize it?

Linwood's words recurred to him. Yes, passion is a fleeting thing anyway, and when that was over the best of her would be left to him, and he would guard—

The current of his thoughts was interrupted by the sound of footsteps approaching along the garden path. He glanced out from his dark retreat; it was Nella and young Linwood. They approached slowly, without speaking, and Canby merely kept silent till they should pass; but, instead, they halted on the opposite side of the bush under which his bench was placed, not ten feet away. Too late he realized his position.

Young Linwood's voice came:

"But, Nella, you have no feeling for me whatever?"

Then a little gay laugh from her:

"Of course! Didn't I say I was awfully fond of you?"

"Oh, fond be hanged!" The representative of youth was evidently ready to explode with impatience. "It's your love I want, Nella. Good Lord, how I hate that word fond! You've got to love me!" His breath caught and he went on: "I didn't suppose anyone in the world could be so lovely, so adorable, as you. I tell you, I can't live without you. Nella, look at me!"

Canby was trying to find a means of escape, but none offered. In the rear was an impenetrable hedge; on either side he was sure to be seen. He had stayed too long, and now must stay longer.

The rustle of a quick movement came from the other side of the bush, and the young man's voice:

"Nella! There, I can't help it! Oh, I've wanted so to hold you in my arms—like this. Ah!" There was the sound of a kiss. "No—please, Nella! I love you, I worship you, I adore you! See, I don't hurt you, do I?"

"No—o. No, you don't hurt me, Mr. Linwood, but—"

"Ah, let me! Nella, you don't know what you mean to me! I never thought—You've just bowled me over! Dearest, let me!"

More kisses. Canby groaned inwardly. To be out of this!

Nella's voice came:

"Mr. Linwood, let me go—please."

"No, I can't! I won't! You must promise me, Nella. Say you love me. I've begged you long enough."

"Mr. Linwood . . . please! Mr. Canby wouldn't like it."

"To the devil with Canby! I want you, Nella, you don't know how I want you. You're a sorceress, a witch; you set me crazy! You've got to promise me; you've got to. I tell you I can't think of anything, of anyone but you. On the train, all day long at the office—everywhere I think of nothing but you. I can't even sleep—I swear I can't! But I don't need to tell you that; you know how I love you. Nella, please—tell me—No! Tell me—"

There was the sound of rustling garments, the scuffling feet on gravel, a little suppressed cry, and then rapid retreating footsteps; and Canby, peering round the corner of the bush, saw Nella's form dimly disappearing down the path in the starlight. She had flown to the house.

Then from the other side of the bush sounded the footsteps of the man she had left. But not along the path; they approached instead on the grass. Was the young idiot actually coming to this very bench?

He was indeed. On the instant, his form appeared from behind the bush and he sat down on the opposite end of the bench without becoming aware of the other's presence; he thrust his hands deep in his pockets, crossed his legs in front of him, and let his chin fall on his chest.

"Well, I'm dashed good!" came his voice.

Canby felt that the situation had reached its limit.

"Hello!" he said abruptly. His voice sounded queer.

Young Linwood jumped up as though there had been a pin under him.

"What the devil!" he exclaimed, wheeling.

"It's I—Canby," returned the other, retaining his grammar in spite of everything.

"Oh!" The young man caught sight of him. He stood for a moment in silent bewilderment. "But what are you doing? How do you happen—"

Canby explained. "I was here when you came up. I thought you'd go on by. You began to talk at once, and there was no escape. I'm sorry."

"Oh, that's all right." Young Linwood looked at him a moment, then sat down again. "Couldn't be helped; not your fault. It happens often, especially in novels. Doesn't bother me any; I don't give a hang if the whole world knows I love her."

Canby was silent.

"You know, I *do* love her," the young man resumed presently. "By Jove, I do; with all my heart. "You heard what I said. Well, every word of it is true. And she won't give me any satisfaction. Most amazing girl I ever saw. She tantalizes me and sets me crazy. I can't understand it. For two days, you remember, I didn't come up here; I was trying to forget her. Duff Lewis and I took two girls down to Long Beach and, Lord, but I was sick of 'em! Couldn't get my mind off of her one minute. I tell you, Canby, I'm hit hard."

It was the first time he had ever called him "Canby" without the "Mister." He had reached the estate of man!

"It's her confounded stubbornness," the young lover resumed presently, changing his tune a little. "She loves me—I know she does, only she won't admit it. It's enough to worry a man to death; because, of course, I'm not absolutely sure."

He stopped suddenly and looked at Canby as though a new idea had just entered his head.

"By the way, I suppose I ought to consult you, sir; you're her guardian. Have you any objections?"

"Objections to what?"

"To my marrying Miss Somi."

"Why—" Canby hesitated. "Have you asked her?"

"Only about ten thousand times."

"What does she say?"

"She says—she says—I don't know what the devil she *does* say! I'll swear I don't know, sir. Confound it all, that's what I'm beefing about! I can't get her to say anything."

"It's just possible she hasn't made up her mind," Canby observed drily.

"Good Lord, how much time does she want? Why, all the other girls—but, of course, that's different. I hadn't asked them to marry me; so naturally they let me kiss them all I wanted. But I can't believe— Has she said anything to you about me?"

"About you? No."

"Not a word?"

"Well, she asked me the other evening if you liked scallops. I believe they were considered for dinner."

"Did she really?" The young man's face brightened, then as speedily fell. "But that's nothing. I'm her guest; she'd do as much for a dog. But she'll marry me, if I have to run off with her. I'd be capable of anything; that is, I mean, if you have no objections, sir."

"None whatever, Tom."

"Thank you, sir."

"What I mean to say is, you're acceptable to me if you are to her,"

Canby continued. "Go ahead and win her if you can. No doubt you'd be as good a husband as the next man. But permit me an observation: don't you think your method is a little boisterous?"

"Boisterous?"

"Well, undignified; er—unreserved."

"Oh! Yes, sir, perhaps; but you can't make love like a clam, you know; you've got to move around a little. Besides, they like it."

Canby grunted. "As you please. It's the way of youth, I suppose." He rose from the bench. "I'll leave you to your rosy reflections. Good night."

He went off toward the house, leaving the young man on the bench.

He went partly because he had heard enough of the youth's chatter, but more on account of a decision that had formed itself in his mind as he listened. Evidently the youth had not yet conquered. It was an open field now and a fair one. He, Fred Canby, would buckle on his armor and enter the lists at once, and at once meant now.

He paced the length of the piazza. There was no one there. The elder Linwood, he knew, had gone up to bed some time before. He entered the house, went upstairs to Nella's room and, seeing a light under the door, knocked on the panel.

Her voice came instantly:

"Who is it?"

"Canby."

"Oh! Come in."

He entered, closing the door behind him. She was reclining in a low fauteuil with an open book in her hand; about her hung the folds of the filmy white dressing-gown she had worn that other night two weeks before, and her dark hair, in two massive braids, dropped from her shoulders. The wonder of her was ever new to Canby, and he gazed at her a second in silence.

Then he began abruptly:

"I've just been talking with young Linwood."

Nella sat up, closing the book.

"He tells me he wants to marry you. He says he has asked you to be his wife. You haven't accepted him?"

Silence.

"Have you?"

"No, I haven't," she declared calmly.

"Have you decided to accept him?"

She seemed to hesitate.

"Decided? No," she replied finally.

Canby breathed. "Then I may speak." He moved forward a little. "You remember, Nella, two weeks ago you said you would marry me if I wanted you to. I refused to accept what I considered a sacrifice. I gave you my reasons then. I no longer hold myself bound by them. I ask you to marry me."

She started to speak, but he raised his hand to stop her:

"Wait; I want to explain. I do this because I see pretty plainly that if you don't marry me you will marry Tom Linwood, and I believe I'd do as well by you as he would. But as your guardian I must put the facts before you: I am forty-one, he is twenty-four. We both come of good families, though mine is considerably better placed socially. I am worth about half a million, not counting Greenhedge, with an income of twenty thousand or so. He is penniless himself, but he is sole heir of his uncle's fortune, which is somewhere between ten and fifteen millions. He will have that when Mr. Linwood dies if he behaves himself. Mr. Linwood is fifty-two years of age and in good health; what he would do for his nephew in the event of marriage I don't know."

Nella's eyes were wide open.

"Is Mr. Linwood so wealthy?"

"He is. No doubt this all sounds mercenary to you, but these things should be taken into consideration when a girl contemplates marriage; and I, being an interested party, can't very well judge for you, so you have to do it yourself. Another thing: You must decide between us strictly according to your own desires. It would be an injury to me—a deep injury—if you permit any feeling of gratitude for what I have done to influence your decision in my favor. You must take the one you want for your husband. You understand that, don't you?"

Nella's face was a study. "Yes, I understand," she said slowly.

"I suppose—" Canby hesitated a moment, then went on: "I suppose you aren't ready to decide? Tom Linwood wants to marry you; so do I. Can you decide now between us?"

His voice trembled a little in spite of himself. If she were willing to take him now, as she had been two weeks previously, he would not refuse the prize a second time. He waited, scarcely breathing.

"I—I—really, I don't know," said Nella at last. "Oh, Mr. Canby, you don't mind, do you? I must think, just till tomorrow. Tomorrow I'll tell you." She had risen from her chair and was standing with her hands clasped in front of her. "I do love you; but I like Mr. Linwood too. I must think over it a little—"

"Of course," Canby agreed. His face was white. "Of course, dear child, you must think."

There was a short silence.

"Tomorrow, then!" said Canby; and, turning, left the room without another word.

VI

He could not get to sleep for a long while, and in the morning he awoke late—late, that is, for him, for he was usually up by six o'clock. Downstairs the house was empty; the Linwoods had supposedly gone, one to the city and the other to the golf links, and Nella was apt to be anywhere. He lingered disconsolately over his fruit and coffee and morning paper, reading the latter through from beginning to end without a single word entering his consciousness. The morning was warm, the air oppressive, everything seemed out of tune; he heard Mrs. Wheeler out in the kitchen berating the cook, and finally, to escape the sound of her voice, he got up and wandered out to the lawn.

Turning a corner of the house, he halted in surprise; for there, stretched out on his back in the shade of a tree with his arms crossed over his eyes, he saw Tom Linwood.

"Hello! You didn't go in this morning?" observed Canby, approaching.

The young man sat up, rubbing his eyes and blinking, and returned a negative with his greeting.

"You look sort of hipped," Canby continued, stopping above him.

The youth nodded. "I feel it." Looking up at the other, he added: "You don't seem very jaunty yourself."

"No. Weather, I guess." Canby sat down on the grass. "Seen anything of Nella?"

"I have."

It appeared from the length of the pause that followed this that young Linwood had said all he intended to say, but presently he continued:

"She's gone off with Uncle Garry. In the Binot."

Canby looked surprised. "Where to?"

"I don't know. Anywhere; nowhere in particular, I guess." Another pause, then he continued: "Rotten car, that Shinton roadster of yours, if you'll pardon my saying so, Canby."

"Say anything you please, my boy. But what—"

"The most I could get out of her was fifty-five. The Binot does eighty, you know. I was after uncle. I might as well have been standing still."

"You were after—" Canby was mystified.

"Yes, after uncle. I didn't want him to insult Nella if I could help it."

"Insult Nella?" Canby turned quickened eyes on him. "Tom, make yourself intelligible, please."

"Oh, I don't mean—that is, it's on account of me," the young man explained. "You see, after you left me in the garden last night I set out to look for Uncle Garry. Couldn't find him anywhere about, so I went up to his room. He was in bed. I should have waited perhaps, but I'd made up my mind to have it over with; so I turned on the lights and woke him up and told him I was going to marry Miss Somi. You see, I was afraid he might object on account of her—that is, she's not—"

"I understand. Go on."

"Well, he sleeps pretty sound for an old man, you know, so I had to shake him up a little and say it over once or twice before he seemed to get what I was driving at. Then he just sat and looked at me—and laughed!"

"Laughed?"

"Yes. I thought he was a little off. Finally he said to me, 'Tom, you're an unconditional ass!' I replied, 'I know it, sir,' and he laughed again. Then all at once he got serious and read me a lecture. He said he knew better than to attempt to argue with words against the celestial trumpet-call of youth. He said he was glad to learn I had begun to talk moon-eyed, because the sooner it began the sooner it ended, but that I was too young yet to play the bass in the matrimonial harmony. He said that while he had all the respect in the world for the primal urge of nature, he preferred not to connive at its premature manifestations. Then he lay down again and told me to get out."

"Well?" Canby was grinning.

"Well, I went. I didn't like it; I wouldn't have minded if he'd let out at me, but I didn't like his sarcasm. I knew he was up to something; and, sure enough, at the breakfast-table this morning, the first thing I knew he and Miss Somi were arranging to go for a drive. I could tell from his manner he meant trouble. But he caught me napping, and pulled the thing off so quick that he had the Binot out of the garage and was off before I got my breath. I went after him in the roadster, but, Lord, I might as well have been chasing a hydroplane in a rowboat."

"But you spoke of insult."

"Sure. Oh, I know Uncle Garry! He's going to try to buy her off. He'd say anything to her, and she's so—so darned sweet, she'd stand for it. He'd throw it up to her about her—oh, about everything. That's what he's doing now. I tell you, Canby, I came nearly busting that roadster up with an axe."

"What time did this happen?"

"Hours ago; about seven o'clock—right after breakfast. What time is it now?"

Canby glanced at his watch. "Eleven."

"They ought to be back soon. I'm waiting around. I'll tell you what, Mr. Canby, I'm going to marry that girl if I have to take—no matter what. I can't live without her; I'm not going back to the office or anywhere else until—Hello, here they are!"

So it was. Through the gate in the great hedge the Binot racer appeared and came spinning along the driveway. Canby and young Linwood rose hastily and crossed over, meeting it as it drew up near the garage. The expression on the youth's face was one of anxiety and determination; on Canby's, curiosity and inquiry.

"Good morning!" cried Nella, leaping out. "Oh, we've had such a fine ride!" She turned to Canby: "We missed you at breakfast. I peeped in your room, but you were asleep."

This was hardly the manner of a girl who had just been subjected to dreadful insults, Canby reflected; and from the bewildered hopefulness on young Linwood's countenance it seemed that he had arrived at the same conclusion. Nella turned her smile, first on one, then on the other, with perfect impartiality; and Canby, who was looking for signs, could find no slightest indication that she had made a decision, either voluntary or forced. The elder Linwood, having relieved himself of his duster, wanted to know of his nephew why the deuce he hadn't gone to his office; but, though the reply was somewhat unsatisfactory, he immediately dropped the question. He regarded the young man with a quizzical, half-amused expression in his eyes; then abruptly turned to his host with a demand for drink, claiming a magnificent thirst.

They made for the piazza, Canby leading with Nella, and the two Linwoods bringing up the rear. It was cooler there, and a faint stir began to be felt in the air, promising relief for the afternoon. Nella and Tom sat in a porch swing, talking by fits and starts; the elder Linwood reclined in a chair and fanned himself; and Canby, who felt that he alone understood the situation, took heart from the rather impersonal quality of the girl's gaze as she let her eyes rest on young Linwood. Still, uneasiness seemed to hover in the air. A keen observer, studying the group, would have noted that each of its members had something on his mind; a subtle lack of repose, a kind of intangible restlessness, made itself felt; there was an undercurrent of uneasy suspense, and you could almost hear the sighs of relief that greeted the call to luncheon.

Canby meant to have a talk with Nella at the earliest opportunity, but they had no sooner gotten up from the table after lunch than he found himself circumvented by young Linwood, who calmly tucked the girl's arm through his and led her away.

Canby watched them go with a sinking heart. He knew that the opposition of the uncle had put the finishing touch to the young man's resolution; he would be capable now of carrying the girl off by main force. Youth could do such a thing while staid middle age looked on and sighed. Middle age did in fact sigh, seeing the two young people disappear around a bend in the garden path; and then turned at hearing the elder Linwood's voice:

"How about a game of billiards?"

But Canby was in no mood for games of any sort, and said so briefly. He wanted to listen to no chatter, either; he only wanted to be alone. With Linwood in one of his genial moods there was only one way to make sure of that, and Canby adopted it. Announcing his intention of paying a visit to his sister at Roselawn, he went out and jumped into the roadster, turned for the gate and was gone.

He did in fact pass the entrance to Roselawn twice that afternoon, but did not enter. He tore along at forty miles an hour, paying no attention to direction or distance, wanting only to move and get away from himself. He was beginning to see that he had indeed acted a fool. Seldom in this sorry life are we given a strong desire and the means of satisfying it at the same time; when the happy combination comes only a madman refuses to take advantage of it. So he had done, Canby reflected. Nella had actually agreed, in so many words, to marry him, and he had refused! Then youth had come—youth, with its fiery eyes and burning words and grace of limb and movement; its awkward phrases and crude inflections that were somehow powerful; its triteness and endless repetition that somehow seemed ever new; youth with all its mastery.

These reflections and a thousand others tossed about in Canby's brain as he drove madly about the countryside all that September afternoon. The thing was eminently just; he wouldn't deny that. The girl of nineteen and boy of twenty-four belonged in each other's arms.

And what a prize she was! Sweetness and intelligence, charm of good mind and body, innocence and goodness, all found their home in her. A prize for any lucky man!

Well, he would soon know. The suspense and indecision would end. This was her tomorrow; perhaps her "yes" was waiting for him now. It was that thought that turned the wheel about and headed him for home.

The dinner hour at Greenhedge was half-past six, and it was just ten minutes before that time when Canby turned in at the driveway. The lawn and piazza were deserted; there was no one in the garden. He left the car in the rear and entered the house. Still no one. Suddenly he heard Mrs. Wheeler addressing him:

"Oh, are you back, sir? Will you eat alone, sir?"

Looking into the dining-room, Canby saw with surprise that no preparations had been made for dinner.

"Why, where is everybody?" he demanded.

"I don't know, sir. Miss Nella said she wouldn't be back for dinner. She said to tell you she left a note for you in your room."

Canby turned slowly toward the stairs with a heavy heart. He had felt this coming all afternoon. It was over. Then the spark of hope, still faintly alive, quickened within him, and he bounded up the stairs three at a time. He ran down the upper hall and dashed into his room. The note was there on his desk, addressed in her quaint round hand: "Mr. Fred Canby." He tore it open.

> I can't help it; really I can't. I'm so sorry. I'm going to marry Mr. Linwood this evening. We aren't coming back. Please, please forgive me; you've been so kind to me— I'll write to you later, and maybe you'll think better of me.
>
> NELLA.

Canby read it over three times, then slowly folded the sheet and placed it in his pocket. Then suddenly he took it out again and tore it into a dozen pieces; after which he walked to the window overlooking the garden and stood there crumpling the bits of paper in his hand. He stood very straight and motionless and his face was white and set like stone.

So youth had conquered! He smiled bitterly. No doubt it was all quite logical and proper and to be expected. Tom had made good; he was after all a worthy representative of the age of adventure. He had picked her up and ran off with her—with Nella, the sweetest and best and dearest girl in the world. She had heard the call of youth and had responded to it, and who was he to begrudge her happiness? An old worthless fossil!

Long after the dinner-bell rang he stood there. Finally he turned drearily and went downstairs, and, after informing Mrs. Wheeler curtly that he wanted no dinner, he went out into the fragrant peace of the garden.

Dusk was approaching; a cool breeze had sprung up and was rustling the leaves of the plants and shrubs. He strolled aimlessly along the paths, seeing nothing, hearing nothing.

But all at once his eyes were opened. Turning a bend in the path, there was a bench before him, and on the bench was seated a young man. Canby stopped short and stared at this young man with an expression of amazed stupidity, as if he had been a ghost. It was Tom Linwood.

"Hello!" said the youth, looking up dismally.

Canby continued to stare like an imbecile. "But what— You—" he stammered at last, and stopped.

Then:

"Where's Nella?" he demanded.

"With her husband, I suppose," was the reply.

"With her hus—! Are you crazy?"

The youth was unmoved in his stony gloom.

"I said, with her husband. That's the proper place for a loving young wife, isn't it?"

Then he burst forth suddenly:

"I don't want to talk about her, I tell you! She's a—she's a— Oh damn it all, I don't know what she is! Yes, I do!" He became dismally ironic: "She's my aunt—my aunt Nella! She's been throwing eyes at that old duffer all along and I didn't know it; and he swallowed her bait. Oh, she's a slick one! They got in the car and Uncle Garry tells me to be a good boy and hands me a note to give to you, and off they go! . . . I forgot; I didn't give you the note, did I? Here it is."

Canby took it and tore it open. There were only a few lines.

Canby:

She belonged to you, but you wouldn't take her; so the prize is mine. We are to be married this afternoon. That young fool Tom was making it too hot for me.

LINWOOD.

Canby dropped weakly on the bench and sat there in an idiotic daze. Coming out of it hours later, he uttered the words:

"Old fool!"

Goodness only knows whom he was talking about.

THE EARLY FICTION OF REX STOUT

—⁓—

"Excess Baggage"	*Short Stories*, October 1912 [3]
"The Infernal Feminine"	*Short Stories*, November 1912 [3]
"The Paisley"	*Young's Magazine*, November 1912 [9]
"Billy Du Mont, Reporter"	*Young's Magazine*, December 1912 [9]
"A Professional Recall"	*The Black Cat*, December 1912 [1, 3]
"Barnacles"	*Young's Magazine*, January 1913 [9]
"Pamfret and Peace"	*The Black Cat*, January 1913 [1, 3]
"A Companion of Fortune"	*Short Stories*, April 1913 [3]
"A White Precipitate"	*Lippincott's Monthly Magazine*, June 1913 [3]
"The Pickled Picnic"	*The Black Cat*, June 1913 [9]
"The Mother of Invention"	*The Black Cat*, August 1913 [1, 3]
Her Forbidden Knight	*The All-Story*, August 1913 to December 1913 [4, 8]
"Méthode Américaine"	*The Smart Set*, November 1913 [1, 3]
"A Tyrant Abdicates"	*Lippincott's Monthly Magazine*, January 1914 [1, 3]
"The Pay-Yeoman"	*The All-Story*, January 1914 [1, 2]
Under the Andes	*The All-Story*, February 1914 [5]
"Secrets"	*All-Story Weekly*, March 7, 1914 [1, 2]

"Rose Orchid"*	*All-Story Weekly*, March 28, 1914 [1, 2]
"An Agacella Or"	*Lippincott's Monthly Magazine*, April 1914 [1, 3]
"The Inevitable Third"*	*All-Story Weekly*, April 25, 1914 [2]
A Prize for Princes	*All-Story [Cavalier] Weekly*, May 2 to May 30, 1914 [6, 8]
"Out of the Line"	*All-Story Cavalier Weekly*, June 13, 1914 [4, 8]
"The Lie"	*All-Story Cavalier Weekly*, July 4, 1914 [1, 2]
"Target Practise"	*All-Story Cavalier Weekly*, December 26, 1914 [2]
"If He Be Married"	*All-Star Cavalier Weekly*, January 16, 1915 [2]
"Baba"	*All-Star Cavalier Weekly*, January 30, 1915 [2]
"Warner & Wife"	*All-Story Cavalier Weekly*, February 27, 1915 [1, 2]
"A Little Love Affair"	*Smith's Magazine*, July 1915 [3]
"Art for Art's Sake"	*Smith's Magazine*, August 1915 [3]
"Another Little Love Affair"	*Smith's Magazine*, September 1915 [3]
"Jonathan Stannard's Secret Vice"	*All-Story Weekly*, September 11, 1915 [1, 2]
"Sanétomo"	*All-Story Weekly*, September 25, 1915 [2]
"The Strong Man"	*Young's Magazine*, November 1915 [3]
"Justice Ends at Home"	*All-Story Weekly*, December 4, 1915 [1, 2]
"Two Kisses"	*Breezy Stories*, January 1916 [9]
The Great Legend	*All-Story Weekly*, January 1, 1916 [8]
"Ask the Egyptians"	*Golfers Magazine,* March 1916 [9]
"This Is My Wife"	*Snappy Stories*, March [issue 2] 1916 [9]

"Second Edition"	*Young's Magazine*, April 1916 [9]
"It's Science That Counts"	*All-Story Weekly*, April 1, 1916 [2]
"The Rope Dance"	*All-Story Weekly*, June 24, 1916 [1, 2]
The Last Drive	*Golfers Magazine*, July to December 1916 [9]
"It Happened Last Night"	*The Black Cat*, January 1917 [9]
"An Officer and a Lady"	*All-Story Weekly*, January 13, 1917 [1, 2, 3]
"Heels of Fate"	*All-Story Weekly*, November 17, 1917 [1, 2]
"Old Fools and Young"	*Young's Magazine*, April 1918 [9]

* Published under the pseudonym "Evans Day"

[1] Reprinted in *Justice Ends at Home and Other Stories* (Viking Press 1977)

[2] Reprinted in *Target Practice* (Carroll & Graf 1998)

[3] Reprinted in *An Officer and a Lady and Other Stories* (Carroll & Graf 2000)

[4] Reprinted in *Her Forbidden Knight* (Carroll & Graf 1997)

[5] Reprinted in *Under the Andes* (Mysterious Press 1985; Carroll & Graf 2000)

[6] Reprinted in *A Prize for Princes* (Carroll & Graf 2000)

[7] Reprinted in *The Great Legend* (Carroll & Graf 1997)

[8] Reprinted in *The Rex Stout Reader* (Carroll & Graf 2007)

[9] Reprinted in this volume

EBOOKS BY REX STOUT

THE WOLFE PACK

If you enjoy the works of Rex Stout, please join the Wolfe Pack—the literary society for everyone who admires the worlds of Nero Wolfe and Rex Stout.

The Wolfe Pack, founded in 1978, is dedicated to the celebration of America's greatest—and largest—detective, Nero Wolfe, and his creator, Rex Stout. The Pack publishes a semiannual journal, the *Gazette*, and sponsors several events each year, including a themed dinner in the spring and our oldest tradition, the Black Orchid Banquet, in New York in December. There are local chapters, called *racemes*, for members outside the New York City area, and we are always looking to form additional racemes.

A two-year membership is $35.00 and includes four issues of the *Gazette* as well as a periodic newsletter notifying you of Wolfe Pack events and Wolfe- and Stout-related news.

To join, please mail name, address, and email address to the Wolfe Pack, PO Box 230822, Ansonia Station, New York, NY 10023, or visit www.nerowolfe.org and select "Membership" to join online and pay with a credit card or PayPal.

For more information, please email: werowance@nerowolfe.org.

MYSTERIOUSPRESS.COM

Otto Penzler, owner of the Mysterious Bookshop in Manhattan, founded the Mysterious Press in 1975. Penzler quickly became known for his outstanding selection of mystery, crime, and suspense books, both from his imprint and in his store. The imprint was devoted to printing the best books in these genres, using fine paper and top dust-jacket artists, as well as offering many limited, signed editions.

Now the Mysterious Press has gone digital, publishing ebooks through **MysteriousPress.com**.

MysteriousPress.com offers readers essential noir and suspense fiction, hard-boiled crime novels, and the latest thrillers from both debut authors and mystery masters. Discover classics and new voices, all from one legendary source.

FIND OUT MORE AT

WWW.MYSTERIOUSPRESS.COM

FOLLOW US:

@emysteries and Facebook.com/MysteriousPressCom

MysteriousPress.com is one of a select group of publishing partners of Open Road Integrated Media, Inc.

THe MYSTeRIOUS BOOKSHOP, founded in 1979, is located in Manhattan's Tribeca neighborhood. It is the oldest and largest mystery-specialty bookstore in America.

The shop stocks the finest selection of new mystery hardcovers, paperbacks, and periodicals. It also features a superb collection of signed modern first editions, rare and collectable works, and Sherlock Holmes titles. The bookshop issues a free monthly newsletter highlighting its book clubs, new releases, events, and recently acquired books.

58 Warren Street
info@mysteriousbookshop.com
(212) 587-1011
Monday through Saturday
11:00 a.m. to 7:00 p.m.

FIND OUT MORe AT:

www.mysteriousbookshop.com

FOLLOW US:

@TheMysterious and Facebook.com/MysteriousBookshop

OPEN ROAD

INTEGRATED MEDIA

Open Road Integrated Media is a digital publisher and multimedia content company. Open Road creates connections between authors and their audiences by marketing its ebooks through a new proprietary online platform, which uses premium video content and social media.

Videos, Archival Documents, and New Releases

Sign up for the Open Road Media newsletter and get news delivered straight to your inbox.

Sign up now at
www.openroadmedia.com/newsletters

CPSIA information can be obtained at www.ICGtesting.com
Printed in the USA
BVOW04s0309030615

402920BV00003B/5/P